The
Hook

Catherine Morrison

For Jamie,
who never once asked 'Why?'
and just went with it.

Chapter One

The plane touched down on the runway. As the brakes screeched into action, a disembodied voice addressed the passengers. "Welcome to New York's John F. Kennedy Airport. The local time is 7 p.m. and the weather not much better than what we left behind in London. On behalf of the flight crew, I would like to thank you for flying British Airways and wish you a pleasant onward journey. Good evening."

As she zipped her laptop into its case, Kate couldn't help but dwell on the word 'pleasant'. There was nothing pleasant about this situation or the mess she had got involved in, and for what – a few quid? But that morning, when she'd read about the impending trial, something told her she had to be there. She knew there was nothing she could do to put things right, at least not without incriminating herself or getting herself into danger, but that hadn't stopped her from coming.

Tapping her black high heel on the seat in front, she decided she had nothing to worry about. It would be enough to see the look on his face when he was found guilty, although it tortured her that it would just be for embezzlement, and not for his more serious crime: murder.

After what felt like an eternity, the plane stopped taxiing, the 'fasten seatbelt' light clicked off and the doors opened, allowing the fresh autumn air to percolate through the stuffy cabin.

She welcomed the cool feel of the air on her

clammy skin, but soon became impatient for the guy in the seat beside her to stop texting and move so she could get out. She wanted to scream at him. He hadn't sat still for the entire flight but now that it was time to go, he was a statue.

Clearing her throat to signal her annoyance did the trick, but she felt obliged to acknowledge him as he begrudgingly let her out into the aisle. She joined the queue which moved slowly towards the open door.

Even though she was a seasoned traveller, the customs and immigration process always made her nervous. She never had anything to hide, but the officers were highly skilled at making her feel like a criminal. She couldn't help wondering if they only recruited people with severe personality flaws or if they actually trained people to behave that way.

Experience had taught her that whichever of the three queues she chose would be the wrong one – and as a bonus she would most likely get the leering old man more interested in staring at her boobs than in doing his job.

After twenty minutes, it was her turn to be interrogated. She was pleasantly surprised to see a young immigration officer call her forward. He was tall, slim, probably in his late twenties and very easy on the eye.

"Business or pleasure?" he asked politely.

As she presented her passport she wondered if they had revised their recruitment process since she had last travelled.

"Pleasure," she replied, but she really meant business.

She fixed her gaze straight ahead. As she waited to be verified, she sensed him scanning her. A quick sideways glance caught him staring at her short skirt and she blushed at the realisation that this – now she was in her late thirties – was the first time she had felt slightly more flattered than objectified by a man so blatantly checking her out. And he was a leg man; how refreshing.

He handed back the stamped passport. "Enjoy your stay."

Her eyes were closed when the taxi stopped with a jolt. She sat up. A quick look out of the window revealed that they had arrived at the hotel. Her heart sank as she opened her purse to pay the driver and realised she only had sterling. In her haste to get to the airport and catch the first flight, she had forgotten to get dollars.

"I'm so sorry, I don't have any cash. Can I pay by card?"

"Cash only, lady," the driver grumbled, unimpressed.

Does he think I was born yesterday? She spotted the credit card machine and tapped on it with her polished fingernail.

"What's this, then, an ornament?"

"Machine's broken."

She groaned. "Is it? Then I suppose you could take me to an ATM to get some cash."

Without turning to face her, he shook his head.

Unamused, she kept her calm. "I'd really hate to have to report you, but may I see your driver number, sir?"

Her demand, in a polite English accent, made him shift in his seat. He turned around and examined the card machine. "My mistake – I can take your card. It wasn't working earlier but it seems OK now."

"That's lucky," she said through gritted teeth, entering her PIN on the handset. She made a point of declining a tip.

He was impatient for her to exit the cab. She'd barely got her feet on the ground when he gestured for her to close the door, then sped off.

She shook her head. There really was no need to be so rude. Next time she would definitely call an Uber.

The hotel was even nicer than the pictures she had seen in the departure lounge when she had booked it. Its glass-fronted facade and elegant signage certainly made it look worth the hefty price tag, but she had checked three price comparison websites and was sure she had got a good deal.

She passed through the revolving door into a large open-plan lobby. About a dozen leather sofas were casually dotted around stylish coffee tables and there seemed to be a nice mix of guests relaxing and enjoying the music played by the pianist in the corner. Behind the reception desk stood a tall, thin man, dressed impeccably in his uniform like a soldier dutifully guarding his post. He was probably in his sixties, with a mane of brilliant white hair.

His name badge identified him as Norman, the manager. He straightened his jacket as he greeted her.

"Good evening, miss. How may I help you?"

She recognised his accent immediately. Although it was somewhat polished, he was unmistakably from East London.

"Miss Turner. I have a reservation."

He smiled, having also recognised her accent.

"Isn't it funny that I've travelled all the way to New York and the first person I meet is probably just from around the corner?" She reached into her purse to retrieve her credit card.

He nodded. "It's always nice to hear a familiar accent but there's a hint of something else in there. Dublin, perhaps?"

She raised her eyebrows. "Oh, you're good, but you're a little too far south. It's Belfast."

"Of course." He looked down at his computer screen. "Yes, Miss Turner, we have you booked in a classic double for three nights."

"Yes." She hesitated. "I don't know how long I'm going to be in town. It might be three nights or perhaps a little longer. Is that OK?"

"Certainly, that will not be a problem. We will do our very best to accommodate you." He checked the computer screen and grimaced. "I'm terribly sorry, but we don't have any classic rooms available."

Is he kidding? She had only booked it a few hours ago. What could have changed since then? She thought it was typical of hotels to try and extort innocent travellers, and was preparing to give him a dressing-down when he continued.

"I'm afraid I'll have to offer you a deluxe room instead – at no extra charge, of course." He winked. "Would you like some help with your bags?"

She picked up her bag to show her minimal luggage.

He offered her the key card.

"Ninth floor, room number 968. The lift is over there. Is there anything else I can do for you?"

"Yes please, I'm in town for…" She looked around the lobby and lowered her voice. "It's kind of a surprise thing so I don't want anyone to know I'm here. There probably won't be any, but if there are any calls for me could you please be discreet?" She bit her lip as she waited for his response.

"Of course, Miss Turner, discretion is paramount. Please enjoy your stay."

"I think I will. Goodnight, Norman."

The room was dark, but instead of reaching for the light switch she set down her bags and walked towards the window. The last time she had been in New York, her accommodation was a friend's sofa in Queens, so she held her breath as she approached, hoping she had a good view – or any view of the Manhattan skyline.

She drew a sharp breath as she was met by the bright city lights which twinkled above and below. Even the top of the Empire State Building was visible. Totally relaxed, she surveyed the city, and at least five minutes passed before she could tear herself away.

Leaning down to the bedside table, she switched on the small lamp and had a look around the room. Beside her at the window was a small coffee table and two armchairs. The bed had crisp white sheets and far too many pillows. It looked inviting and big enough for four. Realising that it was 2 a.m. back home, she resisted the urge to climb in straight away; she wanted to acclimatise to her new time zone.

Facing the bed was a huge flat-screen TV which hung on the wall over a dressing table and a beautiful antique-style chair. A quick look into the bathroom revealed a brilliant white four-piece suite with a corner bath – or was it a Jacuzzi? She was too tired tonight but would definitely figure that out tomorrow.

She returned to the bedroom and tried to find the mini bar. She searched around and eventually found it integrated into the wardrobe. After a quick peek inside she helped herself to a small bottle of chardonnay which she poured into a glass, then pulled one of the armchairs right up against the window.

Promising herself she would unpack before she went to bed, she kicked off her heels, settled into the armchair and took her first sip of wine.

Chapter Two

Her mobile phone buzzed to life on the bedside table and she scrambled to cancel the alarm. It took a few moments for her to remember where she was. With everything that was going on in her head she hadn't expected to sleep so well.

The air in the room was cold and she begrudged having to leave the cosiness of the bed behind, but this was the day she'd been waiting for and she had to get going.

After a long hot shower, she sat, wrapped in her damp towel, at the dressing table and studied herself in the mirror. Her red hair was sopping wet, eyes still puffy from tiredness, and she couldn't work out if her head was fuzzy from jet lag or if it had something to do with the three empty wine bottles on the coffee table.

She took a few deep breaths. After months of being on edge, she hoped she would get the closure she needed. *You can do this*, she thought as she picked up the hair dryer.

Blow-drying her long hair took forever with the cheap hotel dryer, but at least she'd brought her own straighteners to iron out Mother Nature's dismal attempt at curls.

She rolled her eyes as she remembered the humidity of the Far East – all she had needed there was a decent scrunchie or a hat. She'd been in London for the past fifteen months – the longest she'd lived anywhere as an adult – and she was getting a little too used to her home comforts. Perhaps this trip was what she really needed.

She applied some make-up – not much, just a little foundation to warm her pale skin, some neutral eye shadow and a hint of black mascara. She opened the wardrobe and selected one of the three dresses she had hung there the night before. The dark blue dress fitted neatly over her slim figure, just long enough to reach her knees and the plunging neckline just low enough to leave a little to the imagination. Her heart started to beat faster as she slipped into her black high heels, pulled on her jacket and looked at herself in the mirror. It was time to go.

It was raining as she made her way out of the hotel onto the busy street. She immediately regretted taking the time to straighten her hair as she struggled with the cheap umbrella she had just purchased from a street vendor. There was no hope of catching a cab, so she headed towards the subway.

She felt strangely at home as she descended the slippery steps, as if she was back in London on the Tube. Just like the Tube, there were far too many people invading her personal space. *Does no one shower here?* she thought as a pungent odour wafted over her shoulder.

The train screeched out of the tunnel towards the platform. As it ground to a halt, the doors opened and she was practically carried aboard by the crowd that stormed the train. She struggled to keep her balance in the middle of the crowded carriage. Too short to reach the overhead handles, she had to cling to the back of a seat to stay upright.

She emerged from the subway and made her way through the crowded streets, careful not to catch her heels on the vents and broken slabs. As the streets emptied and people poured into the office buildings, she reminded herself to reply to the texts she'd had from co-workers checking she was OK as she hadn't shown up for work that morning.

Turning the corner, she was surprised to see the courthouse alive with excitement. She hadn't expected the trial to be such a big deal.

The NYPD were managing a group of weather-beaten animal rights protestors who were carrying placards and chanting slogans. She was used to such people hanging around outside her office in London. But just because the company she worked for developed pharmaceuticals, it didn't mean they tested them on animals. Testing wasn't her department so she couldn't be sure, but she hoped they didn't.

Why are they here at an embezzlement trial? she wondered as she made her way through the crowd of TV cameramen and reporters.

Her heart raced as she joined the queue for the main door, which was manned by a short, rotund police officer, the opposite of the hottie from Customs the night before. She knew she probably wasn't going to get in, but she had to try.

He was stopping everyone and checking something. What was he going to ask for? Identification, she thought, so she took her passport out of her bag and stepped up.

Without making eye contact, the officer held out his hand. "Authorisation pass, please."

My what? "Oh, I don't seem to have—"

"I'm sorry, ma'am," he interrupted her. "No entry unless you have a pass."

"I must have left it at the hotel," she replied, trying to catch his eye and charm him with a smile.

"Then I suggest you go back there and get it," he snapped.

She upped the ante and placed her hand on his arm, giving it a gentle squeeze. "I've come a long way to be here today. Please, is there any way?"

His eyes widened and he looked at her hand on his arm. She removed it immediately.

"I'm sorry, ma'am. Without a pass, you're just going to have to wait out here with everyone else." He directed her to the crowd of people standing behind the police barrier. "Next, please."

Scowling as she stepped out of the queue, she turned to make her way towards the barrier but stopped when she thought she recognised a face.

He was average height, slim and dressed neatly in a dark grey suit and tie. He had very short brown hair and a day's worth of slightly greying stubble. She presumed he was in his mid-forties. He was very attractive for his age. He reminded her of her grammar school music teacher, who she had wasted many lessons swooning over. All that was missing was the sexy glasses.

The press pass attached to his laptop bag confirmed it was him, although he was much more handsome in person than in his profile picture in his newspaper. She'd seen it every time she'd read the obituary he'd written for his colleague who had committed suicide. *If only he knew*.

She knew she had to invent a way to talk to him –

and quickly, as the queue had begun to move inside. Subtly, she adjusted her boobs and straightened her dress as she made her way towards him. He had set his laptop bag down to check his phone. That was her opportunity. She altered her speed so that she approached as he was distracted, putting his phone back into his pocket. She took a deep breath, intentionally caught her foot in the strap of his bag and threw herself towards him.

She fell into him and he stumbled backwards, almost losing his balance. He just about managed to get his arms under her before she made it all the way to the ground.

Totally stunned and not quite sure what had just happened, he looked down and found what he considered to be a very beautiful woman in his arms. He tightened his grip on her as he steadied himself. After a few seconds he lifted her to her feet and gently brushed her red hair away from her face.

"I'm sorry," he whispered as he stared into her brown eyes.

"That's OK." She blushed. "It was my fault. I wasn't looking where I was going."

They smiled at each other.

He felt the beat of her heart against his chest and suddenly realised he was still holding her. He cleared his throat.

"I guess I should let you go now." Although what he really wanted to do was kiss her.

"Do you have to?" she purred, enjoying the feel of his strong arms around her.

Her words sent his pulse racing. As he let her go, he accidentally ran his hand over her breast.

She gasped.

In an effort to conceal his embarrassment, he cleared his throat and tried to think of a clever line to naturally progress the conversation, but he had nothing.

They stood and stared at each other in silence again until they heard a voice behind them.

"We're closing up here, Mike."

He looked around to see that the queue was gone and the police officer was beckoning him into the building.

"I'm really sorry, but I have to go." He pointed to the door.

She glanced at the door, then back to him. "Do you have to?"

He thought she was beautiful and the thought of walking away from her pained him, but he'd gone out of his way to ask for this assignment, so he had to go and do his job. He just needed a few more seconds with her...

"Come on!" the officer shouted.

His eyes darted to the door and back to her.

She shrugged. "You'd better get inside. Thank you for catching me."

Trying not to break eye contact, he bent down to pick up his laptop. "It was my pleasure. But I haven't had a chance to ask your name..."

She gave his arm a gentle squeeze. "It's OK. I know yours, Mike. I'll see you around."

And she turned on her heel. He was left, speechless, watching her walk towards the barrier. He could do nothing but make his way inside.

"I was ready to close up," the officer scolded him.

"Sorry, Tony."

Mike stopped at the door and turned for one last look. He spotted her behind the barrier. She was still watching him. They exchanged another smile as Tony closed the door.

Disappointed, Kate waited beside the reporters and listened to their chatter. She knew there was little chance she'd get inside, but those bloody protestors hadn't helped matters. If they hadn't been here, she might have been able to slip in unnoticed. She glanced back at the police officer guarding the door. Then again, maybe not.

The rain had started to pick up again, so she decided to leave and come back tomorrow. She might even see that reporter again. She hoped so. But if she didn't, she knew she could find him at the *New York Times* office.

Just as she was about to leave, a ripple of excitement moved through the crowd. A black town car pulled up not far from her. When the door opened, the cameras started shooting and the noise of the crowd rose up around her.

Reporters began to fire questions at the middle-aged man in the very expensive-looking suit who emerged from the back of the car. He ignored all questions and gestured for a second man to exit the vehicle.

The noise increased when a second man stepped out of the car. He was dressed in an unassuming black suit and white shirt with black tie. He looked more as if he was attending a funeral than his trial.

The reporters fired questions and the protestors chanted, but Jack Hudson kept his head down and walked slowly towards the courthouse door. As he approached the barrier he looked up at the protestors, stopping short when he noticed Kate among the crowd. Looking startled, he made eye contact with her. She held his eye for a moment until he was ushered past.

She watched him until he entered the courthouse. When the door closed, her shoulders slumped.

The rain was getting heavier and there was no point in hanging around outside. Perhaps she might be able to watch the coverage on the news back at the hotel. It was America, after all; the trial was bound to be on TV.

Chapter Three

Inside the courtroom Mike managed to get one of the last free seats in the area that had been reserved for the press. He nodded at the familiar faces around him, and assumed that the ones he didn't recognise must be from out of town. There were probably quite a few from Europe because, although the man on trial was American, he was the CEO of an international pharmaceutical company based in New York but which had a sizable office in London, where he spent most of his time.

Both teams of lawyers carefully set out their paperwork in preparation for what Mike thought would be a quick trial. From what he had read, the evidence against the accused was overwhelming.

He felt a nudge in the ribs as he was joined on the hard wooden bench by another reporter.

"Hey, Mike, I haven't seen you for a while. How come they let you out of the office?"

Since his promotion to Business Editor, Mike had spent most of his time at the office, but there had been panic at the early-morning meeting. Two reporters had been struck down with flu – or Monday-itis, as the Associate Managing Editor called it – and he had volunteered to cover this story.

"Ever see *The Shawshank Redemption*?" he joked as they shook hands.

"No way you dug a tunnel in that fancy suit. So, do you reckon we're in for a long trial?"

"No, it's open and shut. I'd say three or four days at the most."

"Just four days? You wanna wager on that?"

Mike shook his head. "No, Alvarez, I couldn't take your money."

The door to the left of the judge's bench opened and the jury filed in one by one. There was an even mix of men and women – strangers grouped together by fate. Visibly daunted by the task at hand, they looked around the courtroom as they took their seats.

Mike opened his laptop bag and took out a notepad and pen, then got his glasses from his jacket pocket.

It wasn't long before the bailiff escorted Jack Hudson into the courtroom. He walked slowly, his head hanging. As he approached his seat, he scanned the room. His gaze fixed on a woman in the second row and she dropped her head to avoid eye contact.

Mike recognised her as Hudson's wife. She had left him when he was arrested.

Hudson spoke quietly to his defence attorneys until they were interrupted.

"All rise."

Everyone in the courtroom leapt to their feet as the judge entered.

He was a short, angry-looking man in his sixties with a full beard but no hair. With a wave of his hand he motioned to the crowd to sit, and the trial began.

The jury were sworn in, then both sides made their opening statements. Mike tapped his notepad with his pen as he listened to the prosecution put forward their case.

Jack Hudson was accused of embezzling

$10,000,000 from his business accounts. The stolen money had been found in an offshore bank account in his name. All the paperwork had been found hidden in his London office.

Mike chewed on his pen as he took notes. He wasn't really listening to what was happening; he was too busy thinking about what had just happened outside. Who was that woman and how did she know his name? Maybe she had heard Tony call him? Yes, that was probably it.

He looked down at his hand and remembered the feel of her breast. He wondered what the rest of her would feel like. She had certainly felt good in his arms. He took off his glasses and rubbed his eyes. What was he thinking? He had just turned forty-eight and had had his fair share of women, but he suddenly felt like a teenager when he thought about her.

As he slipped his glasses back on, he smelt her perfume on his sleeve and sighed. *Why didn't I get her name? Why didn't I give her my card?*

Having realised how distracted he was, he got back to listening to the prosecution. He was trying to concentrate on what was being said when he noticed a small scratch on his left lens. No matter how hard he tried, he couldn't ignore it. His new glasses were in his desk drawer and he would need them tomorrow if he stood any chance of paying attention to the trial. He would have to go to the office later.

Distracted again. He was usually very focused, but that woman had knocked him off kilter. He tried his best to forget about her and concentrate.

A few hours later, the prosecution had finished. Court was adjourned, to resume the following morning.

As the courtroom cleared, Mike was eager to get back outside to see if the woman was still there, but was held back by the string of people wanting to catch up with him. After making lots of small talk and scheduling two games of golf, he finally managed to get outside. He looked over to the barrier where she had been standing, but she was gone.

Disappointed, he hailed a cab and resigned himself to the fact that he would probably never see her again.

Back in the office, Mike held down the button, impatient for the doors to close. He didn't want to be there and was planning to leave again quickly.

When he stepped out of the lift he was greeted by the pretty brunette receptionist.

"Hi, Mi—"

He covered his face with his hand and hurried past. "You didn't see me, Connie. I just need to get my glasses."

"Mike!" she repeated. "Helena Crawford is in your office."

He stopped.

"I told her you probably wouldn't be back today but she's been in there for, like, an hour. Just sitting there, staring. I didn't have the heart to ask her to leave."

"Jeez." He shifted from foot to foot. Helena Crawford was the widow of his former colleague, Alexander, who had committed suicide several months ago while on holiday in London. "I haven't seen her since the funeral. I said I would call, but I never got around to it."

He gave the receptionist what he thought was a reassuring look and reluctantly started along the corridor to his office. Usually quite articulate, he had to rack his brains for something meaningful to say. He really was at a loss for words today. He stopped at his office door, took a deep breath and opened the door.

Mrs Crawford stood up when he walked in. She was shorter and heavier than he remembered. Her once blonde hair was streaked with grey and she had more wrinkles than her fifty-odd years deserved.

"How are you? I'm so sorry I haven't called." He offered her his hand to shake but she pushed it away and pulled him in for a hug instead.

Feeling more than awkward, he returned the hug for what he thought was a reasonable time before he broke her hold.

"It's OK, Mike." She sat down. "You don't have to explain. Everyone's been avoiding me since it happened. People just don't know what to say."

He looked at the ground. He knew exactly what she meant. "Is there anything can I do for you?"

She nodded. "It's taken a while, but I've finally started going through his things. It's really tough…" She reached into her bag and took out a packet of tissues.

He pulled up a chair and sat down next to her. "It's OK, take your time."

She took a few deep breaths. "There are some boxes back at the house – stories he was working on and some notes. I don't want to keep them around, but I'm afraid to throw them away. They might be important. Also, I didn't notice until now that a few withdrawals were made from the kids' college fund just before he died. What did he do with the money? And why would he go all the way to London to kill himself?"

Mike nodded. He'd wondered that too.

"Nothing makes any sense. I wonder if he got mixed up in some trouble or if he was having an affair?"

"I don't think he was having an affair; he wasn't the type," he said in an effort to comfort her, even though that rumour was going around the office.

"Thank you." She touched his arm. "Then he must have been up to something else…"

"Send the boxes down. When I get a chance, I'll look through them to see if there's anything important. And I'll ask around to see if anyone knows anything they haven't already mentioned, but after all these months I doubt we'll find out anything new."

"Thank you, Mike. Alexander always said you were a decent man. I'll have the boxes sent down." She stood up and gave a little sigh as she picked up her coat and bag. He held the door for her and she hugged him again before she left. He watched her walk down the hall, then turned when he heard a voice from the corridor behind him.

"Hey, old man, was that…?"

"Yeah," he said in defeat.

"Rough. Wanna grab a beer?"

Mike nodded. "Yeah, Hooper. Just give me a second." He went back into the office and retrieved his glasses from his desk drawer.

When they arrived at the bar it was already crowded with football fans eagerly awaiting the upcoming game.

"I forgot there was a game later, or I would have suggested O'Malley's."

"Don't worry, I see some free seats." Hooper pointed to a table intended for four but occupied by just two women. "You get the drinks and I'll get the women." He smirked as he made his way to the table.

Mike stood at the bar and watched Hooper. Within seconds the women were laughing and smiling. How did he do it so easily? He groaned as he wondered which woman Hooper would leave with – even if it was both, it wouldn't be the first time.

He knew that Hooper was considered really good-looking, but the trouble was, he knew it. He had just turned forty and dressed in the latest fashion. Tall and well built, he had a generous mop of brown hair and sported a well-groomed goatee. To top it off, he was confident and definitely knew how to turn on the charm.

Hooper gave Mike a smug look as he pulled out a stool and joined the women. Mike sighed as he thought of his earlier encounter. Usually he was quite charming and had done well with women in the years since his divorce, but there was something different about the woman today. She'd taken his breath away.

He arrived at the table with the drinks and nodded politely to the two women as he slid a bottle of beer over to Hooper.

"Thanks. So, what did Crawford's wife want?"

"She was just checking in to see if there was any new information that might shed some light on why he killed himself."

Hooper shook his head while he took a long drink. "You heard the same rumours as me, old man."

"Rumours? I'm only interested in facts."

"Rumours start for a reason. He was off work 'sick' for weeks, then he took off to London and killed himself. I know he seemed like a pretty dull guy, but sometimes it's the quiet ones you have to watch."

"Well, we'll probably never know the real reason, but Helena said he had some unfinished work, so I said I'd look it over after I finish with this trial." He pointed up at one of the TV screens around the bar, which was showing a news report on the trial.

"Yeah, old man, how come you got stuck with court reporting? Have you been demoted or something?"

"Simmons called in sick and I've been wanting to get out of the office, so I told Bob I'd cover it." He took a long sip of his beer. "Would you look at him? He's guilty as hell."

They watched Hudson making his way from the car to the courthouse door. Mike took a sharp breath and pointed up to the screen. "Did you see that?"

"What?"

"The woman in the blue dress. Hudson looked straight at her. Looks like he knows her. I noticed her down at the courthouse today – she was trying to get in past security and when she couldn't she threw herself at me."

"Lucky you. She's pretty."

"More than pretty. She's beautiful – and she smelt great too." He pretended to rub his nose so he could sniff his sleeve; the smell of her perfume still lingered. He bit his lip as he remembered her beautiful brown eyes looking up at him. "But it was obvious she was up to something. I thought she was a pickpocket so I checked for my wallet and cell as soon as it happened. I'm sure he knows her." He rubbed his chin before he took a sip of his beer. "If I see her there tomorrow, I'll talk to her and find out who she is."

Hooper rubbed his hands together. "Get her number for me, would you?"

"What about Gina?"

"Gina? She dumped me, thought I was cheating on her again."

"And were you?"

Hooper recoiled. "No. Not this time."

Mike rolled his eyes. "If I get her number, I'm keeping it for myself."

"What?" His friend looked sceptical. "She's a bit young for you – she's more my type. You'd do better sticking to bitter old divorcees. How's that going, by the way?"

He was offended – not just by the comment, but because Hooper had recently started calling him 'old man'. Hooper was only eight years younger than him, but had had a hard time turning forty. Mike knew Hooper only criticised him to make himself feel better, so he decided to let it slide.

"They're not all divorcees and they're not all bitter."

But Mike was lying. Most single women his age were divorced and the ones not looking for younger men were looking for their next husband, and he didn't fit either category. He couldn't make himself any younger and he definitely didn't want to get married again, but there was a fine line in between and he thought he had mastered how to tread it – at least until today.

He thought back to that woman again and the look they had exchanged when he held her. She *was* beautiful. OK, she was a bit younger than him, but he felt something he'd never felt before and couldn't stop thinking about her.

"Call me crazy, but when I met her today, I think we

had a real moment."

Hooper pointed his index finger at him. "You're crazy."

They laughed.

"It doesn't matter anyway, old man. There's no way a woman that pretty is single – and if she is, there's probably a good reason."

The atmosphere in the bar was buzzing. Fans were ordering food and drinks and settling in for the night.

Hooper looked at his watch. "The game's about to start. I'll get more beers."

Mike nodded and looked back at the television. His ego was dented because even his best friend thought he didn't stand a chance with a woman like that – but that wasn't going to stop him trying.

Chapter Four

The next morning Kate arrived at the courthouse early, wearing a short red dress that stopped just above the knee. Her make-up was flawless and her hair perfectly straight. The crowd was half the size of the previous day, the protestors had thinned out, and there were fewer press cameras. She scanned the crowd, eager to see Mike again. He wasn't there, but it was still early so she was hopeful that that didn't mean he wasn't coming.

Her heart sank as she looked up at the courthouse and saw the same police officer guarding the door. There was no queue this time, so she took a deep breath to prepare herself as she approached.

He sighed loudly when he saw her. "You again? Have you brought your pass this time?" There was more than a hint of sarcasm in his voice.

"The thing is, when I got back to the hotel it wasn't there. I must have left it at my office in London. They're going to Fed Ex it to me," she said reassuringly.

"That's great. When they do, bring it here and show me and then I'll let you in. Next, please." He ushered her away from the door like a stray.

"Damn it," she muttered. Her frustration grew when she saw there wasn't even anyone else in the queue. She started to make her way over to the barrier but stopped when she heard a familiar voice.

"Excuse me, miss?"

She turned and saw a smiling face. It was Mike. He

looked great dressed in a light grey suit, off-white shirt and red-and-white striped tie.

He looked at her, expecting a reply, but she just stared at him. She had spent all night thinking about his striking blue eyes, and she couldn't take her eyes off them.

"Hello," she managed finally, still looking into those eyes. "You look familiar." Playfully, she shook her finger at him. "Aren't you the guy who tripped me up yesterday?"

He squinted at her. "I'm not exactly sure that's how it happened but OK, I'll play along. May I say you look lovely today? Red really suits you."

"Thank you, and how did you know I'd be wearing red?" She pointed to his tie.

He blushed. "I didn't – it must be fate. Aren't you going inside?"

"No. That jobsworth won't let me in. I ... lost my pass."

"You're a reporter too?"

Quickly and without thinking she replied, "Yes."

"Do I detect an English accent?"

"You do." She tucked a stray strand of red hair behind her ear.

That was what he was hoping for. She was *definitely* flirting with him. Now he was free to make his move.

"Oh, man, you've come all the way from England to cover this story and you can't even get into the building?"

"That's right." She played along nervously. "My boss is going to kill me."

"Well, I can't let that happen. Come with me." He

took her by the hand and led her back toward the door.

She felt a flutter when he grasped her small hand – their hands fit perfectly. Her heart began to race as she found herself back at the courthouse door and she avoided making eye contact with the officer, who looked more than annoyed at her return.

"Morning, Tony." Mike gestured to Kate. "She's with me – is that OK?"

Tony shook his head. "I'm sorry, but you know the rules. No pass, no entry."

Mike feigned disappointment. "That's OK, I know there's nothing you can do." He looked at Kate and gave her a reassuring nod then turned back to the officer. "By the way, how did those Knicks tickets work out for your brother's bachelor party? Second row, weren't they?"

The officer's shoulders drooped and he nodded at Mike, regret in his eyes. "They were great. Thanks for organising that for me…"

"Any time," Mike said, feeling more than a little smug. The contacts he'd made at the paper over the years had made him one of the few people in New York who could score good tickets when needed. He was owed more than a few favours.

Tony sighed and looked around to check that no one was watching before he opened the door. "OK, guys, go ahead, but if anybody asks, I didn't let you in."

"Thanks." Mike patted him on the shoulder and Kate gave him a wink as she was led in through the door.

"That was impressive," she said as they walked through the large atrium and made their way into the courtroom. "Thank you so much, Mike." She let go of his hand and gave his shoulder a gentle squeeze. Surprised to feel firm muscle, she squeezed again. Her mind went into overdrive. She hadn't imagined he would be so toned under that suit. She was busy wondering what he would look like without his shirt on and how good it would feel to be pressed up against him again when she was interrupted.

"You're welcome. I seem to be at a disadvantage here. You know my name, but I don't know yours."

"It's Kate." She giggled like a schoolgirl as she offered him her hand.

"Kate, it's lovely to meet you again," he said with a smirk as he accepted her handshake.

She blushed. "Yes, that was quite the catch yesterday. It seems that you're a man of many talents."

"I don't know about that."

"Don't be so modest! That's twice you've rescued me now. I'll probably never be able to repay you."

"It's not necessary—" He stopped himself. What was he saying? She had just created the perfect opportunity for him to ask her out, but he didn't want to come on too strong. He thought quickly. "But since you insist, I suppose I could let you buy me a drink later."

Is he asking me out on a date? She certainly found him attractive, but he wasn't why she was in New York. She didn't need the complication. It took all her willpower to say, "I don't think that's a good idea."

He scratched his head. "You're right. It's not a good idea. I should be the one to buy the drinks."

She laughed, knowing she probably would have a drink with him, but for now she needed to focus on the task at hand. "OK, I'll think about it. So, how did it go in here yesterday?"

She was about to slide into the first available seat when he stopped her.

"Kate, we're down there."

She followed his finger to the benches that had been reserved for the press. Her cheeks began to burn. Maybe it hadn't been such a good idea to lie after all.

As he followed her, he couldn't stop his eyes from scanning her. Her jacket was just a bit too long for him to get a good look at her backside, but he assumed it had to be great as her figure was slim and her legs were perfect. He was imagining how great they would feel wrapped around him when he suddenly remembered where he was and that she'd asked him a question. *What was it again? Oh yes, yesterday.*

"Yesterday? Just the usual. The prosecution presented their case, which was pretty straightforward because the evidence against Hudson is overwhelming. They basically proved in one afternoon that he'd embezzled the millions out of the business, they had the business accounts scrutinised by several auditors and they had all the paperwork for his dodgy bank account. Today the defence is up, and I don't even know why they're bothering. If I was a betting man, I'd say we'll be out of here with a guilty verdict by lunch." He scratched his head. "I still can't believe he pleaded not guilty. If he'd taken the plea deal, he wouldn't even have had to stand trial."

"He's guilty all right, and of much more than embezzlement." She narrowed her eyes. "I just want to see him get what's coming to him. People like him will do anything to make money, and they don't care if they leave a trail of destruction behind them."

He was about to ask her what she meant when the door opened and Hudson entered, his head a bit lower than the previous day.

"Just look at him. He knows he's going to jail," she said with a venomous smile.

As Hudson took his seat, he looked at the crowd and again his eyes fixed on his wife.

Kate strained her neck to see. "Mike, can you see who he's looking at?"

"His wife, Laura. They were married for eighteen years. Do you know, she left him when it all came out?"

"Yes, but I'm surprised she stayed with him that long. He cheated on her all the time."

"Did he? How do you know that?"

"Didn't you know? It was public knowledge where I work."

Then the bailiff instructed everyone to stand as the judge entered, and the courtroom went quiet.

As the trial began, Kate made herself comfortable on the bench. She took off her jacket and crossed her legs. As she did, the hem of her dress crept up her thigh. Mike couldn't help noticing. Just as he had figured out she wasn't wearing pantyhose and her legs were actually as silky as they looked from afar, she caught him looking and nudged him.

He shrugged and tried to suppress a laugh. In an effort to focus on the trial he got out his notepad, pen and glasses. When he slipped them on, he noticed out of the corner of his eye that she was staring at him. He turned to face her.

Nodding in approval, she raised her hand to her

mouth, bit on the nail of her index finger then let out a little sigh. He nudged her like she had done to him.

They were trying hard to keep their composure when they heard Jack Hudson being called to the stand.

Kate's face fell and she focused on the witness stand.

During the questioning Mike noticed that she never once took her eyes off Hudson. When he looked briefly in their direction, Mike saw Hudson flinch when he noticed Kate.

Mike was positive they knew each other, and she certainly had more than a passing dislike of him. It was personal.

After hours of cross-examination, the door was opened and everyone filed out into the large atrium. Not wanting to get embroiled in small talk with the other reporters, Mike directed Kate to a quiet spot near the staircase.

"That went on a bit longer than I thought it would. I was sure we would finish this today."

"Yes, but he *will* be found guilty. He'll get what's coming to him."

He raised his eyebrows. "So how about that drink you promised me?"

She shrugged. "I didn't promise."

"Oh, come on. I practically saved your life yesterday and today I saved your career. The least you can do is keep me company for one drink." He tilted his head and stared at her.

She couldn't resist his beautiful blue eyes. "Well, when you put it like that, how could I possibly refuse? But just one drink." She held up her index finger. He curled his own index finger around hers and tugged on it.

"Well, one might get you hooked."

"You're awfully sure of yourself." She pulled her finger from his grasp.

He nodded. He *was* sure of himself, but only because there was something in her smile that told him he had a right to be.

"Come on, there's a nice place right across the street."

The bar was empty apart from a young couple canoodling in the corner and a table of business people winding down for the day.

"It looks like we've got the place almost to ourselves. What can I get you to drink?"

"A glass of white wine, please."

"Any one in particular?"

"Surprise me," she teased and held out her hand to take his laptop and jacket. His jacket looked expensive, so she hung it carefully over the back of a chair and steadied his laptop against the table leg. She watched him as he waited at the bar. He seemed nice and he was really good-looking. Would it hurt to have a bit of fun while she was here? *Yes, it would*, she told herself. *Don't get distracted. You're not here to meet men*.

He glanced back and caught her watching him. He gave her a little wave and turned back to the bar. *Where the hell's the bartender? What type of wine should I get her?* They definitely had a moment yesterday and today it was more than obvious that there was chemistry between them, but why had she resisted having a drink so much? Perhaps she was married. He had forgotten to check for a ring.

She was aligning the condiments in the middle of the table when he joined her and presented her with a glass of champagne.

"They didn't have any strawberries," he said sadly as he sat down opposite her with a bottle of beer for himself.

"You shouldn't have."

"But I have to make a good impression – it's our first date."

"This isn't a date," she scolded.

"Isn't it?" He raised his eyebrows and she shook her head in return. He held his hands up in defeat. "I know, I'm sorry. Wishful thinking on my part."

She was surprised at him being so forward. Unsure how to reply, she picked up her glass to take a sip when he suddenly said, "So, how do you know Jack Hudson?"

The question caught her totally off guard and she practically inhaled her champagne. She coughed and spluttered as the bubbles fizzed up the back of her throat and ran down her nose. She was mortified.

"Excuse me," she managed, catching her breath and fussing around in her bag for a tissue to wipe her nose.

He jumped up and rubbed her back. "Are you all right?"

She signalled that she was OK so he returned to his seat, chuckling to himself. He waited until she had composed herself before he continued. "I know you know him. I saw him look at you outside the courthouse yesterday and then again in there today. You know each other, but he's surprised you're here."

"Oh, you're good." She pointed her finger at him.

"So that's why you helped me get in there today – to see if you could get any information out of me for your story? You're just using me."

She brought her hand up to her face and pretended to trace a tear running down her cheek.

He flinched. He hadn't meant to upset her. "I'm sorry, I—"

"Mike, that's OK. I did the same to you yesterday." She chanced another sip of her drink – successfully this time.

He sat forward. "You did what?"

"I recognised you. I've read a few of your articles and the exclusive you wrote on Hudson when he was arrested." She didn't mention the obituary. "Yesterday, I thought it was you, but it was hard to tell because you're much more handsome in real life." She leant towards him. "I had to get up close to make sure. I know it was a bit tacky, but I had to make an impression to get you to notice me."

"You made an impression all right, but you could have just said hello."

She blushed. "I never thought of that."

With a roll of his eyes he asked his question again. "How do you know Jack Hudson?"

In an effort to buy some time, she took another sip of her drink. He didn't need to know everything, and he already thought she was a reporter, so that could work. "At the beginning of the year a colleague of mine was doing a story on Hudson – a big one. He told me he'd had a huge breakthrough – and the next day he was dead."

Mike shifted in his seat. "Dead?"

"Dead," she repeated. "I assume now that the

'story' Ray had meant was the embezzlement. I think Hudson found out Ray was on to him and killed him to bury the story."

"Killed him?" He rubbed his nose with his index finger. "No way, that's not Jack Hudson's style. I mean, embezzlement is a white-collar crime and you're talking about murder one. It's a hell of a jump."

She sat back in her chair and folded her arms. Now she was annoyed with him, which he quickly realised and tried to make amends.

"If it is true, what proof is there, who's your source, and what do you have in the way of evidence?"

There was no evidence. That was the problem. The police didn't even suspect foul play. She didn't think it would be wise, or safe, to reveal herself as the source just yet.

She banged her fist on the table. "None. I can't find anything linking him to the murder. I'm not saying he did it himself, but I know he was responsible." She took a deep breath. "I can't prove it yet. But I will. That's why he recognised me. I've been poking around and asking questions, and he knows I'm on to him. I just want to see him go down; I want justice for my friend. So…" – she took a long sip of her champagne – "that's why I need your help. I could do with some resources, and you seem like a pretty resourceful guy. What do you say to a joint exclusive? I'll share my byline with you."

He narrowed his eyes at her. "Well, there's an offer I can't refuse."

"Great." She looked pleased with herself and put her hand on his arm. "And I promise you won't regret it."

"I think I do already," he joked, taking a final gulp of

his beer.

"OK, I've got to go." She finished her drink in one mouthful and began to gather her stuff.

"I can't tempt you with another?" he asked as she stood up.

She was definitely tempted. She didn't really want to spend the evening alone in her hotel room obsessing about Ray and how she'd got him killed. She'd love to have more than another drink with him, but she had to be sensible. "You are very tempting, but no." She slid the strap of her handbag over her shoulder. "Same again tomorrow, then?"

"Only if you have a drink with me again afterwards – actually, two drinks," he added quickly. He had nothing to lose.

"Well, that doesn't sound too painful. You've got yourself a deal. I'll see you in the morning."

She gave him a quick peck on the cheek as she passed, then turned and gave him one last smile.

It nearly knocked him off his feet.

"Bye," was all he could manage as he watched her walk away.

He sat back down at the table, disappointed at the outcome of the evening but happy he had secured a second date. He caught the bartender's attention and signalled for another beer.

Her story was definitely intriguing. He tried to console himself that if he wasn't successful at getting the girl, he'd settle for a good story. But who was he trying to fool? He didn't give a damn about the story; he wanted the girl.

Chapter Five

The next morning, Mike arrived at the courthouse before Kate. Half-heartedly, he made small talk with the other members of the press as he waited impatiently. His eyes widened when he caught a glimpse of her walking up the street. Her stride was confident and she looked even more beautiful than the day before. She was wearing a long black dress with a silver belt round her waist. It made her slim body look taller than he had remembered. Her hair looked different too – not as straight as yesterday but slightly curly in the damp autumn morning.

She waved when she caught him watching and quickened her pace to get to him.

Excusing himself from the conversation, he stepped away from the other reporters. He wanted her all to himself. As she got closer, he tried to determine the correct protocol. Should he shake her hand, or kiss her cheek like she'd done the night before? He didn't want to make a fool of himself, so he decided to act casual and follow her lead.

"Good morning, Kate," he said with a smile.

"Morning, Mike."

She didn't kiss him. They stood and looked at each other in silence until Mike realised it was his turn to speak.

"This way, m'lady."

He led her towards the door. This time it was opened for them by the same officer, no questions asked.

"Thank you, Tony," Kate said. She noticed Mike slip something into his hand.

"Thanks, Mike." Tony nodded.

Once they were inside she asked, "What was that you just gave him?"

"His wife is a real theatre buff. I got him front row centre seats for that new musical, *Cats* or something." He tried to make light of his generous gesture.

She rolled her eyes at him. Not only was he gorgeous, but he was also thoughtful, generous and self-effacing. "That was really kind of you, but please let me know what it cost and I'll pay you back. After all, you were doing me a favour."

"Absolutely not. I was trying to get information from you too so let's call it even." He held the door open for her and they entered the courtroom.

It had been two hours since the closing arguments, and the jury had retired to deliberate their verdict. Mike and Kate had found a place to sit and wait in the busy atrium. He was beginning to type up his story and she was tapping the table with her nails, impatiently checking the time on her phone every other minute.

No longer able to ignore her agitation, he tried to distract her. "It shouldn't be too much longer. Why don't you go outside and get a bit of fresh air?"

She shook her head at him and checked her phone for the hundredth time.

He tried again. "Why don't you go and get a coffee? You could get me one too."

She looked up at him blankly. "What?"

"Coffee."

"Yes, please. Double espresso, no sugar."

He put his hand on her arm. "Why don't *you* go and get us some coffee? It'll take your mind off things."

"Sorry, I wasn't listening. Why the hell is it taking so long?"

He shrugged.

She groaned and picked up her bag. "How do you take your coffee?"

"It doesn't matter now. Here we go." He pointed to the bailiff, who had just opened the courtroom door. He started to pack away his things. "At least that didn't take too long."

She threw him a dirty look and gestured for him to hurry up.

There was little suspense in the courtroom as the judge asked the foreman to deliver the verdict.

Kate held her breath and watched the piece of paper as it travelled from the foreman of the jury to the judge's hand. She braced herself as the former spoke.

"Guilty."

There were gasps and whispers in the courtroom. Kate sighed with relief, a look of satisfaction on her face. She placed her hand on Mike's thigh and gave it a triumphant squeeze. Thrilled by the overly familiar touch, he looked down at her hand, placed his own on top and squeezed back. He fixed his gaze straight ahead, but out of the corner of his eye he saw she was looking at him. When her grip on his thigh tightened, he decided he wasn't going to ask her out for a drink after all; it would have to be dinner.

Jack Hudson looked at his wife in despair as he was led away to await sentencing.

The judge adjourned the court.

"How long do you think he'll get?" Kate asked as they left the courtroom for the final time.

"A few years."

"That's not much for murder," she complained.

Mike tried to reason with her. "But he wasn't on trial for murder."

"He soon will be. Is our deal still on? Are you going to help me do a bit of digging?"

"Yes, but only if you're sure there's something in it. You can come down to my office tomorrow. We'll trade information and see where we go from there."

"Great. You won't regret it."

"You know, you've said that to me once already, and the more you say it, the more I think I'm definitely going to regret it."

He pretended to cower as she playfully hit him on the arm, then glanced at her left hand. "In the interest of trading information, I need to ask. There's no ring on your finger, but that doesn't mean there isn't someone in London waiting by the phone to hear from you. Is there?"

"There isn't." She tried her best not to blush. "And how about you? Is there a Mrs Handsome Reporter I should be jealous of?"

"There isn't." He grinned. "And now we've got that out of the way, would you like to have dinner with me?"

"I'd love to."

Love to? He was taken aback, not just by her choice of words but by the fact she had agreed so easily. He had thought that, due to her reluctance the night before, he would have had to do at least a little persuading. And what about the age gap? He'd better test the waters. "You don't think I'm a bit too old for you?"

"Don't be silly. You're not that much older than me, and I don't think there's an age limit for dinner," she teased.

"And just so there's no confusion, this is a proper date, right?" he said, looking her up and down, lust in his eyes.

She did the same to him then nodded in agreement.

"How come you said no to a date last night but suddenly tonight it's OK?"

"I was trying to be sensible, but the more I see you the less sensible I want to be," she said flirtatiously.

"Good." He gave her a mischievous grin. "I know this great little steakhouse. You're not vegetarian, are you?"

She shook her head vigorously.

"Thank God for that. Now if you don't mind, I need five minutes to type up the story. I've got the basic outline. I just need to fill in the blanks and email it over so it can go in the morning paper."

He looked at her, slightly confused, only just noticing that she didn't have a laptop with her, or a pen and paper for that matter. "Don't you need to do the same?"

Panicking, she thought quickly. "No, everyone will have gone home by now. I'll do it when I get back to the hotel and they'll get it in the morning. But please take your time. I'll just go and freshen up."

Reeling from her lucky escape, she hurried away so he had no time to ask any follow-up questions.

In the ladies' room she stood at the sink and looked at

herself in the mirror. Her usually pale cheeks were bright pink. She wasn't sure if it was because she really liked Mike or because she had nearly been caught lying. It was probably both.

She considered telling him she wasn't really a reporter, but if she told him then maybe he wouldn't help her. She wafted her hands around her face in an effort to cool herself down, then opened her handbag and hunted for her lipstick. Once applied, she ran a brush through her hair and sprayed her wrists and neck with perfume.

She was ready but, before she turned away from the mirror, she gave herself a pep talk. "Remember, it's just dinner, nothing more. And don't drink too much – you know what wine does to you. Yes, I know he's nice but for God's sake don't sleep with him."

At that moment she realised she was not alone; another woman stood right beside her washing her hands. Kate turned slowly. The much older woman was staring at her, open-mouthed. Only then did Kate realise she had been talking out loud. But maybe another opinion was what she needed, so she asked, "Should I sleep with him?"

The woman simply shrugged and left.

Kate rolled her eyes. *Thanks for your help*. She took one last look at herself in the mirror and followed the woman back into the atrium.

Mike was typing with one eye on the screen and the other on the door of the ladies' room. His mind raced as he thought about the night ahead. Normally he wouldn't have any reservations but maybe Hooper was right, she was out of his league: beautiful, smart and younger. But she was sending out all the right signals, so he decided he had nothing to worry about.

Suddenly she was back on the bench next to him. She strained her neck to look over his shoulder at the words rapidly appearing on the screen.

He noticed what she was doing and warned her, "No plagiarism." Then he repositioned the screen so she could get a better look.

"You make that look really easy," she said as he continued to type.

"I'm sure it's just as easy for you. I mean, this case was so predictable it practically writes itself."

She sat in silence. As she waited, she looked around at the courthouse, which was nearly empty. She thought about everyone's journey home. Who or what were they going home to? She thought about Jack Hudson and wondered if he was still in the building or on his way to prison. She felt Mike nudge her.

"OK, that's done. Just gotta send this and…" He made sure she was watching as he hit the send button. He closed his laptop and declared, "I'm all yours."

She rubbed her hands together. "Really? What *am* I going to do with you?"

He slid his laptop safely back in its carry case and stood up. "Anything you want, but let's start with dinner."

The taxi dropped them off in front of an Italian restaurant. Mike held the door and as Kate walked in she was stunned to see a long bar and a large dining area. It must have been a popular place as it was already very busy. As they waited at the maître d' stand the bartender waved to Mike, who waved back.

"I'm a regular here. I hate cooking and they do a great steak."

The maître d' held out his hand as he approached. "Ciao, Michael. Your usual table?"

"No, Giovanni, tonight I think I'll have a table for two," he said proudly.

Kate thought it would be fun to play along. "Oh my…" She raised her hand to her mouth and pretended to be embarrassed for him.

"Va bene, signorina," said the maître d', playing his own game. "Michael is a most valued customer – he brings us *molte belle donne*."

"Giovanni," Mike scolded.

"Più bella di me?" She pouted as Giovanni took her hand.

"Non è possibile, signorina." He brought her hand to his lips and kissed it softly. *"Sei mai stata in Italia…?"*

"Kate. *Ci sono stata qualche volta."*

He took Kate's arm and whispered into her ear as he led her to the table. Mike followed, not entirely able to hear – or understand – what the two were giggling about.

Giovanni pulled out her chair. *"É un piacere conoscerti,* Kate. *Al suo servizio."*

She gave him a warm smile as she sat and he turned to Mike.

"Scusa, Michael. Rosa will be with you soon. Enjoy your evening."

Mike took his seat. "You speak Italian?"

"A little."

"No, *ciao* is a little. What were you two giggling about? If it was about the last time I was here…"

Her jaw dropped. "It wasn't, but now you're going

to have to spill the beans."

He shifted in his seat. "Last month I had a horrific date here. My daughter had been bugging me to get out more, but I work long hours and it's hard to meet women the old-fashioned way. So she signed me up to some online dating thing and convinced me to go on a date." He groaned. "I only did it once and I knew it would be a total disaster so that's why I brought her here. At least I knew I would enjoy the food."

"Is that why you brought me here?" She tutted.

"No, I brought *you* here to show you off."

She narrowed her eyes at him. "But Giovanni said you're here all the time with lots of women."

"Yes, but over the years. I'm not Hooper."

"Hooper?"

"A good friend. He's one of the most intelligent people I know but he thinks monogamy is a type of wood."

They were laughing as the waitress arrived to take their drinks order. Without asking, Mike ordered the same drinks as they'd had the night before.

"So, you have children?"

He nodded. "Yes, one daughter, Claire. She's…" He coughed. "Twenty-six."

Kate gasped. "She's how old?"

"Twenty-six." He gritted his teeth. "And she also has a child…"

"You're a *grandfather*?" She brought her hand to her mouth in a futile effort to suppress her amusement. "You do not look old enough."

"Thanks. I'm just about old enough. I got married straight out of college. My ex-wife and I were already engaged, but let's just say the baby sped things up a little. And don't say *grandfather*. I'm not ready for a retirement home just yet. I'm more a New Age cool Grandpa or Gramps. Check him out."

He reached into his jacket pocket and pulled out a well-used brown wallet to retrieve a picture of his grandson. "His name is Little Mikey and he's not quite a year old. What do you think?"

Proudly he offered her the photo. She made a point of brushing his hand as she took the picture. She studied it. "Aw, Mike, he's absolutely gorgeous." She looked into his eyes. "Just like his gramps."

He genuinely blushed and felt that the night was going exactly the way he wanted it to, even after the revelation that he was a grandfather.

They were so busy staring at each other that they didn't even notice the waitress arrive with their drinks. She shifted from foot to foot as she tried to get their attention. "Are you ready to order?" she asked eventually.

"You go first, Mike, you probably already know what you want," Kate said as she scanned the menu.

"I certainly do." He rubbed his foot against hers and she gave him a coy smile. "Oh, you mean food? I'll have my usual."

The waitress nodded and turned to Kate.

"You have a usual? Well, I'll have the same then, please."

"But you don't even know what it is."

"You told me it was going to be steak and you've obviously got good taste. So I'm sure it'll be perfect, but make mine medium, please," she added as she handed the menu back to the waitress.

"Two mediums. Will there be anything else?"

"A bottle of the cabernet. Thank you, Rosa."

As the waitress left he pointed to Kate's glass of champagne. "You can't drink *that* with steak."

She rolled her eyes. *He ordered it.* "Tell me more about your online dating experience," she said and smirked.

"Ssh, forget I mentioned it. It's so embarrassing. I only did it once, to get Claire off my back. No, let's change the subject. I want to know more about you." He leant towards her. "I find it hard to believe there's no one waiting for you back home. How come a smart, beautiful woman like you is single?"

"Because I am smart, I want to be single." She winked.

He narrowed his eyes at her. "No. Come on, what happened to you? What's your story?"

"Honestly, it's a pretty boring one. I've had some nice boyfriends and some that weren't so nice, but I'm happiest on my own."

They were interrupted by the waitress, who had arrived to pour the wine. Kate welcomed the distraction. She never liked the way people made assumptions about her life. When she was young she had decided not to waste time on relationships or building a career; life was too short for her to be pinned down to one person or thing.

"Enough about me. Tell me about your daughter. Do you get on well with her?"

"Yeah, we're really close. After her mom and I divorced she stayed at my place whenever she wanted. Mostly weekends, but after her mom had more kids she stayed all the time. She and Little Mikey still sleep over sometimes when her husband is out of town with work."

"That's nice."

He noticed that she took a longer than usual sip of wine. "If that changes things and you don't want to stay for dinner..."

She rolled her eyes. "We're not teenagers, for crying out loud, we both have pasts. I was actually wondering why you got divorced, but it's none of my business."

"I don't mind talking about it." He shrugged. "It's nice to get the chance to tell my side of the story. Everyone just assumes my marriage ended because I had an affair."

She grimaced. "Did you?"

"No. Well, not with a woman. I'm a workaholic. I didn't have time for one relationship, never mind two. But it wasn't all my fault. I was what she made me. Audrey quit college and wanted to be a stay-at-home mom, so I worked hard. Then she wanted Claire to go to the best schools, have the best tutors, dancing lessons, horse riding, skiing, music, so I worked harder." He rubbed his temples. "But the list was endless and all of that cost money, so I had to work even harder. The more I earned, the more she spent. I didn't have time to be a husband, a father and a provider and in the end, something had to give. So ... I gave up the husband bit. It seemed the most logical." He shook his head. "You know those families that have it all? I take my hat off to them 'cause it's hard, it's really hard to make it all work."

"You don't need to convince me, Mike." She placed her hand on his arm. "That's exactly why I've avoided all that crap. It's just easier on my own, with no complications."

"So you've never been married? Do you have any kids?"

"No and God no."

He sighed. "I can't believe I'm talking about my divorce on our first date and you're not giving anything away. Tell me about your childhood, then. What are your parents like?"

"Well, my mum was young when she had me. My dad was never in the picture. She was an only child too, so when my grandparents passed away it was just the two of us. We had a good time, though – we were really close."

"Were close? You're not any more?"

"No. She died of a massive heart attack when I was fifteen."

He sat back in his chair and looked concerned. "Fifteen? But you didn't have any other family. What did you do?"

"I was put in foster care." She took a sip of wine.

Stunned, he leant forward. "I'm so sorry, Kate."

"Don't be. It was OK. My foster parents were great – they are great. They have two sons of their own and there was always, like, two or three of us foster kids at any one time. It was different being part of a family, a real change of pace. I stayed with them until I was eighteen. They wanted me to stay longer, unofficially, but I would have been taking up a bed and there was always someone who needed it more than me. I'm still very much in touch with them, especially when I'm back in London."

"*Back* in London? Where are you usually?"

"All over. I love to travel. It's their fault, actually. I

told them I didn't want to go to uni straight away, I wanted to see the world before I had any ties or commitments. So for my eighteenth birthday they gave me a map of the world and inside was one thousand pounds, a plane ticket to Guernsey and a voucher for a week in a hostel there."

"What's a gurney?" he joked.

"Guernsey is a small English island off the coast of France. It's really popular with fruit-pickers and gap-year students so they thought that would start me off on the right foot. And it was amazing. I fell in with a group of French kids and at the end of the week they were headed home so I jumped on the ferry and went with them. I took it from there. I went all the way around the world and didn't set foot in London again for three years. And then I only stayed a few months before I took off again."

He shook his head in awe. "What a gift. Your foster parents sound amazing."

"Amazing doesn't even begin to describe them. Actually, you'd probably get on well with them – you have so much in common. They're in their sixties with grandkids too."

He pretended to be offended. By way of an apology she gave his leg a little rub with her foot. He was busy reciprocating when the waitress arrived with their food.

She continued to tell him about her travels while they ate. He hung on her every word and watched her, mesmerised. She was so animated, waving her hands around to embellish her stories, describing the sights, sounds and smells of the places she had been. At one point she had the couple at the next table laughing along with them – they couldn't help overhearing and getting drawn into her story about the time she and her best friend were so broke that they had to work on a fishing trawler off the coast of Norway for two weeks.

In return he told her a few stories about his days at summer camp, his childhood holidays and the fishing trips he made with his brother. She laughed as he tried his hardest to make his stories sound more interesting, after hearing hers. He even compared the time he got a blister on his big toe as a result of pushing his teething daughter in her buggy the length of Central Park to Kate's shin splints after she spent a summer walking the 500-mile Camino de Santiago.

A glance at her phone showed they had been talking for hours. She looked around to find that they were among the few people left in the restaurant.

"Oh my goodness, would you look at the time? I should really get going."

He gritted his teeth. "That was abrupt. I hope I'm not boring you."

"Not at all. I'm still on London time" – she pointed to the second empty wine bottle – "and I really shouldn't drink any more wine."

He leant in, looking serious. "I thought you wanted to be *less* sensible?"

She gave him a scolding look and he relented, not wanting to push his luck too far.

"I'll settle the bill."

After he had paid, he stepped out onto the street and held the door open, but Kate didn't appear. He popped his head back inside and found her chatting in Italian to Giovanni and some of the waiting staff. He leant against the door and enjoyed watching as they talked like long-lost friends. He thought she was amazing; he could watch her for hours.

After a few minutes she waved and mouthed 'sorry', made her excuses and joined him outside.

"It's stopped raining," she said. "I'm sorry to keep you waiting but I was just hearing a few stories about you. It seems you're quite well thought of in this little town, by this family especially. I can't believe you got Rosa's boyfriend a job at your paper."

He blushed. "I didn't – he got it on his own. I just helped him word his résumé and coached him a little for his interview."

"Either way, it was a lovely thing to do." She looked him in the eye while she adjusted his tie. "Thank you so much. I had a great night."

"It was my pleasure."

He debated whether or not to kiss her then and there. She was certainly standing close enough and technically she had already made the first move by touching his tie. But he decided it would be best to wait and see what she did next.

"And I'm sorry to cut it short, but the jet lag has finally caught up with me. Would you please hail me a cab?"

Damn it, he thought, but was relieved that he hadn't tried to kiss her. Nevertheless, he thought he could still turn the situation to his advantage. "Where are you going?"

"To my hotel," she replied with a puzzled look.

He tried to reassure her. "Which hotel, where? So I can tell the driver."

"I'm not thinking – it's the wine. It's on 7th and

West 46th street."

"That's just a few blocks away. Like you said, it's a nice night. It would be a shame to waste it. May I walk you home?" He offered her his hand.

She thought for a moment before she answered. If he walked her back, he might expect her to ask him in, and she had already made the decision not to sleep with him. *But that was before dinner,* she tried to argue with herself. *And how many glasses of wine have I had?* she argued back. She thought it would be best to make her feelings clear.

"That would be lovely, but when we get there I'm going in alone."

"Of course." Pretending to be offended, he threw his hands in the air. "I wouldn't come in even if you wanted me to." He said it so firmly that he almost believed it himself.

She took his hand and they began to walk along the brightly lit avenue. She felt so comfortable with him, as if she had known him for years. She rested her head on his shoulder and after walking a block he felt bold enough to put his arm around her.

As they walked he told her how he had moved his young family to New York when he got his first newspaper job, and that he could never see himself living anywhere else. He told her the best places to eat and drink in the city and more, importantly, where she could get the best coffee.

When they turned the corner onto Times Square, she sighed.

"Is everything OK?" he asked.

"Perfect. I love the lights. They remind me of when I was young. My mum and I moved to London when I was five. On the first night, she took me to Piccadilly Circus. I'd never seen anything like it before. It was magical. I thought all the stars had come down from the sky to say hello."

"That sounds beautiful. Would you believe, I've never been to London?"

Playfully she slapped his shoulder. "Why the hell not? It's a great city, although it has a totally different vibe to New York. You see this place in movies all the time and it's like you know it before you even get here. But there's a lot more history in London, it's mysterious and exciting. You have to go there."

"I certainly like what I've seen of it so far." He turned towards her and saw the moonlight reflected in her beautiful brown eyes. At that moment he wanted nothing more than to kiss her but he resisted; she'd made her feelings perfectly clear.

She could tell by the look in his eye that he was about to kiss her. She took a deep breath to prepare herself.

"Here we are."

She looked around and was shocked to see the hotel. Devastated that he hadn't kissed her, she soon composed herself. "Thank you again for dinner. It was great."

"But the company was better." He looked down at his feet. "Hey, this is a nice hotel. What room are you staying in?"

It took all her effort to shake her finger at him. "You're not coming in, Mike."

"I know, I've said I won't, but I was thinking maybe I'd give you a call later just to let you know I got home safely."

"It's room 968 and that's really sweet, but I'll be asleep as soon as my head hits the pillow."

"Then I promise I won't call." He took out his wallet and handed her a business card. "I'll see you at my office. Just give me a call when you're in the lobby and I'll come down and get you."

She looked into his eyes and made a point of brushing his hand as she took the card. "I'm sorry I can't ask you in. I think I want to but I'm not one hundred per cent sure it's not the wine. I don't want to do anything I might regret in the morning."

"I understand, but just do one thing for me..."

"What?"

He gave her a little nudge. "Kiss me, Kate."

She clipped him on the arm. "That is so cheesy. How long have you been waiting to say that?"

He was thrilled she got the reference. "Since I found out your name was Kate. But you don't have to kiss me." He extended his hand for her to shake but she grabbed it and pulled him close. The smell of her perfume engulfed him as their bodies touched, and before he'd even had time to prepare himself, he felt her lips on his. As she kissed him softly, her warm breath on his lips sent adrenaline rushing through his veins. But as quickly as it had started, it was over. She had broken the kiss and taken a step backwards.

He stared at her, trying desperately to suppress the urge that was building inside him, then he realised that she hadn't walked away. He took a step towards her and kissed her back just as softly. She threw her arms around his neck and kissed him more intensely. Enjoying the gentle scratch of his stubble on her skin and the firm touch of his hand at the small of her back, she moaned as she accepted his tongue into her mouth. At that moment she wanted to melt into him so they could never be separated. Instead she broke away, leaving him breathless.

She rested her forehead on his chest and they stood in silence and caught their breath. After a few seconds she raised her head and looked him in the eye. "I'll see you in the morning."

Before he had a chance to respond she kissed him quickly on the lips, turned and hurried into the hotel.

Stunned, he could do nothing but stare at the door. Perhaps if he waited, she would change her mind and come back out. So he waited, but after a few minutes when she didn't reappear, he hailed a cab.

Disappointed, he climbed in slowly but kept his eyes on the hotel door, just in case.

"Where to?" the driver asked.

Mike was silent.

"Where?" he repeated.

"If a woman gave you her number but asked you not to call, would you call anyway?"

The driver turned to face him. "No. It's a test. *Women*. Forget the number and wait. She will call you."

"You're probably right, thanks. Riverside Drive, please." He took one last look at the hotel door before the cab sped uptown.

Kate walked through the lobby regretting her decision not to ask him in. She couldn't help wonder how good the sex would be, if a kiss was that good. She got goose bumps just thinking about it. Would it really hurt to let her guard down, just a little?

As she waited for the lift, she decided she had

made the right decision and if she still wanted to sleep with him in the cold light of day, with the very real possibility of a hangover, she would act on it then. *Yes, that's sensible.*

The lift door opened. As she stepped in, she retrieved Mike's business card from her pocket. She studied it and decided to call him to check he got home OK. *It'll be cute, he'll get a kick out of it.*

Just as the lift door was about to close, she heard a male voice.

"Hold the elevator, please."

Is that Mike? Excited, she scrambled to press the button to hold the door but let out a sigh when she saw it wasn't him.

"Nine, please."

"You must be following me," she joked as she pointed to the number nine, which was already illuminated, and turned to face the man as the doors closed.

He was tall with blond hair, probably in his mid-fifties and very well built. She would have found him mildly attractive if the smell of stale smoke from his hoodie hadn't made her feel a little queasy.

"Nice night for a walk, isn't it?" he asked.

"Yes. I'm glad it's stopped raining – that's the first time since I got here."

"Are you here on business or pleasure?"

"A bit of both." She felt her cheeks beginning to burn as she thought about Mike.

"How come you didn't invite him in?"

She was taken aback. "Who?"

"The guy you were kissing out there on the street. It was kinda gross." He sneered. "Why don't you want to sleep with him?"

"I beg your pardon?" she said sharply.

"I'm sorry, Kate. I've had a few drinks and I always get a bit too direct. It did look like a good kiss. All I meant was, he looks old enough to be your dad."

Her eyes widened. *What an asshole!* What was he even talking about? Mike wasn't that much older than her.

"Sorry, there I go again. I'll just stop talking." He smirked.

"I think that would be best," she agreed and turned away from him to face the door.

Then she panicked. *Did he just call me Kate?* No, he couldn't have. The Hudson thing had made her paranoid and she must have misheard.

Fixing her eyes straight ahead, she made sure she had her key card ready and stood in an uneasy silence until the lift doors opened at the ninth floor. She rushed out of the lift, almost trampling over a bellboy, and hurried towards her room, positive she could hear footsteps behind her. She was too afraid to look.

By the time she reached the door, her hands were shaking so much that it took several attempts for her to slide the key card into the slot. She yanked down the handle and flung the door open. Once inside she slammed it shut, locked it and pressed her eye up against the peephole. There was no one out there.

She watched for a moment before panic took over and she reached for the light. She spun around, expecting someone to be in the room with her. She grabbed the iron from the dressing table and held it as she searched the room – everywhere big enough for someone to conceal themselves. There was no one there.

She was about to sit on the side of the bed when she noticed the bathroom door was ajar. Had she left it that way? She lifted the iron once more and walked towards the bathroom, pushed the door open and switched on the light.

Empty.

She returned to the bedroom, sat at the dressing table and looked at herself in the mirror. Trying to steady her breathing, she told herself, *Get a grip, Kate. Why would someone be following you? No one even knows you're here.*

She took two miniature bottles of vodka from the minibar, her hand still shaking as she opened one, put it to her lips and drank it in one go. She shrugged it off as paranoia. The man from the lift wasn't following her, he was just a creep.

Feeling a little foolish, she got undressed, set the alarm on her phone and drank the other bottle of vodka before climbing into bed. There were noises outside in the corridor and on the floors above and below. Feeling alone and uneasy, she turned the television on for company and tried to relax.

The vodka on top of the wine didn't take long to kick in. She closed her eyes and forgot all about the phone call to Mike she had planned to make.

Chapter Six

Next morning, a freshly shaven Mike arrived at the hotel first thing. He nodded as he held the door open for a couple of tourists but shook his head when they didn't acknowledge him. *And I thought New Yorkers were meant to be rude...*

As he walked towards the reception desk, he scanned the lobby for Kate. He tapped out a tune on the desk with his fingers as he waited for the manager to finish a phone call. The manager hung up and greeted him with a nod. "Good morning, sir. How may I help you?"

"Good morning. Can you tell me what room Miss Kate Turner is in, please?"

"I'm sorry, sir, guest information is private."

"Oh, it's OK. I know she's staying here, I dropped her off outside last night."

"Sorry, sir, I can't help you. Hotel policy."

Mike persisted. "OK, please just give her a call and tell her Mike Kelly is here. I promise she won't mind." He put his hands in his pockets and looked pleased with himself.

"Sorry, sir. Is there anything else I can help you with?"

At that moment the manager noticed Kate stepping out of the lift. She caught his eye and gave him a little smile. Then she noticed Mike at the desk and headed towards them.

Unamused at his lack of progress, Mike gestured to

the sofas in the lobby. "I'm just going to take a seat over there and wait, unless you have a policy against that?"

"No policy, but perhaps the young lady behind you is the one you are looking for."

Mike turned to find Kate looking stunning in the blue dress she had been wearing when they first met. Words escaped him and it took all his effort to resist the urge to grab her by the hand and take her back to her room to finish what they had started the night before.

"Mike, what are you doing here? I thought we were going to meet at your office later." She looked at him closely, narrowing her eyes. "You look different – did you shave?"

He touched his face; he didn't think it would be that obvious. "I blew off my first meeting. I thought we could have breakfast."

"Great, I'm starving, but what's going on here?" She gestured to the manager, who was still staring at Mike. She gave him an apologetic smile and he excused her with a nod.

"Well, I asked this guy for your room number and he said you weren't even staying here."

"But I gave you my room number last night. What sort of a reporter can't remember a simple detail like that? I hope you haven't lost your edge."

"My edge? After that kiss, I nearly lost my mind. I thought about calling you all night, but I promised I wouldn't. But it's your loss because you missed out on a really dirty phone call."

She laughed as he took her hand.

"I just couldn't wait to see you. I couldn't stop thinking about you. I really want another kiss."

"So that's why you shaved." She ran the back of her finger down his cheek and under his chin, then brushed his bottom lip with her thumb and finally let her palm rest on his chest. "I was thinking about it too. In fact, I nearly called you." She took a small step closer to him.

"You should have." He took a step closer to her so that their bodies were almost touching. "I'd have rushed straight back down here."

They stared into each other's eyes and their breathing altered. They inched closer... Just as their lips were about to meet, they were interrupted by the sound of the manager clearing his throat. They turned and glared at him.

"Is there anything else I can help you with, miss? Sir?"

As they pulled apart, the manager pointed to the queue that was forming behind them. They blushed and turned back to face each other.

"Come on, I need some coffee." She grabbed Mike's hand and led him quickly out of the hotel.

After a leisurely breakfast and conversation, which consisted mostly of outrageous flirting and sexual innuendo, they arrived at Mike's office.

The *New York Times* building stood proud in the middle of bustling Eighth Avenue. Its impressive glass and steel facade soared towards the sky and glistened in the morning sun.

"I've been past here a few times when I've been in town, but I've never actually stopped to look at this place. It's stunning."

"So you've never been inside?" he asked.

She shook her head.

"Then you're in for a real treat."

He led her through the large glass doors into the busy lobby and walked straight ahead. "Look." He pointed at hundreds of tiny screens fixed to the walls that lined the lobby. The sound of a typewriter could be heard as the screens showed random quotes and headlines from the history of the *New York Times*.

"There must be hundreds of them," she exclaimed as she looked around, trying to read them all.

He enjoyed her excitement. "And check this out..."

She followed his finger to the glass wall, behind which was an open garden surrounded by the building itself.

"Are those real?" she enquired, pointing to the birch trees. "And is that a theatre over there?"

"It's the auditorium. But come on. I'll get you signed in and you can come down and look again later if you want."

They were the only ones waiting for the lift. Mike realised that he was about to get her totally alone for the first time – for a few seconds, at least. He leant over and whispered into her ear, "Wait until I get you into that elevator."

He slid his arm around her waist. She drew in a breath and smiled at him. As the doors opened, he ushered her into the empty lift and they turned to face the door, expectant. He held down the button. As the doors closed, he turned to face her. She held her breath in anticipation of what was to come. As he raised his hand to touch her face, the door opened again and a young man stepped in.

"Oh hey, Mike." He waved.

"Hey, Chuck," Mike replied, his teeth gritted.

Chuck nodded politely to Kate, totally unaware that he was gate-crashing. Mike glanced over at her. She had her hand over her mouth trying to suppress her laughter. He was unimpressed.

The short journey up seemed to take an age. When the door opened on the third floor the three occupants filed out into another small reception area.

"Morning, Chuck, morning, Mike," the receptionist called as they walked by.

"Morning, Connie," Mike replied and pointed to Kate. "This is Kate and she'll be around for a few days."

Kate proudly showed her visitor's pass.

They walked into a large double-height open-plan office. The desks were laid out in a grid fashion with small offices down either side. She was surprised at how busy it was for so early in the morning: people were already talking on phones, fixed to computer screens and some just sat around talking, but pretended to look busy when they saw Mike approaching.

Hooper caught Mike's eye and gave him a thumbs-up as they passed. Mike glared at him. He opened his office door and turned on the light. "Come on in."

She walked in and stopped beside him, then pointed outside to the maze of desks. "Are you their boss?"

"Some of them."

"So you're handsome and successful?" She placed her bag on the floor beside his desk and had a look around the office, which had glass walls. "It's nice that they're sticking with the glass theme in here, although it's a shame it isn't a little more private..."

He gasped. "Are you kidding? At the hotel I knew I

should have suggested breakfast in bed."

"You should have."

Her hand was back on his chest.

"Would you have said yes?"

She shrugged. "I guess we'll never know."

They moved in close to each other again, but this time her breasts were pressed tight against his chest. He rested his hand on her hip.

"OK, lady, here's what's going to happen. I'm going to take you on another date tonight, but I have to warn you that I won't give up so easy. I want you, Kate."

He looked her up and down. He could just see the outline of her bra under her dress. His eyes fixed on her breasts, and he was busy wondering what she looked like in her underwear when she cleared her throat.

"Eyes up, Mike."

He didn't take his eyes off her chest. "Sorry, just stealing a little preview."

"Of what?" She placed her fingers on his chin and tilted his head up so she could lock eyes with him. "So you think I'm going to jump into bed with you on the *second* date?"

"I hope so." He ran his tongue along his bottom lip before he composed himself and said more seriously, "But I'm a gentleman so there's no pressure. The third date will be fine."

"Phew." She pretended to wipe sweat from her brow but was secretly impressed by his candour.

"Will you be OK in here while I'm at my meeting?"

"Yes. I'll just have a little snoop through your stuff."

"That's fine," he said. "I shouldn't be too long."

"I'll get my laptop out. Don't worry, I won't touch any of your stuff."

He whispered into her ear. "But I really want you to touch my *stuff*."

He lingered, desperate to kiss her but very aware of the sets of eyes that were pretending not to stare in at them from the main office. Instead, out of sight, he took her hand and played with her fingers. "Bye."

"Bye," she whispered and with her other hand she caressed the outside of his thigh. He let go of her hand, picked up a folder from his desk and left the office.

Not knowing what to do with herself, she had a good look around. The shelves were untidy with piles of unevenly stacked books. The ones standing upright didn't even seem to be in any order – none that she could make out, anyway. On the floor, heaps of books, old newspapers and journals were delicately stacked like a game of literary Jenga.

His college degrees hung on the wall surrounded by framed newspaper and magazine articles she assumed he'd written. Among them was a portrait of the old *New York Times* building in Times Square. It seemed that he really loved his job – and he was good at it too, according to the awards on top of the filing cabinet.

The desk was tidier than the rest of the office. There was a framed photo of Little Mikey and another of a young woman in her graduation gown – she assumed it was his daughter. She pulled out his chair and sat down, moved the computer keyboard to the side and replaced it with her laptop case.

She thought about the previous night, and their kiss. It was obvious he wanted more to happen, but she wasn't sure if it was such a great idea. It wasn't that she didn't like him; on the contrary, she liked everything about him. But a long-term relationship wasn't something she wanted, and she didn't want to lead him on. She laughed to herself when she realised she was overthinking it. It was a second date, not a marriage proposal.

One of the last to arrive in the conference room, Mike leant up against the wall to let the young woman who rushed in behind him take the last seat at the large wooden table. The room was noisy: over two dozen editors and department heads shouted over each other. There was some laughter and heated debate as they talked through the day's stories and pitched new ideas.

When he was promoted to editor, he used to love these meetings and got really fired up by them, but now he just found them tedious and time-consuming.

"Glad you could make it to this one, Mike, we were going to start without you," someone joked.

"Well, that would have been the second time," he replied with a grin. That morning's meeting was the first he had missed in years.

The noise subsided as the door closed behind Bob, the Associate Managing Editor. He looked agitated as he took his seat. "Let's make this quick. Simmons…"

Everyone went silent as he pointed to a man at the back who looked uncomfortable.

"Way to drop the ball on that medical malpractice piece. Next time double-check your sources – you know what it looks like when we have to print a retraction."

There were jeers and a few paper missiles thrown as Simmons held up his hands in defence.

Bob looked around the room. "And congratulations to Mike, who actually earned his salary this month. He schlepped his typewriter all the way down to the courthouse for the Hudson trial and wrote a pretty decent piece too."

There was a small round of applause and some cheers. Mike gave a quick bow. "Just like riding a bike, Bob."

"OK, let's get to work. Who's got what?" Bob checked his notepad and looked around the room.

"Hey, Bob, I might have a lead on another Hudson story – a lot juicier than embezzlement."

He raised his eyebrows at Mike. "Really? What's the hook?"

"I don't want to say just yet. I met a journalist from London at the trial. She's waiting in my office now and she says she has information on something else he was connected to. I think it's worth exploring."

"OK, you can look into it when you get a minute but don't waste too much time if there's nothing solid in it. The owners will have my ass for wasting resources. It's all about the budget, as you well know."

He turned away from Mike and addressed the room. "What's next? Anyone know if Albright has finished that Central Park thing yet?"

Everyone groaned.

After the meeting, Mike returned to his office to find Kate looking comfortable behind his desk. Elbow on the table and chin resting on the palm of her hand, she chewed on a fingernail while she stared intently at her laptop.

He leant against the door frame and watched in silence as he thought about the night before. They had great chemistry and that kiss had been out of this world, but she was out of his league and they lived on different continents. There was no way a relationship like that would last.

He felt a bit foolish when he realised he was jumping the gun. They hadn't even slept together yet and he was thinking long-term. As she wrapped her lips around her finger, he wanted to storm the office and take her right there on the desk but instead he knocked gently on the door. "May I come in?"

As she looked up an enormous smile grew across her face. She held out her hand and invited him to take the seat in front of her.

"I feel like I'm at a job interview," he joked as he straightened his tie and sat down.

Playfully she tapped her fingers against her cheek and screwed up her face, looking thoughtful. "Hmm, I can think of a *job* I'd like to give you…"

His jaw dropped.

She held his gaze and they sat in silence until there was another knock at the door.

Kate sat up straight and tucked her hair behind her ear as Hooper entered the office. He looked back and forth between them. "I'm not interrupting anything, am I?"

"No, Hooper." Mike was bashful. "Erm, this is Kate. Kate, this is Hooper. He's going to help you out if he can."

Hooper walked over to the desk and extended his hand. "Pleased to meet you. I've heard a lot about you already."

He winked at Mike, who glared at him.

"All good, I hope." She stood up to shake his hand and walked to the other side of the desk, gesturing to Mike that he could reclaim his rightful seat. "Hooper, what do you know about Jack Hudson?"

"Straight to it, eh?"

"Well, there's not much point in tiptoeing around, is there?"

"No, I suppose not. Mike tells me you think he had someone killed?"

"Not just someone, a friend of mine" – she remembered her lie – "a colleague, actually. I don't have any real proof yet, but I know the story Ray was doing on Hudson got him killed. I've got some of the documents he was working on scanned onto my laptop. I've looked at them a million times and I can't see what the story is – it doesn't even seem like embezzlement. I think a fresh pair of eyes might see something I'm missing." She pointed at them. "So that's where you two come in."

Hooper wasn't buying it. "Well, I can't right this minute. I have to tidy up a story for today."

"And babe, I have a pile of work I have to get to this morning; we are trying to put together a newspaper here," Mike said apologetically.

She winced. *Did he just call me babe?* "You can just say no if you want to, guys, I'll be fine on my own."

Mike tried to backtrack. "It's not that I don't want to help, but I'm not a reporter any more. I've got another job to do. But you can hang out here with me, and I'll get you everything we have on Hudson. I'll have to request it from the archives so it might take a day or two."

She tilted her head. It seemed like he had a lot on his plate. "OK. I'll go and get us all some coffee and sandwiches so you don't have to stop for lunch, and the sooner you're finished your work, the sooner you can start helping me." She grabbed her bag and breezed towards the door. "See you later."

Hooper pointed to the closing door. "Jeez, I thought you were bossy. But you're right, she is beautiful: great legs, ass looks nice and tight, but the tits could be a little bigger."

"*Hooper!*"

"Sorry. I forgot she was your girlfriend. Have you slept with her yet?"

"No, I only met her three days ago."

"Exactly! What's keeping you? If it was me, I'd be on her already."

"If it was you, she'd be a distant memory already." He shuffled some papers on his desk.

"Do you think she's right about Hudson having that guy killed?"

Mike checked the door to make sure she was really gone before he shook his head. "I can't see it, but she seems convinced. What harm could it do to let her stick around for a few days? She certainly brightens up the place." He grinned.

Hooper squinted at him. "You really like her, don't you? And I saw the look she gave you. She's into you too."

Mike scratched his cheek. "You think so?"

"Trust me, I know what I'm talking about. But just be careful, old man – women like that usually eat poor saps like you for breakfast." He winked. "Just say the word and I'll be more than happy to take her off your hands."

"Get out of my office!" Mike threw a newspaper at Hooper, who dodged it perfectly and hurried out of the office.

***

That evening they had dinner in a busy Greek restaurant. Mike had finished his meal. He watched Kate push her uneaten food around the plate.

"Thanks again for looking at that stuff for me. Hooper didn't find anything either?"

She tutted when he shook his head. "I was sure there was something I was missing, but maybe not. *Damn it*. I just don't want him to get away with it. I don't know how much time I have to devote to this before I have to go home."

He shifted in his seat. "Just wait and see what else we can turn up. I've requested the stuff from the archives and asked Hooper to make a few calls. I'm sure something will show up."

"There has to be another way to get information. I just haven't thought of it yet."

"You don't give up, do you?"

"No. When I set my sights on something, I usually get it."

Sitting up straight, he adjusted his tie. "Oh, really? Have you set your sights on anything else?"

She sighed and rubbed her temples.

He panicked. "Did I say something wrong?"

There was a slight hesitation before she answered. "No, you said everything right and you seem like a great guy—"

"It's the 'it's not you, it's me' speech?" he interrupted. He was more than confused. After the kiss they had shared last night, all that flirting and inappropriate touching today, he was sure she wanted to take things further. How could he have got it so wrong?

She tried to speak but he held his hand up to stop her. "I'm a big boy. I can take it. I can't say I'm not disappointed, but I'll still help you out with the Hudson thing if you want. Come down to my office tomorrow—"

"Can I speak now? Like I was saying, you seem like a great guy and it's obvious we have chemistry but I'm only in town for a few days and if something were to happen between us, that's all it would be. Just a few days, nothing more." She shrugged. "I just wanted to make sure you were OK with that."

He raised an eyebrow. "So, you're just looking for some company while you're in town?"

She felt her temperature rise. "Exactly. Although I wasn't looking for company but then there you were."

"Lucky me." He grinned. "You're in luck too because I've been told that I'm excellent company."

"I don't always believe everything I'm told so I'm going to need proof of that…"

"I'll prove it right now. Do you want to get out of here?"

"I do." She rubbed her foot against his leg as he had done the night before. "Whose place is closer?"

"Mine," he said quickly. "It's even closer if we catch a cab."

She picked up her napkin and softly dabbed her mouth before tossing it onto her plate. "Cab it is, then."

"I'll get the bill." He stood up slowly without breaking eye contact, then quickly made his way towards the hostess.

Her eyes followed him across the restaurant, and she watched, amused, as he spoke to the young, attractive hostess, totally unaware that she was flirting with him as he settled the bill.

He arrived back at the table and sat down. Looking anxious, he checked his watch.

She raised her eyebrows. "What's wrong? Have you got somewhere else to be?"

"Yes, I do. She's just calling the car service now. It won't be long." He looked at his watch again.

"The car service? Are you trying to impress me?"

"No, I get the feeling you're pretty impressed already."

Kate was gazing into his eyes when the hostess arrived at the table and playfully put her hands on Mike's shoulders and whispered into his ear.

"Mike, your car is here."

Kate glared at her. *That was brazen. Isn't it obvious we're on a date?*

Without taking his eyes off Kate he thanked the hostess and excused himself from the table. Kate stood up. Mike helped her with her jacket and led her to the door. She gave the hostess her most venomous look as they passed.

The door to his apartment flew open and Mike strode in, carrying a giggling Kate over his shoulder. He hooked the door with his foot and jerked it closed behind them. He bent down and placed her feet on the floor, then knelt before her.

"Will there be anything else, Your Majesty?"

She rolled her eyes and offered her hand to help him up.

"All I said was, that was a lot of stairs in these heels. I could have taken my shoes off. You didn't have to carry me up the last two flights."

"Of course I did – I forgot the elevator was being serviced and I had to get you up here as quickly as possible." He scanned her body as he straightened up and moved in close against her. "So where did I get to in the cab?"

"About here." She pointed to a spot just below her collar bone.

He pinned her up against the wall and pressed his lips against that spot, tickling her with his tongue as she ran her fingers through his short hair.

She rolled her head back as he kissed and nibbled her soft skin and moved his tongue down until it met the plunging neckline of her dress. He ran his hands up and down her body, stopping to caress her breasts as he moved his tongue back to her neck. He groaned as she squirmed to break free of his hold.

"I need to powder my nose," she said, almost out of breath.

He pointed at a room to the left of the front door and she kissed him firmly on the lips before hurrying off.

Trying to compose himself, he looked around the apartment. *Oh shit*. He hurried to the living room and shifted a pile of mail and old newspapers from the coffee table and shoved them into a drawer in the sideboard. He picked up that morning's coffee cup and plate and took them into the kitchen. He was busy rearranging the sofa cushions when she joined him.

"This place is fantastic. Have you lived here long?"

"About two years. After my divorce I had a more modest place but that was only because I practically lived at the office. Then one day I took stock. I wasn't paying alimony, college fees or for lavish weddings any more and my money was my own again. I thought it was time to reinvent myself."

"I like the new invention – and I'm not the only one. That hostess was totally flirting with you and she was really pretty."

He took her hand. "Was she? I didn't notice anything but you. May I offer you some wine?"

"Just a small glass."

He kissed her hand and left her in the living room. She had a little look around. He had great taste. A comfortable-looking beige sofa stood in front of the large open fireplace. She traced her finger around the outline of an Edwardian carriage clock which stood proudly on the mantelpiece before making her way to the floor-to-ceiling window. She was enjoying the view when he called from the kitchen.

"Sorry, I don't have any wine, just beer or Scotch."

She thought that was probably a good thing; she wanted to keep a clear head. "Water will be fine, thank you."

When he came out of the kitchen, he stopped dead when he saw her in front of the window. Her red hair glistened with droplets of rain. Her dress, which was just long enough to cover what it needed to, clung to her slim figure, and her bare legs looked firm and silky.

"Beautiful."

"Isn't it?" she agreed. "The lights look like they're dancing in the rain."

"I wasn't talking about the lights," he whispered as he set the glass of water on the coffee table.

She saw his reflection in the window as he came up

behind her. Even though she was expecting it, longing for it, she gasped when she felt his touch. He slid his arms around her waist and pulled her backwards against him. She closed her eyes and let her head roll to the side as she felt his lips on her neck, each kiss sending a ripple through her body. She felt his heart beating against her back. It was just as fast as hers, and she tried to steady her breathing as he moved his hands up and down her body, caressing every inch of her.

She turned to face him, linked her fingers around his neck and pulled him towards her then kissed him, gently at first, then harder. She took her time getting to know the shape and feel of his lips before she opened her mouth and allowed their tongues to meet. As the kiss became more intense she grabbed at his shoulders, sinking her nails into his biceps.

He reached for the straps of her dress and slowly slid them down her arm, tightening his grip on her as he undid her zip and then took his time caressing the contours of her body while guiding the dress to the floor. He helped her step out of it.

She kissed him hungrily. As he responded with equal fervour, she found herself pressed up against the window. She gasped at its coldness, but was left breathless and desperate for more when he broke away.

He took a moment to admire her in her underwear: she was more beautiful than he had imagined. Suddenly he realised where she was standing. He took her by the hand and they switched places so he was in front of the window, shielding her from view.

She placed her hand on his chest and pushed him up against the window, kissing him softly as she undid his tie, pulled it from under his collar and let it drop to the floor. She worked her way down the buttons on his shirt then pressed herself against his firm bare chest as she pulled it from his shoulders.

He squeezed her backside as she kissed his neck and chest, her hands roaming down his back to his waist. She started to undo his belt, but he brought his hand down to stop her.

"Wouldn't you be more comfortable in the bedroom?"

She shook her head. "Later. Right now, I'm going to make you comfortable right here in the living room." She ran her tongue along her bottom lip, grabbed him by the belt buckle and pulled him to the sofa.

Chapter Seven

Mike stirred. A quick glance at his alarm clock showed that it was almost time to get up. He sat up and cancelled the alarm in an effort not to disturb Kate, who was still peacefully asleep beside him.

He turned onto his side to face her and watched her chest rise and fall beneath the crisp cotton sheet that loosely covered her naked body. He thought about the night before. It had been incredible – she was incredible, and he wanted to wake her and talk to her, but he was enjoying watching her sleep.

Reluctant to tear himself away, he lay next to her for a few more minutes and tried to memorise the light sound of her breathing and the shape of her body. He knew it was only a matter of time before she would be gone from his bed – and his life.

After a quick shower he went back in to the bedroom, to find Kate still sleeping. He crept towards the wardrobe and selected his favourite black suit and an off-white shirt with black buttons, and decided that today he would be more casual than usual and give the tie a miss.

He felt great – and not just because of last night. He'd felt different since he met Kate, as if she had awakened something in him. He was happier in himself and less concerned with his greying stubble and thinning hair.

Once dressed, he picked up his watch from the dresser. He balanced his wrist on his knee to fasten the leather strap and, as he was pulling his sleeve down, he noticed Kate was awake and watching him intently.

"Morning," she said softly.

"How long have you been watching me?"

She curled up beneath the sheet. "Long enough. Why didn't you wake me?"

"I thought you could do with the sleep. Last night was quite something." He perched on the side of the bed and took her hand.

"It really was." She looked deep into his eyes as they locked fingers.

"Any regrets?" He'd meant it as a joke, but panicked when she nodded.

"That we wasted an hour eating dinner." She giggled.

Relieved, he brought her hand to his lips and kissed it.

"I hope you weren't going to leave without saying goodbye?"

"I have an early meeting, but I had planned to wake you with a cup of coffee and a kiss but all I have ready is the kiss."

"I'll take it."

As she sat up, the bedsheet crept down to reveal her breasts. Embarrassed, she scrambled to pull up the sheet and tuck it under her arms.

"It's a bit late for modesty, babe. I've already seen everything there is to see … and had my tongue on most of it too."

Her temperature rose as she replayed the night before in her mind. They had given everything to each other; she felt as if she knew him inside and out. She nestled underneath the sheet. "I know, and it was amazing. But you've showered and are already dressed, and I've just realised that I'm completely naked in a strange man's bed. I'm suddenly feeling very vulnerable."

"Vulnerable is not how I would describe you."

He slipped his hand under the sheet onto her thigh and ran his hand slowly along her smooth skin. He stopped to gently caress her breast then moved his hand up to her face. He kissed her softly.

Seduced and aroused, she kissed him back but had to stop herself before she got too carried away. She pushed him away. "I should get up too."

He groaned. "No. I have two meetings this morning, so why don't you make yourself at home and come by the office later? I've left a fresh towel out for you in the bathroom and you can help yourself to anything else you want."

"I did have my eye on that beautiful clock on the mantelpiece," she joked, "but I'll shower back at the hotel. I can't turn up at your office in yesterday's dress – what would people say?"

"That I'm a lucky guy. And you can have that clock, babe. After last night you can have anything you want from me."

He wanted nothing more than to climb back into bed with her, but his inner workaholic wouldn't permit it. He had responsibilities – and above all he had to remember that this was meant to be a casual thing. But on the other hand, if she was only going to be in town for a few days he should make the most of his time with her...

"You know, on second thoughts maybe I could be a few minutes late." He leant over and kissed her.

She caressed the back of his head and groaned as

she pushed him away again. "What I have planned for you will take much more than a few minutes, so either go now and we'll finish this later, or get the hell back in here." She pulled the sheet away.

He stared in awe at her naked body and took a long lustful breath as he summoned up the courage to speak. "I really hate myself for doing this. I've got to go. But that's some image to take with me."

He reached out to touch her.

"No. Later." She covered herself with the sheet and gave him a quick kiss. "Now get out of here." She tried to push him off the side of the bed and he scrambled to his feet.

She held his gaze until he was out of the room, then she pulled the sheet over her head and groaned in disappointment.

On the other side of the door he shook his head. *Did I really just choose work over sex? I need help.*

Content, she lay in bed until she heard the front door close, then sat up and looked around the room for her clothes, before remembering they'd be strewn on the living-room floor where she'd left them.

She hurried to the en-suite and found the towel Mike had left out for her. As she wrapped it around her naked body, she caught a glimpse of herself in the mirror. Her mascara was smudged and her hair tangled, but her cheeks were rosy and she felt great. Had she ever felt this great? Her mind raced back to the night before. Had she been too forward on the sofa, too zealous on the living-room floor and the bedroom ... too *everything* in the bedroom? She shrugged it off. If she had, it was because he had been too ... and neither of them seemed to have any complaints – or self-control, apparently. She splashed cold water onto her face and went to fetch her clothes.

The smell of fresh coffee welcomed her as she opened the bedroom door, and she crept into the living room as if she had no right to be there. It looked very different in the morning light – still modern and stylish but much more homely. She couldn't believe she hadn't noticed the huge bookcase in the corner which, unlike the shelves in his office, looked tidy and organised.

She found her clothes in a neatly folded pile on the sofa with a note on top. She held her breath as she picked it up.

I didn't trust myself to come back in. M. x

She laughed and collected her clothes, but as she walked back to the bedroom she thought he must really trust her to have left her alone in his apartment – but sooner or later she would lose his trust when he found out she'd been lying to him. If she'd had any idea that they'd end up in bed together, she would have told him the truth straight away.

This was turning into a bit of a mess. She'd come to New York with one purpose: to see justice for Ray, not to get carried away with some guy. But deep down she already knew that he wasn't just 'some guy'. She promised herself that she would tell him everything when she saw him later … well, *some* things.

***

They sat at his desk in silence. Four empty take-away coffee cups and two half eaten sandwiches were all they had to show for their morning's work.

Mike stared blankly at this computer screen and tried to concentrate, but every so often he looked at Kate out of the corner of his eye. He couldn't stop thinking about last night: the curves of her body, the coconut smell of her hair, the taste of her on his tongue. His pulse quickened. He wanted to rip open her blouse, hitch up her skirt and bend her over his desk. He took a deep breath and tried to refocus on the computer screen.

She tapped her foot against the side of the desk and half-heartedly flicked through a folder of old newspaper clippings. Once in a while she sneaked a glance at him. Every little hair on her body spiked, as if remembering his touch. She wanted him to touch her again. What she really wanted was to go around to his side of the desk and straddle him on the chair. She closed the folder.

"OK, there's nothing in any of your stuff either. Are you sure this is all you have on Jack Hudson?"

There was no answer. She looked up to find him still fixed on the screen.

"Don't you guys have some sort of archive?"

Still no answer. She shifted in her seat and tried to make eye contact with him. "Mike?" she shouted.

"What?" he responded, finally tearing himself away from the screen. Instantly regretting his outburst, he took a deep breath. "I'm sorry. I'm really busy – I have so much work to get through and all I can think about is last night. It was incredible…"

She offered him a sympathetic smile. "I thought so too."

"I am sorry I snapped and I haven't been any help

to you with this Hudson stuff."

"Don't worry about it, get back to work." Tapping her fingers on the desk, she looked around the room. "You're right. You haven't done much to help me, but I haven't done much either. I've just been sitting here for the best part of two days waiting for something to magically pop out at me. I need to *make* something happen."

Now she had his full attention, he sat back in his chair and took off his glasses. "What do you mean?"

She knew she was in way over her head. She'd done a lot of impulsive things in her life, and this was top of the list. She wasn't a spy, a detective, or even a reporter. But what if she was? She wouldn't just sit around and wait for information to turn up. She'd go out and look for it. But where? She wanted to scream. She scanned the office for inspiration, and spotted a small statue of a black dog on one of the shelves. Was it a dog, or could it be a bull? She sat up in her chair.

"I think a little fresh air will clear my mind. I'm going to do some sightseeing and let you get back to work."

"That's a great idea. Why don't you go up to the park? It'll be lovely there today."

"Actually, I hear downtown is really nice this time of year. I'll probably go down to Wall Street and see that bull thingy – what's it called?"

"The Wall Street Bull?"

"That's inventive."

He smiled at her sarcasm but soon put the pieces together in his head. "Babe, you know that's right by the offices of Hudson Inc., don't you?"

"Is it, Mike? I did *not* know that." She gave him a

mischievous grin. "I suppose if I have time when I'm down there I might just pop by and see what I can find out. It was probably just a coincidence that the embezzlement was discovered when he was in his New York office – but maybe someone there knows something."

He shook his head at her. "I don't know how things work in London, but I'm sure that's not the kind of place you can just 'pop by' without an appointment."

"Well, I'll make an appointment then." She winked.

"Don't get into any trouble." He pointed at her. "I don't want to have to go down to the police station to bail you out."

Reaching out to grab his finger, she teased him, "You would do that for me, Mike? That's so sweet."

"Don't do anything stupid. I mean it."

Without letting go of his finger she got up, walked around and perched on the desk beside his chair. "Nothing stupid, I swear. And I'll head straight back to the hotel when I don't get in." She rested her hand on his knee and made circles with her finger. "Are you going to come by the hotel after work or do you have plans already?"

"I have plans."

Technically he wasn't lying – he had a standing plan with Hooper on a Friday night for beer and wings, but there was a get-out clause if either of them had a better offer. Hers was definitely a better offer.

She pouted.

"I'm teasing. Of course I'll come by – wild horses couldn't stop me. I'll take you for dinner at that French place I told you about."

"Not tonight." She slid her hand up between his

legs and cupped his crotch. "Tonight we order room service."

He flinched as she tightened her grip. "That sounds perfect." As he leant in to kiss her the door opened and Hooper walked in, looking through some paperwork.

"Hey, Mike." He looked up to find them looking at him awkwardly. "Oh hey, Kate." He squinted at her. "I'm sorry, I should have knocked."

"Don't mind me. I was just leaving. I'll see you later." She squeezed Mike's shoulder as she went back round to her side of the desk and picked up her things. "Have a good afternoon."

She winked at Hooper on her way out.

Hooper watched the door close behind her. "What did I interrupt there? Wait..." He leant in close to Mike and examined him. "Yup, you've slept with her. I knew you had it in you, old man." He gave him a congratulatory punch on the arm. "How was she?"

"What do you want, Hooper?"

He rubbed his hands together. "Details."

"There are no details."

"Oh, come on, I always give you details."

"And I always beg you not to."

Hooper's face fell. "I was hoping you hadn't slept with her yet..." He rubbed his goatee. "Cause that makes what I have to say kinda awkward."

Mike sat up straight. "What? Why?"

"She's not who she says she is. She's lying to you."

"Why do you say that?"

"I googled her. I hope you don't mind, but it's something you should have done before you ate up all that bullshit she fed you. It's OK – I get it. You're more like me than you'd admit. You were more interested in checking out her rack than her résumé."

"What's wrong with her résumé?"

"She hasn't got one! According to Google, she doesn't exist. Now, maybe it's just me, but I would have thought that a published reporter would show up on a Google search. But there's nothing. There's also no sign of her on Facebook, Twitter, Instagram or LinkedIn. I don't know about you, but I think that's weird, especially for someone who claims to work in the media."

"Well, maybe she's a private person or hates computers," Mike tried to argue.

"I don't think that's it. Come on, even *you* have a Twitter account."

"Yeah, but the paper made me have it."

"Exactly. So I called the paper she said she wrote for in London, and guess what? They've never heard of her."

"Was it the right paper? Maybe you just didn't speak to the right guy."

"Oh, come on, open your eyes. I spoke to three different people. I did find something out: there was a reporter who worked there who died earlier this year, so that might be the guy she's talking about."

Mike nodded in agreement.

"But it wasn't murder. The guy died of a heart attack in a public park and it was witnessed by about twenty people. Even the police don't suspect foul play. If she's being honest with you, why would she lie about how he died, and why is she trying to implicate Jack Hudson?" Hooper shook his head. "It's obvious that she's up to something, man. She's probably a bitter ex-girlfriend hell-bent on revenge. I'd steer clear if I was you."

Mike sank his head into his hands. She had mentioned that Jack Hudson had a reputation for cheating, and obviously she didn't work for that paper. Hooper, for all his faults, was usually a good judge of character so, as much as Mike didn't want to, he had to accept the fact that she was lying.

"One of the guys I spoke to said he'll ask around about her, but a lot of the staff had already left for the weekend, so he said he'd call me back on Monday. I'm sorry, man."

Mike tried to force a smile.

"Don't be too hard on yourself. You're not the first man to get seduced by a perky set of tits. Just be glad you got to spend a bit of time on that fine ass and forget about her."

Mike clenched his fists. "Don't talk about her like that."

Hooper shook his head. "Oh my God, she's under your skin already, isn't she?"

"No."

He had tried to sound convincing, but Hooper didn't buy it.

"You're going to keep seeing her anyway, aren't you?"

Mike just nodded.

"OK, but be careful. I don't trust her, and neither should you. You'd better be at O'Malley's later. I'll help you drown your sorrows." He clapped Mike on the shoulder before leaving the office.

Mike sighed. If he had any sense, he wouldn't go anywhere near that hotel, but there was something about Kate that made him want to give her the benefit of the doubt. He'd give her the opportunity to tell her side of the story.

***

As she walked down Wall Street Kate scolded herself for not having had the courage to talk to Mike – but it was only because she didn't know how much to tell him. She wanted Jack Hudson to get what he deserved, but she wanted to keep her part in it quiet. Mike was a such a great guy. She didn't want him to find out what she'd done. She resolved to talk to him when he got to the hotel. As for how much she would tell him … she'd play it by ear.

The Bull glistened in the afternoon sun and Kate stopped to watch a group of Japanese tourists laugh and joke as they took selfies around it. She marvelled at the buildings that speared up into the sky and wondered what exactly went on inside: money changing from one rich hand to another, each businessman getting richer at the expense of the average hard-working person.

She was bowled over by the lavish decoration in the lobby of the building where Hudson Inc. had their offices. Exactly how much money were these companies making that they could afford to waste it on marble floors and extravagant pieces of art?

She rooted through her bag as she approached the security barrier, where she was stopped by a female security guard.

"Do you know where you're going, ma'am?"

"Yes, thank you, to the eleventh floor. Hudson Inc." She spoke confidently as she found the item she was looking for in her bag. She waved the Hudson Inc. security pass at the guard.

The guard let her past.

I hope this works, she thought as she reached the barrier and swiped the card through the machine. She could barely hear anything over the sound of her heart thumping, then she heard the mechanism click as the card activated, but was that a positive click or a negative one?

Slowly she opened her eyes and breathed a sigh of relief when she saw the green light inviting her to pass through. She made her way into the lift and was able to stop her hand shaking long enough to extend her finger and press the button for the eleventh floor.

The lift opened onto a large reception area. Four black leather armchairs sat around a large oak table strewn with newspapers. She noticed two copies of the *New York Times* and quivered as she thought about Mike; the two were now inseparable in her mind, much like she and Mike had been the night before.

The reception area was empty apart from a man checking his phone at the end of the long reception desk and a tall blonde standing behind it.

"Can I help you, miss?"

"Yes please, I'm here to see Mr Davenport."

The receptionist checked a diary. "Certainly, what time is your appointment?"

"I don't actually have an appointment, but we're friends. I'm sure he'll see me."

Looking over her glasses with a degree of scepticism, the receptionist enquired, "You're a friend of Mr Davenport's? Then that shouldn't be a problem at all." Without taking her eyes off Kate she shouted, "Mr Davenport, this lady says she's a friend of yours."

Oh, shit. Kate's heart sank as the man standing at the bottom of the reception desk turned to face her. *Of course that's him.* How had she not recognised him? She'd seen his photo so many times. She steadied herself and tried to summon her sexiest smile.

He walked towards her, smirking. "Really? I think I would remember having a friend that looked like you. I'm sorry, *do* I know you?"

"Yes," she replied, feeling more than a little flushed. "Well, we haven't actually met, but my name is Kate. Kate Turner, from the London office."

"The London office?" A smug grin crossed his face. "Of course, you were Jack's assistant. Kate, it's *great* to finally meet you" – he kissed her hand – "to put such a beautiful face to the voice that's been haunting me on the other end of the phone. Did you come to New York to see the trial?"

She flinched. *How does he know about that? He must be guessing.* "No, not for the trial. Actually, I forgot about that until I got here and saw it on the news. I'm in town for a friend's wedding and I had some time to kill so I thought I'd do some sightseeing. I was over there looking at that bull thingy when I realised that this is where our New York office is, and I thought it would be fun to call in and see how you guys do it over here."

"I'm so glad you did. Would you like a coffee?"

"That would be lovely, Max. I—"

"Mr Davenport, you have that meeting," the receptionist snapped.

"Yes, Noreen, thank you." He tutted and turned

back to Kate. "I'm sorry, I actually do have a meeting to go to. This thing with Jack has everyone on edge. How about dinner instead? It's Friday – we could make a night of it."

She knew from his reputation that he was offering more than just dinner … and even if she didn't already have plans with Mike, there was no way she'd ever go there.

"Oh, Max, I'd love to, but I already have plans. What do you guys call it, a bachelorette party? Perhaps you could give me your card? I'll call you when I'm free."

"Are you going to be in town long?"

"A few days."

"In that case," he handed her his card, "I look forward to hearing from you."

"I look forward to calling—"

"Mr Davenport, they're all waiting for you in the conference room."

"Yes, Noreen," he said rudely. "Goodbye, Kate." He walked off along the corridor and disappeared through large wooden doors.

Kate slumped. That was awkward. What was she even doing here without a plan? She made a mental note to get better at planning ahead.

"So, you were Mr Hudson's assistant?" Noreen asked, suddenly a lot more friendly.

"Yes, but they reassigned me when he was arrested."

"That's terrible about what he did. Did you have any idea?"

"No, but he was always up to something." She leant

in. "If his wife knew the half of it…"

Noreen nodded furiously. "Yes, they're the same here, Kate, and I wouldn't bother with that one if I was you" – she pointed in the direction of the large wooden doors – "he's the worst of them all."

Kate screwed up her face. "I don't intend to."

They giggled like old friends.

"Apparently he's gone through more mistresses than I have pantyhose. In the three weeks I've been working here, I've seen all sorts. Oh, and there was a woman here on Monday – older than the rest, and a bit plump. She went into his office all friendly and a few minutes later I heard shouting. Then when she was leaving, I heard her tell him that he couldn't treat her like that and his days were numbered. How crazy is that?"

"That's pretty crazy, Noreen."

Disappointed, Kate looked around reception. She would have liked to get into Max's office for a snoop around. She hadn't expected to be in and out so quickly. Then she noticed Noreen looked agitated. "You OK, Noreen?"

"It's a bit embarrassing. I really need the ladies' room and my cover won't be here for another thirty minutes. They really hate it when I leave the desk unmanned, especially with the details of this top-secret new drug finally being announced next week."

"I forgot about that. They always hype these things up but it's probably just a spot cream," Kate joked.

Noreen laughed – a little too much, Kate thought. Her joke hadn't been *that* funny. Sensing an opportunity to buy more time in the office, Kate approached the desk. "I can cover for you if you want to use the ladies' room."

Noreen looked around to check that no one was coming. "Are you sure? That would be great."

"I'm always happy to help out a colleague," she said as she swapped places with Noreen.

"Do you mind if I run downstairs for a cigarette too?"

"Not at all. Take your time. I can handle this." She watched Noreen leave and rubbed her hands together. *OK, let's see what we can find out.*

Automatically, she logged on to her own email account. She'd only received a few since she'd left, none of which were important apart from one from Human Resources which told her she no longer had a job. She exited the email program and stared blankly at the screen, deflated.

What exactly did she think she was going to find? A secret file on the desktop with all the information she needed? There was nothing relevant on the reception desk either – unless Noreen's nail polish was the vital piece of the puzzle. It was a nice colour though; she noticed her own nail polish was beginning to chip.

She was trying to figure out which of the offices was Max's and if she had time for a quick look around when she heard the lift doors open.

A courier approached the desk.

"Letter for a Mr Davenport. Sign here, please." He held out a tablet for her to sign.

"Sure." She took the letter and the tablet and thought for a second before she signed.

Noreen x.

She winked at the courier as she passed it back and he smiled back at her as he waited for the lift. When the doors opened again, Noreen came out.

"Thanks, Kate. Anything exciting happen?"

"Nope." She looked at the letter in her hand. The logo on the envelope said *Biomes*. "Just this letter for Max." She placed it on the desk.

Noreen grimaced. "He's been waiting for that. I'd have been in trouble if I wasn't here to sign for it. You saved my skin."

"Any time, Noreen. I'll see you around." Kate called the lift, disappointed that she hadn't been able to speak to Max and find out what he knew. She resolved to give him a call on Monday – once she had made a plan.

***

Mike stared at Kate's hotel room door, summoning the courage to knock. Hooper was right: she was lying to him and it would be best just to finish things then and there, leave it as one great night. It wasn't as if they had a future together.

Finally, he knocked. When the door opened, Kate greeted him with a huge smile. She looked incredibly sexy in the skirt and blouse he'd been wanting to rip off her all day.

This is going to be harder than I thought.

"I was expecting you ages ago. I was starting to think I'd been stood up," she joked as she offered her lips for a kiss, but he just walked past her into the room.

"I'm sorry. Something came up at work," he said quietly.

"Well, I'm glad you're here. I need to talk to you

about something." Realising that he hadn't yet made eye contact with her, she tried to catch his eye. He was definitely distracted. She ran her hand down his arm.

"Are you OK?"

He looked at her hand as it rested on his arm. If she had touched him like that six hours ago it would have driven him crazy, but now he just felt like an idiot. Hooper was right; she'd bewitched him. He'd taken everything she told him at face value and questioned nothing. Whether or not she had a hidden agenda, she had lied to him, and he wasn't sure if he could forgive that.

He tried to smile. "Yes, it's just been a really long afternoon. What did you want to talk to me about?"

Sensing his unease, she thought maybe now wasn't the best time to come clean. She'd wait until he was in a better mood. "Not now, Mike, you look like you need a drink. Why don't you make yourself comfortable?"

She pointed to the armchairs. As he walked to the window, he noticed her laptop was open on the bed. He tried to have a look at the screen, but she closed it as she followed him.

He sat down and watched as she bent over to open the minibar, biting his lip when her short skirt revealed her skimpy underwear. He had to pull himself together.

"So how did you get on down at Hudson Inc. then?"

She froze, her head in the fridge, and wondered if she should tell him. It wasn't as if anything had happened.

"You were right. I couldn't get in, so I just came back here. Beer or wine?" She waved a small bottle of each at him.

"Any Scotch in there?"

"That sort of a day?"

"Yeah. So, tell me a bit more about yourself. What college did you go to?"

She panicked. "Erm, London … City of London."

"Do they have a good journalism school there?"

"Yeah, I guess it's OK." She poured the tiny bottle of whisky into a glass.

"It must have been hard studying for your degree with all that travelling you did."

What degree? She reached into the minibar again.

"This paper of yours back in London, do you like it? How long have you been working there?"

She poured a second tiny bottle of whisky into the glass; she had a feeling he was going to need it.

"Hooper's spoken to you, hasn't he? I thought he was being weird with me earlier."

Mike hung his head. He couldn't believe he felt guilty confronting her when she was the one doing all the lying.

She handed him the glass and pulled the other chair over beside him. "I just assumed you'd told him about last night and he felt awkward. But obviously he rang the paper in London, and they said they'd never heard of me."

"Yes." He took a sip of his drink and set it on the coffee table. "And he googled you, tried to find you on social media, but found nothing. What aren't you telling me, Kate? Is your name even Kate?"

"Hold on." She sighed and reached for her bag. She took out her passport and offered it to him. He opened it at the picture page and had a quick look.

"Thank you, Katherine."

"Just Kate. Nobody has ever called me Katherine

except my mum, and I like it that way. And you already know I'm not a reporter. When we met, you assumed I was and I just didn't correct you. It was just a lie of omission. I would have put you straight at the time if I had any idea that this would happen." She looked him in the eye. "Honestly, I planned to tell you the truth tonight. But the story I told you about the reporter being killed *is* true. Ray Freers was his name and he wasn't a colleague. He was an ex-boyfriend."

Mike swallowed.

Kate rolled her eyes. "A *very* ex-boyfriend, and now he's *very* dead. We'd kept in touch and met for lunch occasionally. He told me about a story he was doing, he said it would be huge and great for his career. The next day, I read in the paper that he was dead. When I heard it was a heart attack, I began to suspect that he had been murdered. He was only thirty-five, he was healthy, he ate well, went to the gym, really looked after himself. I thought his death might have something to do with the story he had told me about, so—"

He held his hand up to stop her. "Healthy people die from heart attacks all the time. It's tragic, but it's a fact."

"I'm aware of that! My mum was one of them."

Oh, shit! He wondered if he had room in his mouth for his other foot. "I'm so sorry."

She placed her hand on his leg to reassure him. "But Mum had a real heart attack; she wasn't murdered like Ray. I need you to believe me. No one else suspected it was murder, so I went looking for proof. I went down to his office, blagged my way in and went through his things. There was all this stuff about Hudson Inc. and some new product they were developing. I worked out he had found out something he shouldn't, and that's why Hudson had him killed. When the embezzlement story broke, I realised that must have been Ray's story! Hudson killed him to try and bury it, but it got out anyway. When I heard Hudson's trial was starting, I knew I had to be here. I felt as if there was something I could do. I just don't know what. You pretty much know the rest from there."

Mike downed the rest of his drink.

"I know it's a lot to take in. You can leave if you want to. We can talk tomorrow – or not. Whatever you want." She could barely breathe as she waited for him to speak. The thought of never seeing him again made her nauseous. She'd never felt like that before.

He took her hand. "I don't want to go, Kate. But that was a lot to take in – and a lie of omission is still a lie."

She looked down at her feet. "I know. I didn't intend on lying to anyone but when I saw you at the courthouse I thought you might be able to help me. I had to get your attention somehow, and when you held me in your arms, I couldn't believe how much I liked it. I thought we had a real spark. Then on the second day you approached me, and it was pretty obvious you felt the same. I didn't want you to think I was Susie Psycho running halfway round the world on a whim, so when you thought I was a reporter I let you."

"Then what do you really do for a living?"

"I don't really have a profession as such, but I've done lots of things in lots of countries."

She folded her arms as if she was finished but he looked her in the eye and waited for the answer to his question.

"But currently I'm a PA," she said softly. "Correction, I *was* a PA. I've just been sacked for running off to New York without booking time off work."

She was aware that she hadn't told him *her* part in the events that led to Ray's murder, or any specific details about how it happened, but that didn't change the fact that he was dead and she was doing everything she could think of to bring his killer to justice. And Mike was so disappointed in her already, when all he thought she had lied about was her job title.

It would be OK. She was confident there was no way he would ever find out what she'd done – only she, Ray, and the other dead reporter knew about that.

Mike's eyes widened. "So, you're a secretary? That is so sexy."

"A personal assistant." She tutted. "Stereotype, much?"

He grinned, then grew serious. "But no more lies – just the truth from here on in. Don't make a fool out of me for trusting you."

"I won't, and that wasn't my intention."

He raised his eyebrow. "Then what was your intention towards me?"

She placed her hand on his thigh and slid it up to his crotch. "Purely sexual."

"I can live with that."

She got up from her armchair and perched on his knee, sliding her other hand around his neck. She gazed into his eyes while she moistened her lips with her tongue.

He drew in a breath as her grip on his crotch tightened. As she leant in to nibble his earlobe, the familiar smell of her perfume brought memories flooding back from the previous night. He ran his hands up and down her back as she traced her lips down his neck, biting him gently between kisses. Completely aroused by the feel of her tongue on his skin, he gathered a handful of her hair and gently tugged her head back so her eyes met his.

Both feeling an inexplicable intimacy after just one night together, they kissed, not slowly or tenderly but with a lust and hunger for one another that couldn't wait. He scooped her into his arms and carried her to the bed, where he laid her down then kicked off his shoes and removed his jacket.

Her heart raced. She was aching for him and couldn't wait to feel him inside her. He was unbuttoning his shirt when she grabbed him by the shoulders and pulled him onto the bed beside her.

"There isn't time," she gasped, hitching up her skirt and climbing on top.

On her knees, with him between her thighs, she undid his belt and zip and, with a little help from him, manoeuvred his clothes out of the way. Feeling his erection, she suddenly realised that the only barrier between them was her already wet black lace thong, and that was the wrong barrier.

He pulled at the thong and she reached over to the bedside table to grab a foil packet from the top drawer. She peeled off the top and handed it to him. He took the packet and, as he slipped his on, she slipped hers off.

He held her backside tightly as she lowered herself onto him, and she moaned as he thrust inside her. She placed her hands on his stomach to steady herself and set the pace, feeling him deeper inside with each movement.

He reached up to undo the buttons on her blouse and caressed her breasts over her black lace bra. He could feel her heart pounding as they moved together in perfect rhythm.

Remembering what she had enjoyed the night before, he offered two fingers, which she took into her mouth, then he brought them down to massage her clitoris while his other hand squeezed her backside.

She arched her back as she increased the pace, keeping him exactly where she wanted him. She was close to orgasm.

She leant over him and held his shoulders so she had full control. Ready to explode, she moved faster and harder, moaning and digging her nails into his shoulders. She tried to suppress a scream as she let go and collapsed on top of him.

"That was great, Mike," she whispered, gasping for breath.

Quickly, he rolled her onto her back and climbed on top. He looked deep into her eyes and smiled. "That was all you, babe. I haven't even started yet…"

She drew a sharp breath as he thrust into her again.

Chapter Eight

Mike was staring into space when Hooper burst in to the office, his cheeks red.

"Where the hell have you been?" he demanded. "I've been trying to call you for days."

"I spent the weekend with Kate."

Hooper shook his head. "You could have called. I was worried when you missed our tee time on Sunday. Then when you didn't show up for work yesterday, I thought something awful had happened to you. I was ready to come over to your place but Bob said he'd talked to you, said you were in bed sick."

"He was half right." Mike smirked. "I spoke to Kate and it's not as bad as—"

Hooper cut him off. "Yeah, I know. She tracked me down at my desk just now and tore me a new one in front of everyone. It was embarrassing. She was all high and mighty" – he put on a high-pitched voice and attempted an English accent – "why did I go behind her back? If I wanted to know something, why didn't I just ask her?"

Mike shrugged. "Well, she does have a point."

"What? How can you stick up for her when she's been playing us since day one, you especially? I know you like her and it's nice to see you with a spring in your step, but there has to be more to it than she's telling us, otherwise why would she have gotten so angry at me?"

"Maybe she feels threatened by you. You haven't exactly been nice to her. Look, I spent the whole weekend with her and really got to know her. She's amazing. I think she's genuine."

At least, he hoped she was.

"For the record, I still don't trust her. You've developed a blind spot where she's concerned – you're acting all out of character. I've never known you to miss a meeting or call in sick. Please don't do anything stupid."

"OK, OK." Mike tried to pacify him. "What time is it? Call your contact in London and see what you can find out about this reporter, Freers."

"It was the first thing I did when she left my desk. My guy says he wasn't sure if he had a girlfriend, but he did tell me that Freers' office was broken into on the night he died. Nothing of any value was taken so the paper just thought it was a coincidence."

Mike took off his glasses and rubbed his eyes. "OK, she did tell me she went to his office. She just omitted the 'breaking in' part." He tried to shrug it off as a misdemeanour. "Where is she now?"

"She went to get coffee. Maybe she's a spy or something, like a female James Bond. Maybe she killed that reporter and you're next."

Mike rolled his eyes. "I think your imagination is running away with you. Don't worry, I'll keep a close an eye on her for now" – he winked – "and get this. She's not a spy, she's a secretary."

Hooper caught his breath. "A secretary? That is so hot."

"I know."

They were so busy forming lewd images in their minds that they didn't notice Kate walk into the office holding two take-away coffee cups.

"What's hot?" she asked, looking between the two men, who stood in silence looking guilty as hell.

"It's OK, guys, I know you're talking about me but this coffee's also hot, so here." She smirked as she handed one coffee to Mike and then pinched his bum with her free hand. She offered the other cup to Hooper. "I got one for you too – a peace offering."

Reluctant he took the cup. "Thanks, Kate," he managed. "None for you?"

"I had a double espresso and it's long gone. I think we got off on the wrong foot. It's OK that you don't trust me. I haven't given you any reason to, and I know you're just looking out for your friend. So, can we start again, please?" She offered him her hand. He looked at Mike before he shook it.

"Just make sure he doesn't miss golf this Sunday."

Mike smiled at him, happy that he and Kate were finally getting on together.

"Great, so we're all good then, guys?"

Mike and Hooper looked at each other and then at Kate, then nodded in unison.

"So, what's our plan for today then?"

Hooper grimaced. "I have to go down to the UN and I just know I'm going to run into that translator I slept with last month. She's called, like, ten times."

Mike shook his head. Hooper was dodging an ever-increasing number of women in the city. "And I've got a meeting in five with Bob, who's trying to cut the budget again. I swear I—"

"Do you mind if I just hang out here in your office? I have to go back through everything you have on Hudson. I must have missed something."

"That's fine, but stay out of trouble." He picked a

stray hair off her shoulder, intentionally brushing her breast. "I'll be back in an hour."

"Then can I get into trouble?"

She moved in close and was about to kiss him when Hooper coughed. "Guys, this is a place of business."

Mike gave her a kiss on the cheek and whispered into her ear, "Hold that thought."

He signalled for Hooper to follow him out of the office.

As they walked down the corridor Mike raised the coffee cup to his lips and was about to take a sip when Hooper grabbed his arm, almost spilling the hot liquid over them both.

"Wait, you don't think she'd—"

"What, poison the coffee?" He looked at Hooper as if he was crazy.

"Well, we didn't see her drinking any."

Mike prepared himself and took a long slow sip. He swirled the coffee around in his mouth a few times before he swallowed, then paused for a moment and looked up to the ceiling before declaring, "It's just coffee."

Relieved, Hooper was about to take a sip of his coffee when Mike grabbed his arm. "But she *likes* me." He walked off, chuckling to himself.

Hooper's face fell and he pulled the cup away from his mouth. He examined the cup, took off the lid and sniffed the contents, then put the lid back on and disposed of it in the nearest bin.

***

"I can't tell whether or not you enjoyed that," Mike

joked as he pointed to Kate's empty plate.

"That was the best chicken Caesar I've ever had. I'm not complaining, but why are you treating me to lunch when a sandwich at the office would have been fine? Are you going to eat that?" Without waiting for an answer, she slid her plate to the side and replaced it with his barely touched risotto.

He watched in awe as she devoured his lunch. She certainly had a healthy appetite, and not just for food. He thought back to the past few days and how incredible they had been. He dreaded the day she would tell him she was leaving. He prepared himself to reveal his true reason for getting her out of the office. He had a question to ask her. He wasn't going to propose. Not marriage, anyway, but something that he knew Hooper would say was equally stupid and impulsive.

"I knew you'd really like this place and, well, I need to talk to you about something." He bit his lip.

"Is everything OK?"

He nodded and took a deep breath. "I've really enjoyed these past few days with you…"

She squirmed in her seat. *Was he ending things?* "Spit it out, Mike." She tried to sound calm.

He reached over the table and took her hand. "I've been putting off asking, but I need to know how much longer you're planning on staying in town." His jaw tightened as he waited for her response.

"Oh." She gave a nervous laugh. "I've been thinking about that too." She looked at him and wondered how to phrase her answer. If she was truly honest with herself, she'd admit that she had feelings for him – feelings she'd never had for anyone before. That really scared her. Her mother's death had affected her more than she let most people believe. It took over a year of therapy before she could forgive her mother and let go of the anger she felt towards her for leaving her on her own. To ensure she was never hurt like that again, she had decided to avoid commitment and keep relationships casual. She had vowed never to let anyone get close enough to hurt her. But in just a few days she had let Mike get closer to her than anyone had been before. And from the way he was looking at her, she knew he had feelings for her too. Even so, she was sure that commitment wasn't what she wanted, and she didn't want to give Mike false hope. Her head was telling her to go back to London and forget about him. But her heart was telling her something else.

Mike stared at her, trying to figure out what she was thinking, but her expression gave nothing away. She was taking too long to answer. He had already decided that he wasn't going to like her response when she smiled.

"Well, I got sacked from my job so I don't have that to rush back to, and I don't think there's anything else that can't wait … so I guess I could stick around for a while if you want me to."

He tried his best to subdue the huge grin that was trying to take over his face, but it was impossible. "I was hoping you'd say that. Did you know that your hotel is right around the corner from here?" He raised an eyebrow.

"Oh, so that's why you didn't touch your food? You were saving yourself for dessert? Didn't you get enough of that last night?"

"No, I can't get enough of you. That's why I'm

110

taking you there to collect your stuff. You're coming to stay with me."

She laughed and sat back in her chair, shaking her head furiously. "No."

His face fell. "No?"

She nodded. "No, that's a terrible idea."

"No, it's a great idea! If you lived here, it would be a totally different situation, but that hotel can't be cheap, and we've barely spent a minute apart since we met." He grabbed her hand. "I really like it that way."

Deep down, she liked it too, but she couldn't let herself get carried away. "That's really sweet, but I'll just go to a cheaper hotel – in Queens, maybe."

"You're not going to Queens. What's the point in wasting money on a shitty hotel when you know you're going to spend all your time at my apartment?" He batted his eyelashes at her.

She couldn't believe that she was even contemplating saying yes. "It's crazy. You're crazy."

"I know, right? But it feels like it makes sense, to me anyway."

She groaned and rubbed her temples. His apartment was far nicer than any hotel she could afford. If she wanted to stick around for a while, this would probably be the only possible way, but she had to make clear that it was in no way intended to be a permanent arrangement.

"OK. But I want to say that I'm doing this under extreme duress and that I have" – she held out three fingers – "three conditions."

Smiling, he gestured for her to continue.

"One, this isn't a commitment. This isn't me saying 'I love you' or us agreeing to spend the rest of our lives together, it's just two people who enjoy each other's company spending time together, *casually*." She looked at him for his approval but he grimaced.

"It can't be completely casual – there has to be a small degree of commitment."

"No, there doesn't."

He held his hands out to calm her. "All I mean is that I don't want you bringing any other guys back to my apartment."

"Oh, right. Well, I guess I can agree to that."

"So, your first condition is null and void. Next?" He looked smug.

She narrowed her eyes at him. "You have to let me contribute financially."

"Absolutely not. I won't hear of it."

She threw her hands up into the air. "Then it's a no."

"Come on, Kate, my bills are my bills. It would be different if you were staying forever, but you're not, so I don't want your money. I can afford to keep you."

"Oh, you want to keep me, do you?" she teased.

He went quiet and looked down at the table. "For as long as I can. What's your other condition?"

"This is the serious one." She pointed at him. "Promise me that if things get weird between us, say if you change your mind or I change my mind, we have to be honest with each other and call it a day, no hard feelings."

"I don't think that third one is going to be a problem either, babe. I really like having you around." He stroked the back of her hand. "So can we just say that you are moving in with me unconditionally?"

"OK, but it's definitely not moving in. I'm just

staying with you while I'm in town."

"I'll let you have that one." He winked.

They were busy playing footsie and staring into each other's eyes when they were interrupted by a voice from a nearby table.

"Looks like you slept with him after all. Lucky guy."

Stunned, they turned to see a man in a white shirt and blue jeans. Kate immediately recognised him as the man from the lift.

"I beg your pardon? I take it you've been drinking again," she replied with disdain.

Mike turned back to her. *How did she know him?* "Who the hell is this?"

She looked defensive. "I don't know! Some pervert who stands and watches people in the street then follows them into lifts." She turned to face the stranger. "But whoever he is, he'd better watch his mouth."

"Sorry, guys. I didn't mean to interrupt your lunch. I'll see you around." He threw a twenty-dollar bill on his table and left.

Unconvinced, Mike asked again, "Who was that?"

She held her hands out in a pleading fashion. "I don't know. He's just some jerk staying at the hotel. The night you dropped me off outside, he got into the lift behind me and at first I thought he was hitting on me but then it just got creepy. He said he saw us kissing out on the street. He said it was gross, that you were too old for me. I couldn't get out of there fast enough, and I haven't seen him again until now. I promise I'm telling you the truth."

"OK then, I'm going to talk to him." He threw his napkin on the table as he stood up.

She grabbed his hand. "What do you think you're going to do, defend my honour? He didn't do anything. Please sit down. He's just an asshole and I'm not going to be staying at that hotel any more so it's not a problem. Forget about him." She looked at him to check he had calmed down. "Let's just go and get my stuff and we'll never see him again. We've got time for dessert if you still want it."

As she got her bag and summoned the waiter, Mike looked out of the window.

The guy in jeans was standing on the corner smoking a cigarette and talking on his mobile. When he finished the call, he threw the still-lit butt on the ground and hailed a cab.

***

That evening as she was placing her bag on the bed, she looked around and wondered if she'd made the right decision. She had feelings for Mike and loved every minute she spent with him, but this was a big step for anyone – and for her it was huge.

She knew she was being impulsive by agreeing to stay with him – totally crazy, actually – but she felt so comfortable with him. Perhaps being in such close quarters would bring her to her senses. Even though the last thing she wanted to do was hurt him, she had to be true to herself. She wouldn't stick around if it wasn't working. That would certainly be easier than admitting to her feelings for him.

She looked for the cupboard where he said he'd cleared some space and opened it. It was completely empty. *How much stuff does he think I have? I didn't bring much, actually. Now I'm staying a while longer, I should really go shopping – and a decent hair dryer will be top of my list.*

In the en-suite she placed her cosmetics bag on the shelf above the sink, took out her toothbrush and rolled her eyes as she placed it beside his. As she examined the toiletries, which were neatly organised by type, her mind raced back to the shelves in his office. There was no way this bathroom had been organised by the same person. She made a mental note to ask him what day the cleaning lady came. He *had* to have one – there was no way he could get towels that soft by himself.

She picked up a bottle of aftershave and put it to her nose. Not pleased with the scent, she closed it quickly and put it to the back of the shelf. She selected another and sniffed. That was it. The one he had been wearing the day he caught her at the courthouse. She closed her eyes as she remembered the moment.

She was putting her shampoo in the shower when the doorbell rang. *Surely he's not back already?*

She had barely opened the door when a bag was shoved into her hand. The woman doing the shoving looked up and seemed to be just as startled as Kate.

"Who are you, and where's my dad?" she demanded. Without waiting for an answer, she barged past Kate and pushed a buggy into the apartment, leaving her other things at the door.

Kate looked down the corridor towards the lift, desperate to see Mike. When he didn't appear, she picked up the abandoned bags and followed her visitor into the living room.

"I'm Kate and I assume you're Mike's daughter."

She offered her hand.

The other woman looked around the room. "And where is Mike?"

"He went out to get some things. He should be back in a few minutes." She checked the clock. *He'd better be.*

"And who are you again?"

"I'm Kate, a friend of Mike's. I'm staying here for a few days while I'm in town."

She narrowed her eyes. "What sort of *friend*?"

Kate ran out of patience at the woman's rudeness. Her tone became less friendly. "Just a friend. Sorry, I didn't catch your name." She already knew it was Claire.

"Claire."

Kate shook her head, crouched down to the buggy and smiled. "And you must be Little Mikey. It's nice to meet you, Mikey."

He cooed and offered his rattle.

She took it from him, shook it a few times, pretending to be amazed at the sound, and passed it back to him. She looked up at Claire. "Oh, he's so much cuter than in photos."

"When did you see photos of him? And I've told Dad not to call him Little Mikey – his name is Michael. It makes me so mad when he calls him that."

As Kate stood up from the buggy, her smile faded away. She glared at Claire, trying desperately to hold her tongue.

Perhaps realising that she might have been a bit out of line, Claire relented. "I'm sorry. It's just that Michael has been ratty all day – I can't even hear myself think. My husband is out of town at a conference and I just fancied seeing my dad. I called his cell and left a message, said I was coming to stay the night."

"I guess he didn't get the message."

"Yeah, by the looks of it he's had other things on his mind. How old are you, by the way?"

"I beg your pardon?"

"I'm sorry." She held out her hands. "I haven't eaten or even had a chance to go to the bathroom in hours. I don't mean to be rude, but aren't you, like, my age?"

Kate rolled her eyes. As much as she would have liked to think so, there was no way she looked that young. "No, I'm not," she said firmly and bent down to the pram to talk to Michael. "Would you like to play with me while your mummy uses the bathroom and your..." – she couldn't quite bring herself to say 'grandfather' – "and Mike will be back soon with dinner. I'm sure there will be plenty to go around."

She looked back at Claire, who looked nervous.

"Don't worry, babies love me. Come here, Little Mi— Michael."

She stretched her arms out and he cooed as he went to her willingly. "We're friends already. Go, take your time." She checked the clock again as Claire reluctantly left the room.

Mike stumbled into the apartment. He balanced groceries, a bag of take-out and two bottles of wine as he struggled to get his key out of the lock. He spotted Kate in the kitchen doing the dishes. He tiptoed in, set the stuff on the table and crept up behind her.

"Honey, I'm home!" He slid his arms around her waist and kissed her neck.

She turned and, just as she opened her mouth to

speak, Claire walked into the kitchen. "Dad, that is so inappropriate."

Mike jumped and turned to face his daughter. "Jesus, what are you doing here? You scared me half to death."

"Well, if you'd checked your messages, you'd know. Steve's out of town, so is Mom, and I've been on my own with the baby for days. I've just put him down in the guest bedroom. I needed a bit of adult company and I thought we could do with a catch-up … by the look of it, I was right." She frowned as she gestured towards Kate, who, feeling awkward, had made herself busy cleaning the counter tops.

"Be nice, Claire," he warned, pulling his mobile from his pocket. "Hey, a message."

"Wait until I tell Mom you have a new girlfriend."

"I doubt she'll care," he said. "How is Audrey anyway?"

"She's fine. She and Rodger are in Hawaii."

"Again?" Mike rolled his eyes. It was bad enough that his ex-wife had married a surgeon, but his daughter had married one too. He felt like being an editor at one of the biggest newspapers in the world didn't seem a worthy profession.

"Oh, wait, she said she still hasn't got your RSVP for Steve's thirtieth birthday party yet. It's this Saturday, Dad."

"I'll pass, thanks. Why does she keep inviting me to those things anyway? You know, your wedding was the start of it. I knew I should have skipped that but seeing as I paid for the whole damn thing, I thought I'd at least show my face." He winked.

"Come on, you like Steve."

"Yeah, but he just likes me for the Knicks tickets. No, I'm not going. I always feel like a walking target at those things."

"I'll go with you," Kate said, linking arms with him. "I won't let anything happen to you."

A devilish grin crossed his face. "On second thoughts, call your mom and tell her I'm bringing someone."

"Really?"

"No. I'm not going. But I am going to take a peek at my grandson. Would one of you lovely ladies get me a beer?"

"Sure, Mike."

"Yes, Dad."

They spoke simultaneously and Kate blushed as Claire shook her head.

"Be nice, Claire. I mean it," he warned as he headed towards the bedroom.

"I'll get the plates." Claire managed a smile.

Kate managed one back. "I'll get the wine."

They tidied up the baby stuff and settled at the table. Kate filled the wine glasses and Claire began to unwrap the food as they waited for Mike in silence. Unable to bear the tension any longer, Kate decided to lighten the mood with a little small talk.

"I love your blouse. The blue really suits you."

Claire looked down at her favourite blouse. That's what she thought, but nobody else had ever passed comment on it before. "Thank you." She thought it would be polite to return a compliment. "I like the colour of your hair." She should have stopped there. "Is it from a bottle?"

"That's a very personal question," Kate said sharply, running her fingers through her hair. "And it's natural."

"Sorry." Claire suppressed a giggle and then said more seriously, "I know my dad dates and I have been telling him to put himself out there more. You seem nice, but I actually meant for him to find a woman closer to his own age. No offence," she added.

Kate rolled her eyes. "Although I may look twenty-six, I'm not. I'm closer to Mike's age than yours. It's not an issue..."

"What's not an issue?" Mike asked as he joined them in the kitchen. "Kate, I hope my daughter isn't giving you the third degree?" He glared at Claire as he sat down next to Kate.

"No, Mike, we're just making small talk," Kate said, squeezing his knee.

"So, Kate, you don't actually live in New York?"

"No, I'm currently based in London, but I've travelled quite a bit."

"Yeah, Claire, Kate's been all around the world. She has some fascinating stories."

"Oh, really?" Claire dismissed him and directed her questions back to Kate. "And are you planning on staying in town long?"

Mike looked at Kate, who had shifted in her seat. "Enough with the interrogation, Claire. Kate and I are seeing each other and that's the end of it. Can we please just have a normal conversation while we enjoy our food?"

Her cheeks reddened and she looked down at the table. "I was just asking. I didn't mean to be rude."

"That's OK, Claire," Kate offered as Mike patted her thigh in an effort to comfort her.

"I'm sorry, Kate, you too, Dad. It's just that this was the last thing I was expecting tonight." She tried to change the subject. "This food looks great."

They ate in awkward silence until Claire, halfway through her second glass of wine, felt bad and decided to extend an olive branch.

"So, did you really go all the way around the world?" She sounded genuinely interested. "I've never even left the States. Where have you been?"

Kate smiled. "Erm, all over Europe, I guess. France, Spain, Germany, Scandinavia, Italy, Croatia. You know, this could take a while. It would probably be easier telling you where I *haven't* been. I've never been to Russia, didn't fancy the Middle East. I've been to China, India, Indonesia, Japan, Australia, New Zealand. I spent quite a bit of time here in the States when I was in my twenties, and a few countries in South America, although funnily enough I've never been to Canada."

"Really? That's somewhere I could take you," Mike offered.

Kate gasped. "That would be great. I hear Niagara Falls is really romantic."

Claire grimaced and Mike choked on a noodle.

Kate looked between the two. "Have I missed something?"

"Erm, my mom and dad went there on their honeymoon," Claire said awkwardly.

"Let's give that a miss then, Mike." Kate laughed. "Shame."

"Did you go all these places by yourself, Kate? That's really brave."

"Sometimes. Other times I tagged along with people that I met. If I was happy somewhere, I stayed until I wasn't and then I moved on. I didn't stay anywhere I didn't want to be."

She winked at Mike, who smiled back then looked at Claire, happy that she was being a bit nicer to Kate.

While they ate, Claire continued to ask Kate about the places she would like to visit and Kate told some stories about the things she'd done and mishaps that had happened along the way. After dinner, they chatted over coffee.

"And what did you do for money in all these places? You're not secretly rich, are you?" Her eyes lit up.

"Definitely not." Kate laughed. "Whenever I wanted to stay somewhere, I just found a job. You know – barmaid, waitress, cleaner, telemarketer. I was a croupier in Monte Carlo for a year, that was fun. Oh, you'll like this, Mike. I spent a season picking grapes in the Côte de Sézanne in France. I learned about grapes and their different combinations, what wine goes best with what meats, et cetera, and I actually learned that it's perfectly fine to drink some white wines, especially champagne, when you're eating steak."

He sighed and rolled his eyes. "Why didn't you say something?"

"Because I didn't want to embarrass you on our first date." She gave him a loving smile which turned into a laugh when he actually blushed.

"I hate to cut the evening short," Mike said, trying to suppress a yawn, "but ladies, it's getting late. I think it's bedtime."

They agreed, stood up and started to collect the dishes. Kate loaded the dishwasher.

Mike kissed Claire on the cheek. "It's good to see you, honey."

She threw her arms around him. "You too, Daddy."

All of a sudden Kate felt uncomfortable, as if she was intruding on a family moment. "Just leave all this and I'll clean it up in the morning. Goodnight, Claire." She made her way out of the kitchen.

"Wait for me," Mike called and she stopped to wait. He put his arm around her waist and they walked towards the bedroom.

Claire called after them. "Goodnight, and for the love of God please go straight to sleep."

"OK, honey," Mike replied then turned to Kate and whispered, "No way."

They smirked as they went into the bedroom and closed the door.

Chapter Nine

Mike stood at the kitchen door and watched Kate feed Michael. She was telling him the story of Goldilocks as she spooned porridge into his mouth while trying to dodge his newly weaponised beaker.

Michael exploded into excited babble when he noticed his grandad at the door.

"Morning, sleepyhead," Kate said without turning her head.

"Morning, babe, you were up early."

"I heard Claire and Michael were awake. I thought she could do with a few minutes to herself, so I sent her to take a bath."

He was taken aback. "That's really thoughtful of you, especially since she wasn't very nice to you last night."

"It's OK." She shrugged and didn't mention that it was so she didn't have to be alone with her.

"No, it's not. I'll speak to her. But you two seem to be getting on well. How come you're so good with kids?" He kissed her on the cheek.

"There were loads of babies around when I was with my foster family and I used to get extra pocket money for helping out with changing nappies, feeding and stuff. For most of my life it was just me and my mum, so I enjoyed the company."

"Good morning, Little Mikey," crooned Mike.

The baby cooed back.

Kate slapped Mike on the arm. "Don't call him that, Claire doesn't like it."

"It's OK."

"No, it's not. You're winding her up and she's cross with you already."

"Why, what have I done?"

"Not to be crude, but me. You said yourself it's been a while since you introduced her to anyone and she turns up here to see you've got a gorgeous woman staying with you who's maybe just ten years older than her. She's bound to be a little jealous so just give her a break."

"OK, babe." He pulled her hair to the side and nuzzled her neck.

"Jesus, Dad, not in front of Michael," Claire snapped, appearing at the door.

Shaking him off, Kate stood up to put the bowl in the sink.

Mike lifted the baby out of the chair and kissed him. "Morning, Michael." He winked at Kate. "Did you have fun sleeping over at gramps' house?"

The baby gurgled.

Kate held up the coffee pot. "Can I top anyone up before I go?"

"No, thank you," Claire said politely.

"Go? I'm not ready yet," said Mike, who was only half dressed.

"I forgot to tell you, I'm going shopping this morning. I didn't expect to stay so long so I need to get a few things. I'll meet you down at the office later if that's OK?"

"Sure, babe, but take this." He handed the baby to

Claire and took his jacket off the back of the kitchen chair. He took his credit card from his wallet and offered it to Kate.

When she saw what it was, she shook her head. "No thank you, Mike."

"Take it," he repeated. "I saw your hotel bill and you wouldn't let me contribute."

"Because it was my bill."

"Yes, but all that champagne from room service was my idea. Just spend my half of the bill plus a little extra. I want to treat you. Please?" He batted his eyelashes at her.

"OK. Thank you." Graciously she took the card, intending to spend very little.

He whispered the PIN in her ear. "Got it?"

"Got it. I won't go mad, I promise. See you later." She was about to kiss him on the lips but at the last moment remembered who they were with and redirected her lips to his cheek. She turned to Claire. "It was nice to meet you, and you too, cutie pie. Bye-bye, Michael." She waved at him and he waved his chubby little hand in return.

Claire used the fact that she was holding Michael as an excuse not to shake hands. "Yeah, nice to meet you too."

Claire waited until she heard the door to the apartment close, then looked out to double-check that Kate had actually gone before she turned to her dad.

"I held my tongue last night, but what the hell are you doing? It's bad enough she's staying at your place, but now you're giving her your credit card?"

His jaw dropped. "Held your tongue? Is that what

you call it? Kate made a real effort with you and you were nothing but rude in return."

Claire relented, but only slightly. "I'm sorry. She does seem nice but she's not your type. I don't want to see you getting hurt, and isn't she a bit young for you? How old is she, anyway?"

Mike bit his lip. "I don't know. Like, thirty-four, thirty-five, maybe?"

"You don't even know how old she is?" she shouted. "Well, it doesn't matter. She's not right for you, Dad, it's never going to work. What about that dermatologist Steve introduced you to? She was lovely – and your age. Plus, you got loads of replies on that dating app – did you even meet any of them?"

"Yes, I did, and the less said about her the better." He sighed. "You don't have to worry about Kate. I know what I'm doing."

"Do you, Dad? Or are you just getting carried away because you met a pretty girl? Think about it."

"I'm going to finish getting ready."

He stormed out of the kitchen, not entirely sure if he was really mad at Claire or just annoyed because she might be right. Kate really did seem too good to be true: smart, beautiful and kind. OK, she was a bit younger than him, but surely not enough to warrant everyone's comments. He realised that he'd had the opportunity to find out her age when he looked at her passport. It hadn't even crossed his mind to look. Not the actions of an investigative reporter. Maybe Hooper was right – could she be clouding his judgement? *No!* He shook it off and went to get dressed.

***

Kate burst out of the department store onto the busy street, narrowly dodging a collision with a bike messenger. She felt her phone buzz in her pocket and smiled when she saw it was a text from Mike.

Credit card company called, wondering why I'm buying women's lingerie. Can't wait to see it! x

She texted a reply:

There's not much to see! ;)

All of a sudden, she got that uneasy feeling she usually got on the Tube when someone was too close to her. She was about to turn around when a hand grabbed her arm. She froze and drew a sharp breath as she felt another hand on her shoulder. The smell of smoke caught her nose as she heard a male voice behind her.

"Finally, I've got you on your own. Keep walking."

She tried to resist, but he pushed her forward. A car pulled up beside them.

"Get in," he instructed, taking a last drag on his cigarette and throwing the butt onto the ground.

"No!" She tried to break his hold.

He pulled the car door open, pushed her head down and forced her inside. He got in beside her and pulled the door shut.

She flinched as his shoulder touched hers, then recognised him as the man from lunch the day before and from the hotel lift. She pulled frantically at the door handle. When it didn't budge, she panicked and looked around for something she could use as a weapon.

Nothing.

"Who the hell are you, and why are you following me?"

"I'm not following you, Kate, I—"

"And how do you know my name?" she snapped.

"Let's just say a friend of mine has asked me to keep a close eye on you."

"Does this friend have a name?"

"No, but he has a message for you. He wants you to forget everything you think you know and get the hell out of town."

She took a deep breath and tried to sound brave. "Not a chance."

"Kate, you're a pretty girl." He ran his finger along her arm. "It would be a real shame if something awful happened to you."

She shrugged him off, but her voice wobbled. "Are you threatening me?"

"No."

The look on his face said otherwise.

"I'm just giving you a little bit of friendly advice. You're in way over your head here. I'd cut my losses if I was you."

She took a moment to think and replied with more confidence. "OK, let's compromise."

"You're in no position to compromise, sweetheart." He laughed.

"I'll stop looking into Jack Hudson but I'm not leaving town."

He sat back and thought for a moment, then he nodded. "OK. But I want you to call off your reporter boyfriend. He seems like a nice guy and you wouldn't want him to get hurt, would you?"

"He doesn't know anything! Just leave him out of this."

He sneered. "You know, I actually believe you. OK, you can go now, but just remember: *stop*." He ran his hand up her thigh and leant in close. "Because if I have to come and speak to you again, I might not be such a gentleman."

She slapped his hand off her leg. He smirked as he opened the door. Stepping out of the car he extended his hand to her, but she glared at him, ignoring his offer of help. Once out of the car, she pushed past him and hurried down the street.

He watched her go then took his mobile phone from his pocket. He placed a call as he got back into the car.

"I just talked to her. I gave her a bit of a scare, like you asked. Yes, I think it worked. But get this, she's not even on to you. She thinks I work for Jack. The reporter shouldn't be any trouble either. He probably knows less than her. I'll keep an eye on her for the next day or two, to be sure."

***

The door to the office opened. Mike looked up, expecting to see Kate, but was surprised to see an intern carrying two storage boxes.

"Where do you want these, Mr Kelly?"

"What are they?"

"Don't know. I was just told to bring them to you."

"Just put them over there. Thanks, kid." He pointed to the only free space on the floor in between two huge piles of old newspapers.

As the intern placed the boxes on the floor, Hooper strolled into the office.

"Hey Mike, where's the wife?"

"She was shopping but she's on her way. And don't say stuff like that in front of her. We're meant to be keeping it casual."

"Casual, you? You've never done anything casual in your life. You're always so serious. Just be careful…"

"Stop it! I've already had it from Claire this morning, and I don't need it from you too."

"Claire knows?" Hooper made a face. "What's in the boxes Ted brought in?"

"Don't know. Feel free to have a look."

There was a note taped to one of the boxes. Hooper ripped it off and held it up for permission to open it.

Mike nodded.

"It's the stuff Crawford's wife said she'd send down. Do you really think you're going to find anything in there to explain why he killed himself?"

Mike groaned. "I don't expect to find anything. She was upset about having the stuff around. She thought it might be important, but it's probably nothing. Do me a favour? If you've got a minute, start looking through it."

Hooper removed the lid from the first box and took out several piles of paper. "Bank statements." He scanned through them and found one with a sticker attached. "This must be the account she was talking about. It's just deposits month after month and then three withdrawals really close together. The last one was the day he died." He looked at another pile of papers. "Hmm, that's a coincidence…"

"What?" Mike asked, not turning his head from his computer.

"There's stuff in here from Hudson Inc. – product development information and profit and loss accounts." He set them to one side. "Ooh, some photos." He flicked through them and his eyes widened. "Oh my God."

"More coincidences?" Mike asked.

Hooper waited until he had Mike's full attention. "You're not going to like this." He handed over one of the photos.

The blood drained from Mike's face when he saw it. "Why the hell does he have a photo of Kate?"

"I dunno, but there's a few of them. It looks like he was watching her. I knew she was up to something. Now do you believe me?"

Mike buried his head in his hands. His mind raced as he tried to replay every conversation he'd had with Kate. He already knew that she'd lied to him once, but he believed her when she said she was now telling the truth. How could he have been so stupid? He hadn't listened to Hooper or Claire, and he'd even shrugged off his own misgivings. He was so angry – not just at Kate but at himself. How could he have been so gullible? He'd let her stay in his apartment, he'd given her his credit card and she'd even been alone with his grandson.

He got up from his desk and wandered aimlessly around the office, shaking with anger.

"What are you going to do?"

"I dunno." He continued to pace and resolved that as soon as she arrived, he would have it out with her. Not like at the hotel where he had practically rolled over for her like a well-trained puppy. He was done with her and her lies and he was going to ask her to leave.

Hooper glanced out of the window and saw her walking down the hall. "Shit, Mike, here she comes." He scrambled to get the documents and photos back into the box and was placing the lid on top when she came through the door.

Without even looking at her, Mike turned to Hooper. "We'll finish this later."

But when he looked at Kate, he saw that she was pale and shaking. His anger quickly turned to concern, and he rushed over to her. "Are you OK? What happened? Hooper, get her some water," he instructed as he pulled out a chair for her. He knelt in front of her and took her hands.

She looked him in the eye. "We really need to talk."

Then Hooper arrived back with the glass of water. "I'll leave you to it." He had turned to leave the office when Kate spoke.

"Hooper, you should probably hear this too."

Her hand was shaking as she brought the glass to her mouth. She took a few sips and looked nervously at Mike. "Please don't be cross with me."

His heart was thumping and his head was spinning but he tried to remain calm. He got up and sat on the edge of his desk. "Start talking."

She shifted in her seat. "I haven't been one hundred per cent honest with you. I haven't been researching Jack Hudson; I know him personally."

Mike groaned and looked at Hooper, who wasn't even trying not to look smug.

"Remember I told you I was a PA? That was true. I just didn't tell you that I was Jack Hudson's PA.

Everything started in January. A few of us PAs went out for drinks after work, celebrating because Jack had just given us a bonus. A guy started hitting on me at the bar, tried to get my number. After a while I had had enough and left, but I got the feeling I was being followed and when I turned around, he was there. He said he needed to talk to me alone, that he was a private investigator Hudson's wife had hired because she thought he was having an affair – which he did, by the way. She wanted concrete information for her solicitor before she confronted him. He said he just needed a bit of information and he would give me one thousand pounds to give it to him. He insisted that it was trivial information, he said no one would ever find out. I was having a bit of a cash flow crisis at the time so ... I said yes."

Mike and Hooper looked shocked.

"I know what you must be thinking, but I thought I was helping that poor woman get rid of her cheating husband! So what if I made a few quid in the process?"

She looked at them for approval, but didn't get it. She sighed.

"It was all pretty innocent. He gave me a date and time. All he wanted to know was who Hudson was meeting. He gave me his number and five hundred pounds in cash. I had to text him the details and he said he would meet me at the same bar the next night and give me the other five hundred. I thought even if I did it and he didn't show up I would still be five hundred quid better off for doing next to nothing. So the next morning I went in early and checked the calendar and texted the guy the information."

Mike rubbed his temples. "And was he meeting a

woman?"

"No, it was just a normal business meeting, nothing important, so I thought the guy might not even pay out. But that night we had a drink and he gave me the other five hundred." She took a deep breath. "Then he asked me for another favour."

"Jesus, Kate, what have you got yourself into?"

"He needed access to the building. He wanted ten minutes alone in Jack's office. If I could figure out a way to get him in there, he'd give me five thousand pounds."

Mike and Hooper glared at her.

"I knew it was too good to be true, but it seemed so easy – I mean, I practically ran that place. I could pull it off with no questions asked … so I said yes."

Mike opened his mouth to speak, then sighed and let her continue.

"I know it wasn't the best decision I ever made, but it went perfectly. Jack was out of town at a conference in Germany, so I scheduled an 'electrician' to come in and fix the blinking light above his desk. It was that easy. The PI was in and out in less than ten minutes and I had five grand in cash."

"Weren't you worried he'd query why the light wasn't fixed?"

"No, Hooper, because I changed the light bulb!"

"So, what did he do in there?" Mike asked, still unsure whether or not to believe her.

"I have no idea. He asked me to stay at my desk and keep watch in case someone came past."

"You really expect us to believe that?" Hooper scoffed.

"Yeah, I do. And I know he found something

important because the other times I'd met him we'd had a bit of chit-chat, about the weather and so on, but he left in a real hurry. The next time I saw his face, it was on the cover of a newspaper."

"Newspaper? What was the article about?"

"You should know, Mike. You wrote it."

He screwed up his face. "What? I don't write many articles any more, but I think I'd remember writing one about an English private investigator."

"Oh, I never said he was English. It turns out he wasn't a PI either, and that article you wrote was an obituary."

He thought for a second. "Alexander Crawford?"

She nodded. There was a dead silence in the office until Hooper spoke.

"I don't really understand what's going on here. Crawford killed himself."

"No, he didn't. I talked to him the day he died, and he was on to something. Hudson must have found out he'd been digging around and got to him. He made it look like suicide, the same way they made it look like Ray had a heart attack."

"That's a big reach, babe. Is there even a connection between Crawford and Ray? They're both reporters, so I suppose they could have been looking into the same story."

"You could say that." She looked at the ground. "I'm the connection and I'm the reason Ray got killed."

Mike and Hooper glanced at each other, then back to Kate.

"What I told you at the hotel wasn't a lie; it was a version of the truth. Ray and I had dated but lost touch years ago, then one day he turned up at my office to interview Jack. After the meeting we got talking and swapped numbers and agreed to meet up sometime. That was two days before I met Crawford. When I found out he was dead I knew I had to do something, so I rang Ray and told him what I've just told you. He said he'd look into it and the next day he was also dead. And the reason I'm positive that it wasn't a heart attack is because … I was there when he died." She went quiet.

Mike, who couldn't believe what he was hearing, tried to stay calm. "Keep going…"

"Ray called me and said he'd found something at the hotel where Crawford was staying and he'd tell me about it over a drink. He told me to meet him at a park not far from his office. I got to the park first and I was sitting waiting for him when I saw him enter through the other gate. I got up and started to walk towards him, then I saw a guy coming up behind him. He was wearing a hoodie, so I didn't see his face, but he reached into his pocket and took out a needle. He jabbed Ray with it and walked on past as if nothing had happened. Ray fell to the ground, and I froze. Other people rushed over to help him and called an ambulance, but he was already dead. I watched the man walk away. He didn't seem like he was looking for anyone else so I just stood there, too scared to move. Then I panicked. Whatever Ray had found out was worth killing him for, and if he had my name or any information about me in his office and someone came asking questions it might have led the killer to me. I knew where his office was, so I knew I had to get in there and remove all traces of myself."

Hooper shook his head. "So you did break in?"

"Of course I broke in! Two men were dead and I

thought I might be next. I broke in, took all his paperwork and went home."

Mike picked up Kate's glass of water and took a sip. "What did you do then?"

"I thought about going to the police, but I knew they wouldn't believe me – and even if they did, the killer might find out and come after me too. So I just went to work the next day and every day after that. I kept my head down and I listened but I didn't actively do anything to help those poor families. A few days later, Hudson was arrested here in New York for the embezzlement. The night before the trial, I jumped on a plane. I thought if I saw him go down for that, it would be some kind of justice. But I know his sentence won't be long enough, not for what he did."

She took the glass of water from Mike and finished it. "But now I know what I need to do next. I have to speak to Jack Hudson. I know him quite well so I might be able to get something out of him or force him to slip up and give away some info." She looked at Mike, who remained silent. He drew a deep breath and turned to Hooper.

"You've got some contacts in the DA's office and the Justice Department. Can you see if you can get Kate in to visit Hudson in prison?"

Hooper glared at Mike. *Was he serious?* "I'll give it a go, but I can't promise anything."

"I'd owe you one." Mike turned to Kate. "That was some story, babe."

"I—"

"Kate…"

Not knowing where to start, he took off his glasses and rubbed his eyes. "Is there anything else you need to tell me?"

She looked at the floor. "No."

"Are you sure? Because I asked you for honesty last week at the hotel and you didn't even tell me half the truth. What else aren't you telling me?"

"Nothing. I'm so sorry I didn't tell you everything, but I didn't want you to find out what I'd done, what a terrible person I am."

"You're not a terrible person, you're amazing."

"Oh yeah." She rolled her eyes. "Taking bribes, breaking and entering, getting people killed. Oh, I'm a modern-day Mother Teresa." She put her head in her hands. Mike put his arm around her.

"If you hadn't taken Crawford's money, he would have found someone else to take it, that's how these things are done. But maybe that person would have just walked away from all of this – you're trying to put it right. I'm going to help you get to the bottom of this, but you can't lie to me any more."

Hooper coughed. "I'm going to make a few calls." He shot Mike a concerned look on the way past. Mike returned what he hoped was a reassuring smile then focused back on Kate.

"Why did you decide to tell me all this now? What's changed?"

"Remember that guy from lunch yesterday?"

He recoiled. "You said you didn't know him."

"I don't, and I didn't see it at first, but I'm sure he's the guy that killed Ray. I didn't see his face at the time but he's the same height and same build. Just now, he forced me into a car and threatened me."

"He did what? Did he hurt you?" Mike was angry with himself. "I knew I should have gone after him

139

yesterday."

"He didn't hurt me. I'm just a little shaken up. And he didn't just threaten me…" She rubbed her eyes.

"Hey, don't worry." He tried to reassure her. "I've been threatened before – it comes with the job. What did he want?"

"For me to stop digging around, to call you off too and to get out of town."

He looked her in the eye. "Is there anything else? If there's anything you haven't told me, now is the time."

She bit her lip. "Actually…"

He rolled his eyes.

"When I said I didn't get into Hudson Inc., I lied. I did."

He sighed. "More breaking and entering?"

"No!" She hit him on the arm. "I used my key card from the London office. I swear I didn't think it would work but it did, and I got to speak briefly to Max Davenport. He's the new CEO."

"Who did you tell him you were?"

"Me. I was Jack's PA. I used to speak to Davenport all the time on the phone. We always had a sort of flirty back and forth so I tried to use it to get into his office, but he was on his way to a meeting."

"About that flirty back and forth … did you sleep with Ray and Crawford?"

The question caught her off guard. She hadn't thought of Mike as the jealous type. "Yes and no."

He gestured for her to elaborate.

"I didn't sleep with Crawford. I only met him those three times and it was all business. Was he your friend?"

"We worked together for a few years; he was a

good guy. So, you *did* sleep with Ray?"

"Yes, Mike, I slept with him loads of times. I told you that we used to date. It was years ago. I've made no secret of that fact that I've slept with a few guys – not as many as you probably think, mind you, but it doesn't make me a bad person."

He took her hand. "I know you're not a bad person. You're amazing and I'm crazy about you."

She blushed. "Whatever this is between us, I never intended to trick you or use you. The only reason I'm here with you is because I want to be. I have no ulterior motive."

He was visibly relieved. "Thank you, Kate. I don't really want to admit to being Mr Insecure but I'm really glad you said that because there has been a little doubt in the back of my mind. What would a beautiful woman like you see in an old man like me?"

"Are you crazy? You're a ten."

He looked at her as if she was insane.

"OK, maybe a nine, nine and a half." She winked.

"I'll take it." He puffed out his chest.

"I'm serious, Mike, you're gorgeous. You've got a great body, you're taller than me but not too tall, you have the most amazing blue eyes and a beautiful smile. You're funny, kind, successful … great in bed."

It was his turn to blush. "I know all that is true, but everyone thinks I'm too old for you."

"OK," she said sharply, "let's nip this in the bud right now. How old are you? Forty-five, forty-six?"

"I'm forty-eight."

"Oh." She screwed up her face. "I'm nearly thirty-eight so let's call it an even ten years. That's nothing, Mike. And why do you care what anyone else thinks?"

"I don't. Forgive me for thinking that you're too good to be true."

"You're forgiven. Everything is out in the open now so I don't want to hear the age thing or the honesty thing being mentioned again because you know everything about me – well, everything that's relevant to the current situation. But what are we going to do about Jack Hudson? That bloke manhandling me into the car proves that we're on to something. I really need Hooper to get me in to see him. I know I'll be able to get something out of him."

"I thought you told the guy that you were going to stop digging."

"Sometimes I just tell people what they want to hear," she said flippantly.

"Jesus, Kate, you're a paradox."

"Not you, Mike. You're not people. Are we clear?"

"Crystal. I think." He scratched his head and pointed at his newly acquired boxes. "Crawford's wife sent those down. They contain everything he was working on when he died."

"You're kidding? I'll start there now." She jumped up and hurried over to the boxes, ripped the lid off one and started looking through the paperwork.

He approached and picked up the photos. "I'm really glad you were totally honest with me, because he has some photos of you." He gave them to her and watched as she flicked through them.

"You look beautiful in this one – in all of them. How do you always look so beautiful?"

Blushing, she threw the photos down and wrapped her arms around him. "Are we OK? Remember the third condition. If you want me to go, I will."

"You're staying where you are. I need to keep a close eye on you." He looked her up and down. "A very close eye."

***

Mike couldn't stop thinking about her story as he cleared away the dinner dishes. She had got herself into a mess – and a dangerous one at that. He debated trying to get her to talk to the police, but it had all happened months ago and in another country, so there was no point unless they could find some new information. Maybe he should try to talk her out of pursuing it altogether. That guy could have hurt her – or worse. But he knew he would never be able to talk her out of it and she would just get angry at him if he tried. Hell, it would probably make her even more determined. He knew her well enough to know that she had a real stubborn streak.

He found her sitting on the floor between the fireplace and the sofa, surrounded by paperwork. He watched as she studied each page, her expression changing as she read. He knelt down behind her and massaged her shoulders. "I thought you'd finished for the night. There's plenty time for that tomorrow."

She groaned. "All this trouble for five grand. What was I thinking?"

"What did you spend it on anyway?"

"It's ironic, actually. I *was* going to use it to go travelling. I'd been in London too long and the walls were coming in on me." Her voice faltered. "But after everything happened, I was afraid, so I tried to forget about it. Then the day before the trial I just had this overwhelming urge to be here, to see Jack Hudson get sent down, so I used it to pay for the flight and the hotel. And now I know where it came from – Crawford's kids' college fund." She turned to him and rested her head on his knees. "Holy crap, I am a horrible person."

He stroked her hair. "I know you're not."

They sat in silence for a few moments then she sat up and gave him a seductive smile. "Do you have five grand I could borrow? I'll pay you back … eventually."

"I'll give you five grand," he said softly.

"Actually, with the exchange rate, it's probably more like seven. You put Claire through college – what would seven grand get you anyway?"

"Probably just textbooks. It really is just a drop in the ocean."

"Then I'll find another way to make it up to them." She narrowed her eyes. "Would you really have given me five thousand dollars?"

"I've already told you, you can have anything you want from me."

She glanced at the clock on the mantelpiece. "I think that's the wine talking. It's late. You'd better go to bed."

He climbed to his feet. "You're not coming?"

"You go on in, I'll be there in a sec."

He leant down and gave her a kiss, then she watched him walk into the bedroom. She rearranged the papers into neat piles and stared at the boxes. There had to be something in there. She wasn't sure how much more of this she could take. That guy had really scared her and she deeply regretted having got Mike involved. It was all such a mess, a far cry from her once carefree life. Trying not to think about it, she got up from the floor, picked up the empty wine glasses and took them into the kitchen. She washed them and left them on the side to dry, filled the coffee pot with water and set out two clean mugs for the morning.

When she got to the bedroom Mike was already asleep, flat on his back with his arms behind his head.

She watched him. She was really falling for him, but already part of her felt that this relationship wasn't a good idea. They had only known each other a little over a week, which she had spent lying to him, and she had already caused trouble with his daughter and got him threatened by a killer. Imagine what could happen if they were together for a month... Plus, even if things worked out between them, it was obvious that she would have to be the one to give up her life and settle down with him in New York. She wasn't sure she could do that. It was all too much to think about, so she resolved to put it to the back of her mind for now.

Climbing into bed naked, she nestled into his bare chest and draped her arm around his waist. Enjoying the feel of his warm skin against hers, she lay and listened to his heart beating until his breathing became heavier and he started to snore. She tried to stir him by tapping him on the chest. "*Mike.* Mike, you're snoring again."

She rolled her eyes when it did no good, then slid her hands beneath him and pushed him over onto his side. He grunted, but it did the trick. His snoring subsided. She moulded herself around him until she was comfortable, tuned herself into the sound of his breathing and adjusted her own to match.

Unconsciously his hand found hers and he brought

it up to his chest, squeezing it tightly. She squeezed back and thought about nothing other than the rhythm of their breathing until she too was asleep.

Chapter Ten

Mike watched Kate scrutinise every word on the page in front of her, wishing he could be that immersed in his own work, which was piling up on the desk beside his computer.

She looked confused.

"What is it, babe?"

"I found these in Crawford's box." She waved some papers at him. "It's financial information on a company called Biomes. When I was down at Hudson Inc. last week, I saw a letter for Max from the same company. I'm trying to figure out what they're about, but I can't make head nor tail of all this stuff. Something big could be staring me in the face but I can't see it because I don't know what the hell I'm looking for. Is there anyone here at the paper who knows anything about finance?"

"This is the *New York Times* – we know about everything. Up on the next floor are the Wall Street guys, financial analysts, that type of thing."

"So maybe I should run up there and see if someone could translate these for me."

Frowning, he leant towards her. "Don't take this the wrong way, but you're not authorised to be running around here talking to everyone, and I need to get some other work done." He took her hand and looked her in the eye. "We're getting nowhere because it's too hard for us to concentrate when we're together. I should be working but I just sit here staring at you, wishing that I had blinds on my window and a lock on my door."

She giggled. "I'm sorry, Mike. I don't want to get you into any trouble."

"It wouldn't be trouble but it's only a matter of time before Bob starts questioning where the big story is and why we've been wasting time and resources."

"Don't worry, honey, it's fine." She tidied up her half of the desk. "I've enjoyed spending all this time with you, but you are right, we need to be more professional. Who's Bob again?"

"He's the Associate Managing Editor."

"Top brass? Don't worry, I'm just going to run upstairs to see if there's anyone I can talk to and then I'll take all this stuff home and read it there. No need to bring a take-away. I'll throw dinner together." She glanced out of the window to see if anyone was watching, then gave him a quick kiss.

As she turned away he took her hand. "Take a cab, babe. I don't want you walking or taking the subway alone. You're not safe with that guy on the loose."

She tutted. "I went all the way around the world on my own. I think I can make it to your apartment in one piece."

He held his tongue and watched as she put some of the papers from the box into her laptop bag.

Before she left, she turned to him. "It's sweet of you to worry, but that guy took me by surprise. That won't happen again. And don't worry about Bob, either. I'll handle him." She hurried out of the door.

"What do you mean, babe?" He called after her. "*Kate?*" He buried his head in his hands. *I'm fired.*

***

The phones were silent and the office was nearly empty, but Mike was still busy at his computer; he'd barely made a dent in his pile of work. As he looked at his watch and tried to decide how much longer to work, it finally dawned on him. He sat back in his chair and thought about all the years he had spent working late, putting in that extra hour – he'd even sacrificed his marriage for it. It was far worse after his divorce. He was always first to arrive and one of the last to leave, he was there at weekends and on holidays, stopping for take-out on the way home to an empty apartment.

Enough was enough. It was Friday night and there was a gorgeous woman at home – why was he keeping her waiting? He was tidying up to leave when there was a knock on the door.

"Have you got a minute, Mike?"

"Yeah, Bob, what is it?"

"Word around the paper is that you and Kate are seeing each other. Is that right?"

"Yeah, you could say that." He would never have suspected that Bob would be the next in line to give him unsolicited advice about his love life.

"Good for you, Mike, she's a great girl. Is she what happened to you on Monday?"

"Yeah, sorry."

"Don't be sorry, we've all been there. Just don't make a habit of it." He winked. "She dropped by my office before lunch."

What the hell did she say to him? "She did?"

"She gave me the pitch and I thought it was a great idea, so I told her to run with it."

Mike loosened his tie. "Run with what?"

"What do you mean? She said it was your idea."

"What was my idea?" He swallowed. "I mean, we had a few. I just can't remember which one we settled on."

"Her freelance work. The series of features about her travels around the world? We talked it over for an hour. She's done some 'out there' stuff and has a unique perspective on things. I think she'll be really popular, especially with the online readers. You know full well that readership is down, and I think she could breathe some new life into this paper. She can have the desk next to Sulzberger but I'm not paying her a cent until I read something I like." He tapped his index finger on the desk. "Great job, Mike. We need that sort of forward thinking round here at the moment. I gotta go. You hold on to that girl. She's going places."

"Thanks, Bob."

He watched Bob leave then sat down at his desk and tried to make sense of what had just happened.

***

Mike stood at the door and watched Kate dance around to 'Hotel California'. He'd never seen his kitchen so alive with energy – there were bowls and plates everywhere, plus empty wrappers, containers and a huge pile of dishes in the sink.

Totally unaware that she had an audience, she stirred a pot on the hob while singing along.

He enjoyed watching her for a while before turning the music down.

She spun around. "I didn't hear you come in." Her eyes widened when she saw the huge bouquet of wild flowers in his hand. "Are those for me?" She clapped her hands as she approached.

"They are you." He smiled. "At least, the best representation of you that I could find: incredibly beautiful and really wild."

Blushing, she took them from him and kissed him on the cheek. She held them to her nose and took a deep breath, then sighed before setting them on the table and beginning to hunt through the cupboards.

He bit his lip as she bent down to the cupboard under the sink. He'd never seen her wearing jeans before and her ass looked great. He composed himself and pointed to the mess on the counter. "Where'd you get this stuff?"

"From the store – there's one right at the end of the street," she said sarcastically as she continued to look through the cupboards.

"You didn't need to go to all this trouble when you've been working all day."

Frustrated, she threw her hands in the air. "Vase?"

"No, why would I have a vase?"

"Why would you buy me flowers if you don't even have a vase?"

"Because I'm an idiot and didn't think it through..." He went to the small cupboard beside the fridge and pulled out a plastic beer pitcher.

"Perfect." She took it to the sink and filled it with water. As she arranged the flowers in the pitcher, she pointed to the pot on the stove. "Stir, please. So ... am I going with you to this party tomorrow night or not?"

He looked at her blankly then put his nose down into the pot and took a deep breath.

"Your son-in-law's thirtieth birthday party?"

"No, I'm not going to that."

"Why not?"

"Because I really don't want to."

"Don't be so selfish! It's not about what you want. Claire wants you there." She pointed a handful of flowers at him. "I don't have to go with you, but you are definitely going, you need to be there for your daughter. It won't hurt for us to spend one evening apart. I'll still be here when you get back."

He sighed. "I'm definitely not going by myself, but are you sure you want to go and make small talk with my ex and her new family?"

"Will there be alcohol there?"

"Yes."

"Then I'll be fine." She laughed. "I'll run out in the morning and get something nice to wear."

"No, that sounds like a lot of hassle for you. Let's just leave it." He raised the spoon to his lips and nodded in approval.

"What? Shopping in New York City, Mike, that's what every woman dreams of."

He shook his head. "I can't believe you've talked me into this. It's black tie so you'll need an evening gown or a cocktail dress." He set the spoon down and got his credit card from his wallet. "Please say yes. I don't want you to incur any expense on my behalf."

"Perfect." She offered him her hip. He slid the card into her back pocket and gently caressed her bum. "I'd say this is a little bit like that scene in *Pretty Woman,* but I'm not a prostitute."

"And unlike *Pretty Woman,* this card has a limit." He wrapped his arms around her waist and rested his chin on her shoulder. "But it's a generous limit so get a dress, accessories, whatever you need. And definitely get something for a little party of our own after." He nibbled her earlobe and ran his hand up to caress her breast.

"OK." She struggled to carry the flowers to the table with him wrapped around her.

He waited until she had put the pitcher in the middle of the table then spun her around, lifted her and perched her on the edge of the table. He wriggled his knee in between her legs and used it to spread her thighs apart, then wrapped his arms around her. "Will dinner keep?" He moved in for a kiss.

Trying to evade his lips, she teased, "No, *you* will."

"Oh, come on, I missed you this afternoon." He tried to kiss her again and she squirmed to avoid him.

"Well, that's what you get for throwing me out of your office."

"I didn't…" He gave her puppy dog eyes.

"I'm kidding." She pulled him to her and kissed him. "But I've put a lot of effort into dinner."

"I know – it smells amazing." He took her hand and kissed it as he helped her back to her feet. "In other news, Bob came by my office before I left and said you two had been talking."

"Yes, he's a great guy. I thought you said he was a huge pain in the ass?"

"He told me you'll be working at the paper. How the hell did that happen?"

She grimaced. "I hope you don't mind, but I didn't want you getting in trouble and I thought it would be easier for me to make a few contacts and do a bit more digging without having to explain myself all the time. I'll have my own work space so I'll be out from under your feet and you can work without distraction." She looked pleased with herself.

"But he's going to expect some stories, and you do know you're not really a reporter … don't you?"

He thought it was best to check, just in case she had some sort of split personality disorder she had 'omitted' to tell him about.

"A minor technicality. You know I've got loads of stories and I'm not bad at writing so I'll get something down on paper and then, with the help of a good editor to make it sound more newspapery, it's job done." She rubbed her nose against his and kissed him.

"I'm not that kind of editor, babe, but I know what you mean."

She pointed to her laptop on the coffee table. "I started one this afternoon, so have a little read through before dinner and let me know what you think. You've got ten minutes."

He was dubious but curiosity got the better of him, especially after hearing the word 'newspapery'. He shuddered. "I think I will."

Impatient, she helped him off with his jacket and ushered him towards the living room. "Oh, and I spoke to Chen up in Finance. Can you believe he just took all that stuff for me? He's going to read it over the weekend and give me an abridged version on Monday. What a sweetheart."

Not at all surprised that she had charmed someone else into helping her out, he settled down on the beige sofa, pulled the coffee table closer, adjusted the angle of the screen and picked up the waiting bottle of beer.

The smell of Thai food coming from the kitchen soon made sense. Captivated, he read her story about a hike to Wat Chaloem Phra Kiat, deep in the mountains of Northern Thailand. It was good. She never ceased to surprise him. He called to her in the kitchen. "You've got a real talent, babe."

"You have to say that! You're sleeping with me."

He rolled his eyes. "I've got integrity, you know. I'm serious. It won't take much to polish this up and make it printable."

"Thanks. When you're done, go to the desktop. There's a folder, *Story One*. It's pictures for the online version."

"This is great, but why did you tell Bob it was my idea?"

"It was your idea! You inspired me, you—"

The doorbell rang.

"Are you expecting someone?"

He shook his head.

"OK, keep reading. I'll get it."

Praying it wasn't his daughter, Kate opened the door, relieved to find Hooper shifting from foot to foot.

He squinted at her. "I thought I'd find you here."

"Of course you would, I'm staying here now. Come in."

"You are?" he asked, puzzled. "Since when?"

She pointed towards Mike at the coffee table as she walked back to the kitchen. Hooper followed and tried to get Mike's attention by waving at him. Mike, not even taking his eyes off the screen, waved back half-heartedly.

"What are you cooking? It smells amazing."

"Thai curry," she replied.

"I love Thai food," he said wistfully. "Mike and I usually grab a beer and some wings on a Friday night. I suppose I'll just have to go on my own."

That was a guilt trip if ever she'd heard one. "Would you like to stay for dinner?"

He nodded and went to the refrigerator. He was startled to see it was full of food. He helped himself to a bottle of beer. "Where'd all this food come from?"

"Why are you here, Hooper?"

He tapped his nose and made her wait until he had opened the bottle, put it to his lips and taken a long drink. He set the beer on the counter and made a show of patting down his jacket pockets, finally revealing a folded piece of paper. He handed it over and eagerly awaited her reaction.

Uncertain, she looked at the content and gasped. "Thank you so much!" She threw her arms around him and kissed him on the cheek. He recoiled. Then Mike joined them in the kitchen.

Kate waved the paper in the air. "Hooper's guy came through! It's a visiting permit for Hudson, it's for…" She realised she hadn't read any further than the title of the document, so she read on. "Tuesday. Thank you, Hooper." She looked at the permit again before she noticed that the pot on the stove was boiling over. "Oh shit." She set the permit on the counter and lifted the pot. "Guys, it's ready, sit down."

"You're staying for dinner?" Mike looked at Hooper, then smiled at Kate, thankful they were getting along.

She winked back at him. "He doesn't even seem worried that it might be poisoned."

Hooper's face fell and he whacked Mike on the arm. "You told her?"

Kate gave Hooper a reassuring pat on the back. "It's OK. Poisoning's not my style … it's way too subtle.

When I want you dead, you'll know about it."

She set a plate with a ball of steamed rice before each of them and revealed her menu. "This is *gang daeng*, red curry with chicken, coconut milk and lime leaves. *Pad Thai*, basically noodles with beansprouts, but you'll like what I've done with it. *Som tam*, it's a papaya salad but I made it extra spicy so it might be rough on your little tummies if you're not used to it. And I threw together some spring rolls and made my patented sweet chilli dipping sauce."

Mike was astounded. "You did all of this in one afternoon?"

"I didn't make the filo pastry – life's too short. Dig in, guys." She set herself a place at the table, sat down and watched as they filled their plates and took their first taste.

They chewed slowly. The flavours of the curry – coconut, lemon grass, spices – exploded in their mouths. They looked at each other and took another mouthful.

"Is it OK?"

"OK? I think this is the best food I've ever eaten."

"Yeah, babe, this is pretty great. Where did you learn to cook this stuff?"

"Thailand." She shrugged as she filled her plate. "I worked in a kitchen for a few months chopping vegetables and doing dishes but I paid attention and picked up a thing or two."

"This certainly is a thing or two." Mike looked at her with affection.

Hooper noticed the intimate look and joked, "This is all very cosy. Have you guys set a date for the wedding yet?"

Mike nearly dropped his fork and kicked Hooper under the table while Kate glared at him.

"Not yet, Hooper, but we'll be sure to let you know." She took a long sip of her wine and changed the subject. "Where's Hudson's prison?"

After dinner they relaxed in the living room. Kate lay on the sofa, her feet on Mike's lap, listening intently as he told a story about a high school football game. Hooper sat in the armchair and watched Mike rub Kate's feet while she nodded along to his story, even though it was obvious that she hadn't got a clue what he was talking about.

When Mike got to the climax of his story, Hooper laughed but Kate stared at them blankly. She didn't get it.

"On that note, I'm going to bed. I'll need all my energy for my shopping trip tomorrow."

Sensing that was his cue to leave, Hooper sat up straight. "I should go."

"Don't go on my account – you'll probably want some time alone with Mike to talk about me." She giggled. "Do you guys want another beer while I'm up?"

Sheepishly, they nodded as she picked up her wine glass and the empty beer bottles and took them into the kitchen. She returned with two fresh beers and handed one to Hooper.

"Don't forget your leftovers."

"Thank you, Kate."

She turned to Mike and held his beer behind her back. "You don't get yours as easy." She leant down to him and pursed her lips.

He stretched up and kissed her. "Goodnight. I'll try

not to wake you."

"Wake me if you want to," she whispered as she disappeared into the bedroom.

Hooper looked behind him to make sure she was gone before he spoke.

"You two seem pretty loved up, but I thought this was meant to be a casual thing. It's been, like, a week and you've moved her in – why didn't you tell me?"

"Because I didn't want that look you just gave me. I know it's totally crazy. I met her eleven days ago but I feel like I've known her eleven years." He sat up and looked serious. "And don't use that word 'love' around her and definitely no more marriage jokes," he warned. "She's got a thing about commitment."

"If she's so against commitment, should you really be pursuing this? You're just leaving yourself open to get hurt and I don't want a repeat of the Barbara fiasco."

"This is nothing like what happened with Barbara. I know it might not work out but I'm willing to take that chance. I think she's worth the risk. She's beautiful, smart, funny – everything about her is amazing."

"Yeah, even her lies."

Mike sighed. "She made a mistake and she's trying to put it right. I really admire her for that."

"Well, I have to admit that I'm warming to her a little, and she sure can cook."

"No kidding. We went to the market on Sunday and got a load of stuff and right before my eyes she turned it into beef Wellington – she made *that* pastry from scratch. And Monday morning it was eggs Benedict, which was phenomenal." He looked nervous. "And you should probably know that Bob's given her the go-ahead for some freelance work for the paper."

"What? Why, how?"

"I don't know exactly what she said to him, but he told me tonight before I left."

"But she's not really a reporter – can she even write?"

"Actually, she's pretty good. And not a word to Bob that she's not really a reporter."

Hooper shook his head. "Now she's got us lying for her?"

"Just a white lie. She'll be able to pull it off."

"Is there anything she can't do?"

Mike shook his head. "Not that I've seen so far."

Chapter Eleven

The party was in full swing when Mike arrived in the ballroom. Dressed impeccably in a tuxedo, he fiddled with his cuffs as he looked around the room at the mix of well-dressed socialites, medical professionals and members of Audrey's extended family.

People were already dancing to instrumental versions of classic love songs played by a six-piece band on a platform. There was no sign of Kate, but he noticed Claire waving from the back of the room. He joined her and she greeted him with a beaming smile.

"Hi, Daddy." She threw her arms around him. "Thank you so much for coming. No Kate?"

"I had to see a guy about some tickets, and she was running late so she's going to meet me here."

Claire's face fell. He took her hand.

"I know you're having trouble with this but please be nice to her. She's important to me."

"OK, Dad, I'll try. I just don't think she's right for you." She managed a smile. "But come over here. There's someone I want you to meet."

She ushered him over to a woman in her early fifties and introduced them. She said that Mike was a keen golfer and because the lady was thinking of taking up the sport, they should have lots to talk about. It was obvious that she was trying to set them up.

Mike shook his head. How could Claire have the audacity to do that when she knew Kate was on her way?

"I'll leave you two to chat." Claire scurried away.

The woman stroked his arm. "It's lovely to finally meet you, Mike. I've heard a lot about you."

"I'm sorry..." He had been so busy getting annoyed at Claire that he hadn't caught her name. "I think Claire has got her wires crossed. I'm actually seeing someone."

"She didn't mention it..."

"She's having trouble with it; she doesn't approve."

Her grip on his arm tightened. "I've been there. Last year I was seeing this guy and my kids just didn't take to him. They made his life hell until he dumped me. It was such a shame too – he was a lawyer, really well off. I can't get used to this role reversal where my kids think they can tell *me* what to do. That's OK, Mike, I actually had my eye on a guy tonight" – she pointed over to a group of men at the bar – "the one on the left, he's a surgeon. Good luck to you." She headed off towards the men.

Relieved at his lucky escape, Mike spotted Claire and made a beeline for her.

"How could you do that, knowing that Kate is on her way?"

"I'm sorry, Dad, but I didn't think it would hurt for you to keep your options open, just in case."

He was about to remind her that he was more than capable of choosing his own dates when they were joined by another man, who put his arm around Claire's waist and extended his hand to Mike.

They shook hands.

Mike slipped him an envelope. "Happy birthday."

"Thanks, Mike." Steve grinned as he put what he hoped were great Knicks tickets into his jacket pocket.

"And thanks for coming. I know how much you hate these things. I can't wait to meet your date. Believe me, I've heard all about her." He gestured towards an annoyed Claire, who was glaring at him.

Mike felt a hand on his arm and turned, expecting to see Kate, but found his ex-wife instead. Almost a head taller than him, she was slim with short brown hair and looked elegant in a flowing white ball gown and pearls.

"You're looking well, Mike." She kissed his cheek. "Where's Kate?"

"She's running a bit late. Oh, she's…" he glanced at the door, "she's just arrived."

They all turned to see Kate in the doorway dressed in a rich burgundy off-the-shoulder cocktail dress. The hem framed her slim legs and her stilettos made them look longer. Her usually straightened red hair had been transformed into soft curls that framed her perfectly made-up face. She looked elegantly minimal, with her only accessories a silver choker and small black clutch bag.

Anxiously she scanned the room. When she met Mike's eyes, a warm smile spread across her face and all her insecurities melted away. She held his gaze as she walked towards him and the rest of the group, radiant and full of confidence.

"I'm so sorry I'm late." She kissed him softly on the lips and turned to face the others. Mike took her arm for support, not entirely sure which of them needed it most at that moment.

"Everyone, this is Kate. You've met Claire."

Kate waved to Claire, who had to be nudged by her husband before she responded with a smile.

"And this is my son-in-law Steve, the birthday boy."

"It's a pleasure to meet you," Steve said genuinely as he shook her hand.

"And this is Audrey, my … Claire's mom."

"Hi, Kate, it's lovely to meet you." She extended her hand.

"It's lovely to meet you too, Audrey. Well, to meet all of you." She looked around the group. "I love your dress, Audrey, is it Dior?"

Audrey nodded.

"It looks beautiful on you."

They stood in silence until the slightly awkward mood was broken up by another man who arrived at Audrey's side. He was taller than her, slim with black hair and dressed in a traditional tuxedo.

"Kate, this is my husband, Rodger."

"It's a pleasure to meet you, Kate." He kissed her hand.

"You too, Rodger. Is Michael here too?"

"He's over there with his uncles. Those are our sons, Jake and Ethan." He pointed to the children's table in the corner and she spotted Michael playing a game of peek-a-boo with two young boys.

"You two have a lovely family. If you don't mind, I'm going to go and say hi to Michael. Please excuse me." She squeezed Mike's arm as she left.

Audrey watched Mike watch her go. "She seems lovely, Mike."

"She is. I hope this isn't too awkward." He took a deep breath and braced himself for the advice that was about to start pouring in.

"Not for me," Steve offered irreverently, and Claire elbowed him in the ribs. "Ouch."

Audrey touched Mike's arm. "It's fine. I'm glad you could both come. Oh, look at that!" She pointed over at Michael, who had leapt into Kate's arms. "Michael seems to be taken with her."

"I hope he doesn't form too much of an attachment," Claire joked.

Having had enough of her jokes, Mike turned, intending to reprimand her, but before he could open his mouth to speak, he was beaten to it by an angry Audrey.

"Where are your manners, young lady? Show your father some respect."

Claire gave her mother an angry look and stormed off. Steve and Rodger sloped off quietly too.

"So how long have you and Kate been together?"

"Not long. Actually, we're just good friends."

"Claire said you're living together?"

He was taken aback. "We're not living together; she's just staying with me while she's in town."

Audrey held up her hands. "I wasn't judging. I saw the way you looked at her when she arrived. In all our years together you never looked at me like that."

"We were just kids, Audrey." He sighed.

"I know but I always hoped you'd get married again, that you'd be happy, like me and Rodger."

"Hey!" He waited until he caught her eye. "It's OK. That was a long time ago. I'm not your responsibility any more; I can take care of myself." He took a deep breath. "Would you please excuse me? I need a drink."

"Me too."

He put his arm around her shoulder and they walked together to the bar.

By midnight, guests had started to leave but the band were still playing for the half dozen couples that occupied the dance floor. Mike and Kate were sitting with Audrey and her family around a circular table littered with empty glasses and beer bottles.

Michael was sound asleep in his father's arms. The other children were watching iPads and the adult conversation mostly revolved around sports.

The band began to play 'The Way You Look Tonight'. Kate turned to Mike.

"I love this song. Would you like to dance?"

He screwed up his face. "Dancing isn't really my thing, I'm sorry, I wouldn't feel comfortable." He rested his hand on her knee.

"That's OK." She looked down at the table and ran her fingers up and down the stem of her champagne flute. Envious of the other couples on the dance floor, she was taking a sip of her drink when she heard someone clear their throat.

"I would *love* to dance with you, Kate."

She looked up to find Audrey's eldest son, Jake, offering his hand.

"What a gentleman." She swooned as she allowed him to help her up.

The youngster winked cheekily at Mike as he led Kate onto the dance floor.

Mike watched them dance. She was elegant, graceful and effortlessly leading the young man through what looked to be his first ever dance. He looked across the table to his daughter. She was deep in conversation with her husband as their child drooled on his shoulder. Other family and friends were laughing and chatting, and it suddenly dawned on him that this party hadn't been so bad after all.

He looked back at Kate, grateful that she'd talked him into coming. And even though she was probably feeling just as out of place as he was, she was handling the evening perfectly. He was suddenly racked with guilt when he realised that all she had asked of him in return was a simple dance.

He finished his drink and excused himself from the table. He walked out onto the dance floor and tapped Jake on the shoulder.

"Get out of here, squirt, I can handle it from here."

The youngster looked disappointed when Mike offered his hand to Kate.

"May I?"

Kate kissed Jake on the cheek and curtseyed. "Thank you, handsome, that was the best dance I've ever had."

Jake blushed as he headed back to the table.

She turned her gaze to Mike, knowing that it had taken a lot for him to change his mind, especially in front of the current company.

He took her hand, put his arm around her waist and pulled her in close. They began to move in time to the music.

Bringing his lips to her ear he whispered, "I don't think I told you that you look incredible tonight." He saw her blush. "I'm serious. Just look around – everyone in the room is staring at you."

A quick look around revealed that at least half the eyes in the room were fixed on them.

"They're probably wondering how I got so lucky." She nestled her head on his shoulder and they danced slowly until he whispered into her ear again.

"I really want to kiss you, but I'm afraid I might not be able to stop."

She tilted her head and looked deep into his eyes. "Would you be comfortable doing that in front of all these people?"

"Yes, and I hope they're all watching."

He ran his hand through her hair, looked into her brown eyes and kissed her. As she kissed him back, his hold on her tightened. That was the moment he realised that he would never be able to let her go.

The band were packing up to go home. Kate waited patiently with Mike's jacket while he finished catching up with an old friend.

Audrey joined her and they smiled awkwardly at each other before Kate spoke.

"It was a great party, thank you."

"You're welcome. Do you mind if I say something?"

"No," Kate said politely, wondering what was to come.

"I was more than shocked when Mike called to say he was coming and a little worried when he said he was bringing someone. I've never met anyone he was seeing before, but I can already tell that you're good for him. I've known him a long time – we dated in college, we were married for thirteen years and we've been divorced a little longer, but I hardly recognised him tonight. He's so … relaxed. I know you talked him into coming. And that's only the third time I've ever seen him dance."

Kate was taken aback. "Thanks, Audrey. I was a little worried too. I wasn't sure what to expect and Claire didn't exactly give me a warm reception when I first met her."

Audrey rolled her eyes. "Don't worry about Claire. She's used to sharing me with Rodger and the boys, but she usually has her daddy all to herself. It's not personal; she hates anyone he's seeing. She did have a few nice words to say about you and she told me that you've done a lot of travelling. I wouldn't mind hearing a few of your stories, because I want to talk Rodger into taking a trip for our anniversary next year. Maybe you could give me some advice?"

"Of course. We could have a cup of coffee or grab lunch sometime?" She frowned. "Claire said something nice about me?"

They were laughing when Mike approached them. He put his arm around Kate's waist. "You ready to go, babe?"

Kate nodded and handed him his jacket, which he immediately draped around her shoulders. He shifted his glance between the two of them.

"I hope you two are not comparing notes?"

Audrey and Kate giggled.

"No, we're going to meet for lunch to do that. Goodnight, Audrey, and thank you again."

"It was lovely to meet you, Kate. Mike can give you my number."

They hugged as a bewildered Mike looked on.

As they walked away, he whispered, "You guys are on hugging terms?"

"Yes, I think I just made a new friend." She linked arms with him and rested her head on his shoulder as they walked out of the ballroom.

"That's great, babe." He kissed the top of her head. "But did it have to be my ex-wife?"

Chapter Twelve

Very early on Tuesday morning, they were woken by Kate's mobile ringing. Startled by the sudden noise, they sat up in bed and looked around the room. *Who on earth is ringing this early?* Kate wondered, reaching for her mobile phone, which said 04:57.

Mike put his head back down on the pillow and closed his eyes.

She answered the call. "Hi. Yes, I'm fine. Lunch? I can't, I'm still in New York. Yes. I'm sorry I didn't call. I got distracted."

She looked over at Mike, who had a smug grin on his face.

"I'm not sure when I'll be back. Actually, can you do me a huge favour and go down to Heathrow and pick up my car? I'll post you the key and the ticket." She shook her head. "On second thoughts, don't worry. It'll probably cost more than it's worth to bail it out of the short-term car park." She grimaced. "I know, but it was closer to the terminal and I was late for my flight. I had to flirt my backside off to jump my way through the queue at security... Yes, OK. Is Diane there?"

She sighed and watched Mike pretend to not to listen.

"Hi, Mum, how are— No, nothing's wrong, I just decided to stay a bit longer." She fiddled with her hair. "There *might* be a guy. Of course he's handsome. No, I will not. Mike. An editor at the *New York Times*. Oh, and I'm working there now too – as a freelance." She rolled her eyes. "No, it was not nice of him to get me a job. I got it for myself. It's still early here – can I give you a call later today? OK, bye Mum, love you." She rubbed her eyes as she ended the call. "Sorry, that was my foster parents."

He put his arm around her and kissed the top of her head. She snuggled into him.

"I figured. You call her Mum?"

"She became like a mum to me. I initially said it as a joke but she liked it, and I suppose I do too. She only had boys of her own and she treats me like the daughter she never had. She wants me to send her a photo of you. She's so embarrassing." She glanced at the alarm clock and circled his nipple with her finger. "So … we've got a while before we need to get up."

He looked at the clock and back to her. "Really? You're insatiable. I'm still exhausted from last night."

Giggling, she slid her hand down to his crotch and gave a quick squeeze. "I'll go easy on you then, and afterwards I'll make you a nice breakfast so you have plenty of strength for tonight."

He turned onto his side to face her. "I want to talk to you about that." He brushed the hair away from her face. "You do too much for me. You're not my maid. The cleaning and the cooking are fantastic, but I hope you don't feel obliged to do that stuff because you're staying here."

She squinted at him. He was right – she had been doing all those things without even realising it. She felt more at home with him than she realised.

"I don't... I guess I like looking after you."

"Good. Because I like it too, but you're going to have to let me look after you as well. So tonight you're going to put your feet up and I'll cook."

She shook her finger at him. "No, I'm too much of a control freak for that. Anyway, I thought you hated cooking."

"I don't mind cooking, I just hate cooking for one."

"Then I'm looking forward to it, but I don't eat fish – anything but fish." She pretended to gag.

He laughed. "So, did I eavesdrop correctly? You've no real plans to go home?"

"No immediate plans, but I have to go home sometime."

"Why?"

"Because my visa's only ninety days…"

"I know, but there are ways around that. It's not like you have anything to go back to."

"Excuse me?" She sat up and glared at him. "I have a life. People who care about me."

"That's not what I meant, babe. I just—" He stopped himself. He knew he was starting an argument he couldn't win. There was nothing he could say to change her mind, and the more he tried the more she would try to resist.

The last thing she wanted was to have 'the talk'. Even though she really didn't want to, she heard herself say, "Do we need to talk about this?"

He looked her in the eye. "I know this was meant to be casual and you're supposed to go back to London, but then you got the job at the paper, and you just threw away your car … I thought you'd changed your mind."

She rubbed her head. "Then you're overthinking it, Mike. Let's just take it one day at a time. OK?"

"OK." He turned onto his back and stared at the

ceiling.

It was obvious to her that something had changed, for him anyway. How had she not seen it happen? She felt awful that he felt so insecure. She rested her head on his chest and thought about how to reassure him.

"Don't worry, I'm not going anywhere yet." She grimaced. *That probably won't cut it*.

They lay together in an uncomfortable silence and listened to the sounds of the world waking up outside. The word 'yet' plagued him. He stroked her hair and sighed. He knew ninety days wasn't long enough.

She kept her eyes closed and tried desperately not to focus on his breathing – it made her too conscious of her own. But it was no use. She was uncomfortable and had to get out of there.

"It's a long way to the prison so I'd better start getting ready. I'm going to have a shower."

As she got out of bed, she half expected him to try and pull her back in, but he didn't. She turned to him. "Would you like me to make you some coffee first?"

He lifted his head from the pillow and smiled back. "No, thank you." He put his head back down and closed his eyes.

She stood and stared at him. She didn't like seeing him upset, but she didn't know what else to do. Settling down wasn't what she wanted so she couldn't let him believe it was. Her head was spinning. She didn't want to leave, but she didn't want to stay either.

Knowing she hadn't left the room, he opened his eyes. She stood at the foot of the bed, staring at him.

"What are you thinking?" he said, sitting up.

She bit her lip. "That I wish I hadn't met you, Mike Kelly." She took a deep breath. "You've complicated my life."

He let out a little laugh and beckoned her over. She joined him at the side of the bed and he took her hand.

"Good." He brought her wrist to his mouth and kissed it.

She ran her other hand through his hair as he worked his way up her arm, kissing her soft skin while his other hand caressed the small of her back.

She whispered into his ear, "I really do have to shower. Why don't you come with me?" She motioned for him to join her and walked off towards the en-suite.

He followed close behind.

***

The prison was much more modern than she had expected – and not at all like ones she'd seen in the movies. Not sure of the protocol, she watched the other visitors and decided it would be a good idea to pick one of the more experienced-looking ones to be her unwitting guide. She saw a Chinese woman, probably in her seventies, who looked to be more than used to the procedure.

She quickened her pace to follow her through the entrance gate and to the main door where she was asked to show her identification and visiting pass. Her mobile and handbag were sent through the X-ray scanner while she had to walk through a state-of-the-art body-scanning machine. Kate held her breath. Even though she knew she had nothing to hide, the whole process made her feel as guilty as the man she was visiting.

She collected her belongings and continued to

another reception area where she showed her documents again, signed the visitors' register and took a seat.

This was it: she was about to come face to face with Jack Hudson. After all these months, she would be able to call him a murderer to his face. She put her hands between her knees to stop her legs from shaking, then the Chinese woman was called forward. She nodded in polite recognition to the guards as she moved to the next room.

Kate wondered who the lady might be visiting and how many times she had been through this rigid and unpleasant process. Then her name was called, and she approached the door.

"Bay Four, please, ma'am." The guard held the door open and she walked into the visiting room.

This room was more like what she had seen in the movies. A line of twelve booths faced a huge glass wall which ran the width of the room. On the other side there was a matching row of twelve booths. Phone handsets were fixed to the wall to the right of each bay.

Unlike the deafening silence of the waiting room, this room was noisy: there was talking, crying, even laughter. She approached the empty Bay Four, sat down on the grey plastic chair and looked through the glass to the door on the other side.

She glanced over at the woman she had followed. She was sitting opposite a man of approximately the same age – most likely her husband. Their phones were still hanging on the wall; they were just looking at each other.

Kate stared at them, wondering if they were in love or had been in love at some point. She thought about

Mike and imagined them being separated by a glass wall. Could she bear not being able to touch him, or feel his touch? What if they were separated by an ocean and she couldn't see him every day? When the time came, would she actually be able to walk away? No sooner had she thought about having the freedom to walk away than she remembered she was in a prison. A feeling of claustrophobia washed over her. What if deciding to stay with Mike made her feel imprisoned?

On the other side of the glass, the door opened. She was so consumed by her thoughts that she didn't notice Jack Hudson enter the room.

He was average height, average build and actually average in every way. He had no distinguishing features and only looked like a criminal thanks to his orange jumpsuit. He looked withdrawn as he made his way to his seat, but his expression changed to anger when he saw who his visitor was. He picked up the handset and tapped it on the glass to get her attention.

She tried to compose herself as she picked up the phone. She took a deep breath and gave him a little wave. "Hi, Jack."

"What the hell are you doing here?" he demanded.

"What, a girl can't just stop by and see her ex-boss in prison?"

He shook his head and pointed his finger at her. "It was you, wasn't it? Who hired you?"

"You hired me, Jack."

"Not as my PA! Who hired you to set me up?"

Confused, she sat back in her chair. "I didn't set you up."

"Of course you did. Then you came to the trial to see me squirm and now you're here to gloat. Who hired you? Laura?"

"Your wife? No, she didn't hire me! And I'm not here to gloat, I'm here to prove you had my ex-boyfriend killed."

"What?" He sounded horrified. "I didn't have anyone killed. What the hell can I do from in here?" He gestured to the prison guards.

"Not from in here – months ago in London. Ray, the reporter you talked to."

She saw his eyes widen. *He knows I'm on to him.*

"Ray Freers? I didn't know he was your boyfriend, and he wasn't killed. The poor guy had a heart attack."

"No, he didn't! I saw it happen. He was murdered – and by the same guy you sent to threaten me."

"I have no idea what you're talking about. I don't know anything about a guy threatening you, and I definitely don't know anything about murder."

"It's a bit of a coincidence that a few days after Ray talked to you, he's dead, don't you think? I know he did some digging and found out about the embezzlement, so you had him killed to bury the story."

He shook his head. "You've got this all wrong. I didn't want to bury his story – I was giving him his story!"

She squinted at him. "You told him about the embezzlement?"

"No. I didn't even know about the embezzlement until I was arrested for it. I told you, I'm innocent." Looking defeated, he rested his head on his hand.

She thought she saw a tiny flicker of something that looked like sincerity and thought back to her first drink with Mike. He hadn't believed her story at first but gave her the benefit of the doubt. Maybe she should afford

Jack the same courtesy.

"OK. Let's ignore the fact that you've been found guilty by a court of law." She rolled her eyes. "Convince me you're innocent. Start with Ray. You said you were giving him a story – what was it?"

"A world exclusive. You know that new drug we're developing?"

"The top-secret spot cream that no one was allowed to talk about? Sure."

"That's the one. But it's not a spot cream. It's a cure for Alzheimer's and dementia." He held up his hands. "Sorry, the lawyers said I'm not allowed to use the word 'cure'. It's a treatment. It significantly reduces symptoms and gives patients a greater quality of life. Usually a drug like that would be so expensive that it would be out of reach for the millions of patients that desperately need it, but I found this company, Medibond, that has developed a ground-breaking new technology to manufacture the active pharmaceutical ingredient. We're working on the details of the licensing and technical agreements and we hope to manufacture it for a fraction of the usual cost. And we're going to pass those savings on to the customer. It'll be the first affordable drug of its type – and it's going to revolutionise the industry."

Kate thought that sounded amazing – well, everything but the pharmaceutical company not wanting to make any more money. That didn't sound plausible at all.

"Why on earth would you sacrifice that amount of potential profit?"

"When I got the job as CEO of GB Inc., I found out they had been investing huge amounts of money into the research and development of this drug. It almost bankrupted them. That's how I was able to acquire a huge percentage of the stock, and it became Hudson Inc. as you know it now." He looked her in the eye. "Kate, my grandfather had dementia. I saw what it did, not just to him but to my whole family. This is my chance to do something worthwhile, to really make a difference."

"That all sounds very admirable, but how did Ray fit in to all this?"

"A few years ago he wrote a story about the hypocrisy of the industry. It really stuck with me. I wanted him to have the world exclusive. He just had to wait until the drug had been approved by the regulatory authorities."

Kate nodded. That corroborated what Ray had told her and removed Jack's motive for his murder. She must have missed something else.

She tapped her foot on the floor. "What happened in the days between you talking to Ray and getting arrested?"

"You already know that, Kate. I went to Germany for the conference and then came here to New York. Did anything strange happen in London while I was gone?"

She grimaced. "There was another reporter snooping around, an American. He claimed to be a private investigator, but it turns out that he was actually a reporter for the *New York Times*. His name was Alexander Crawford. You didn't talk to him too, did you?"

"No, I've never heard of him."

"He was very interested in you." She hung her head, ashamed. "He paid me to give him some information about you – it was about the meeting with Medibond. He also paid me to let him into your office to do some snooping around."

"For what?"

"I don't know, but he ended up dead too. They say it was suicide, but I don't buy it. Give me a minute. I need to think."

She hung up the handset and racked her brains. Two dead reporters and the only link between them – that she knew for sure – was that she had talked to them both. If Jack really was as clueless as he seemed to be, there had to be someone else involved.

She took a deep breath and picked up the handset. "Tell me about the embezzlement. What happened?"

"You were at the trial; you know what happened."

"Remind me."

"An audit exposed the missing money and the forensic accountants found it in my bank account. But I didn't take it – I didn't set up that offshore account."

"But the expert at the trial verified that it was your signature on all the paperwork."

He looked down at the table. "You know me – sometimes I sign stuff without really looking at it."

She shifted in her seat. That was exactly how she had got him to approve bonuses for her and the other secretaries…

"Then why didn't you mention that at the trial?"

"Because my lawyer told me not to. He said it might incriminate me on some of the other things I'd signed."

"Oh, like what?" She held up her hand. "Actually, I don't want to know."

"My lawyer was useless. He wanted me to plea bargain so we wouldn't even go to trial. He said I'd lose the company but I wouldn't go to prison. But I couldn't plead guilty to something I hadn't done. I asked Max if I should fire him and get someone else but he said that—"

"Max?" She rubbed her head.

"Yeah, he recommended the lawyer to me. Said they were old friends from college."

Now her head was spinning. If Max Davenport had got him the shitty lawyer, maybe *he* was involved.

"Could Max be involved in all this?"

"No – they looked at him for embezzlement too, but they didn't find anything."

She rolled her eyes in frustration. "Not the embezzlement, the setting-you-up part."

"Why would he? He's my business partner."

"Exactly! So if anything happens to you, for example you go to prison, he takes over running the company, leaving him free to do whatever he wants." She remembered her visit to the New York office and the letter that had arrived. Noreen had been really uptight about it. She screwed up her face. "I was down at the Wall Street office the other day. I heard they're using a company called Biomes for the new product."

"Biomes? No. They tendered for it but not only were their costs huge, their audit findings were never great. They're on the verge of going out of business, so there's no way we would have given them the contract."

"Well, we did."

"No, I had everything ready to bring to the board for approval. We were using Medibond. Max wasn't overly happy about it but once I'd explained to him that we could bump up the margins on a couple of other products, and the good will it would generate would be great for the company, I talked him round."

"Did you?" She gritted her teeth. "I used to think you were smart, Jack. Max set you up."

Jack slumped in his chair. "I hate to admit it, but I think you might be right."

"You know I'm right."

Kate stared at Jack in silence. If she *was* right, he was innocent and he had just been trying to be a philanthropist – sure, he would still make some money from the sale of his new drug, but he obviously wanted to help people. Max? He was probably still in the business of making money – and stood to lose billions if Jack made his deal. It was entirely possible that Max had Jack set up to get him out of the way. But would he kill to protect a deal like that? People had killed for less, hadn't they?

"I'm going to help you. I'll get to the bottom of this, but I need a few more answers—"

"I don't mean to be rude, but what do you think you can do? You were just my assistant, and you weren't even qualified to do that. I only gave you the job because you were pretty and I thought you might sleep with me."

She pointed her finger at him. "That attitude is why I never slept with you – never mind the fact that you're married." She leant in close to the glass. "And excuse me, *not qualified?* I was the best damn assistant you ever had and I'm going to prove it by getting you out of here. And when I do, you're going to owe me big time, Jack." She folded her arms and sat back in her chair.

"Is there anything I can do? Should I talk to my lawyer?"

"So he can tip Max off that we're on to him? No

way. Speak to no one but me." She looked at the clock. "I've got to go."

"Thank you so much for doing this. Please be careful – if you're right and people are being killed over this, you could be in danger."

Kate looked through the glass at him, sincerity in his brown eyes. She felt guilty for having accused him of two murders when he had actually been trying to do something pretty amazing.

He leered through the glass. "And thanks for wearing that dress."

"You're an asshole, Jack." She slammed the phone down and grabbed her stuff.

***

She burst into the apartment and looked around at the empty living room, then ran into the kitchen to find Mike and Hooper drinking beer at the table.

"Great, you're both here."

"What did you find out? You sounded excited on the phone."

Mike leant up for a kiss but she bypassed him, threw her arms around Hooper and kissed him on the lips.

Hooper pushed her away. "What the hell was that for?"

"Thanks to you, we've got our first real break in the case."

"Don't you mean the story? You're not a cop, or are you?"

"Case, story, whatever. Jack didn't do anything. He was set up."

They listened intently while she told them what had happened at the prison.

"We need to start from scratch. This whole thing started when I met Crawford, so I need to know what he was doing in London in the first place. Mike, you said the paper didn't send him."

"That's right."

"So, he was working for himself. He used his own money to travel, he paid me five – no, six – thousand pounds for a story. Would either of you go to those lengths to get a story?" She looked back and forth between the men, who shook their heads.

"No, not unless it was the scoop of the century, and affordable medication is hardly Watergate, babe."

Hooper added his two cents. "And Crawford was a lazy reporter. He did easy stories; he wouldn't go out of his way for anything."

"That helps. So, if he wasn't there for a story, what was he doing? If it was me, I would only use my own money if I was invested in something, if I was going to profit from it in some way…"

They nodded so she continued.

"Crawford asked me for information about the pharmaceutical deal, so what did he do with it?"

She waited for one of them to answer but they just stared at her. She shook her head in disbelief. "Come on, guys, you're meant to be reporters. Where's your investigative spirit, Mike?"

"He … gave it to Davenport?" Mike said tentatively, then with more confidence he said, "He's working for Davenport."

"Yes, ten points to Mike. And the last thing we know Crawford did was go into Hudson's office, so what was he looking for? Hooper?" She pointed to Hooper, who thought for a moment before he answered.

"I don't know."

"Zero points for Hooper." She turned back to Mike. "What did he find?"

"Nothing?"

"Yes! He found nothing because he wasn't *looking* for something. He was *planting* something."

"He planted the evidence to get Hudson convicted of the fraud? But you told me he'd found something in the office, that he looked like he had a lead."

"Uh-uh. Looking back on it now, it makes sense. He'd done what he came to do. He didn't need me any more so no pleasantries. He left quickly because he knew he was going to be getting a huge payoff. Either something went wrong, or Davenport wanted him out of the way too."

"It's certainly plausible." Mike nodded, impressed with her detective skills.

"I'm going to go through those boxes with a fine-tooth comb to find out how we can link Crawford and Davenport, and I need to speak to Crawford's wife about his trip to London. What's her address, Mike?"

"I'm not sure I—"

"Don't give me any of that GDPR bullshit."

"I'm not, I don't think it applies here, but she lost her husband and thinks it was suicide. It still could be, so you can't go around there talking about murder unless you have some solid evidence, which you do not."

"Don't worry, I'll be discreet. After all, she might be in on it too…"

"Oh come on, why would she ask me to look at that

stuff if she was involved?"

"You're probably right."

They locked eyes.

Hooper noticed and shook his head. "OK, Lois and Clark, it looks like you two have this covered. I've got a hot date. See you tomorrow."

"Good luck."

"Kate, look at me, I don't need luck." He finished his beer and strutted out of the kitchen.

She watched him go then sat on Mike's knee, kissed him and snuggled in close. "That little chat we had this morning has been on my mind all day."

"Mine too," he said with caution, "but you're right. Let's not get hung up on stuff and just enjoy the time we have together."

"Exactly. We're OK, aren't we?"

He nodded.

"So…"

He drew a breath as she raised her eyebrows. He'd seen that look before. It meant she wanted him.

"What are you making for dinner?"

"Oh shit, I forgot."

Chapter Thirteen

Kate hovered at the office door. "Hi, handsome, are you busy?"

He pointed at the mess on his desk and sighed. "Always. But for you I can make time." He beckoned her in. She grinned as she pulled out the chair opposite him and made a show of crossing her legs so her skirt crept up her thigh. He noticed and took a breath. "I didn't expect you back so soon. How did it go?"

She screwed up her face. "She wasn't at home."

"She wasn't home?" He took off his glasses and sat back in his chair. "Or she was home and you talked to her, but you'd rather keep it to yourself for now?"

"You still don't trust me, do you?"

"Of course I trust you but let's just say ... I've learned to expect surprises."

She made a face at him. She knew she hadn't really given him any reason to trust her, but she felt compelled to say something. "Well, it might *surprise* you to learn that I didn't want to waste the day waiting. I wanted to get back here to finish my story so we can get it into the paper. And that is just a sugar-coated way of saying you don't trust me."

"Come on, babe. You're living in my apartment, I vouched for you here at the paper, I let you be around my grandson *and* I gave you my credit card. Now do you want to rethink what you've just said?"

She sighed. "OK, sorry. You know, I've never actually thanked you for everything you've done for me."

He dismissed her with a wave of his hand and she gave him a cheeky grin.

"No, really, Mike, you're pretty amazing. And about that credit card … I barely used it."

"I know. I checked my balance. I expected it to be at least double what was on there. Are you sure you know how to shop?"

She laughed, then looked around at all his paperwork. She felt bad that he was so busy. She wanted to help, but didn't know how. She leant across the desk. "I'm going to my desk now and I'm really busy, so I don't want you coming over to bother me or making up excuses to get me back in here."

"I won't. I'll be in meetings all afternoon." He looked defeated.

"Are you all right?"

"I envy you." He pointed out to the main office. "Part of me wishes I was still sitting out there. I used to really enjoy my job but now it's all paperwork, meetings and budgets. I've just been thinking about it all recently. Am I too old to have a mid-life crisis?"

She gasped and brought her hand to her chest. "I've been called many things but never a mid-life crisis."

"You know that's not what I mean."

"I know, but why don't you take a leaf out of my book? If you don't like your job, ditch it and get a new one. We could go travelling…" She pointed north. "Canada's just up there."

"You want me to just ditch a career that I've spent the last thirty years building?"

"Yes! What's the point if you're not happy?"

"You make me happy." He looked her in the eye, expecting a reply, but instead she broke his gaze, picked up a piece of paper from his desk and began to read.

He coughed to get her attention. "I know you're desperate to keep this casual, but this is the part where you *could* say that I make you happy too."

She sighed. *Does he really need that sort of validation?* After a few seconds she noticed that he was still watching her.

"You make me happy. There. I said it." She threw the paper onto the desk in protest.

"Come on, you could at least say it like you mean it."

"I do mean it. I wouldn't be here if I wasn't happy." She frowned. "But this kind of conversation is happening more and more often. You're putting too much pressure on me."

"There's no pressure, I promise. But it is OK to be happy, Kate," he said with a loving smile.

"Whatever." She dismissed him with a wave of her hand and stormed out of the office.

He flinched as the door slammed behind her. *That girl has issues.*

Later that afternoon as Kate walked along the corridor, a woman walking towards her altered her course to meet her. The woman was pretty, blonde, a bit taller than Kate and at least ten years older.

"Excuse me, Kate, can I speak to you for a minute?"

"Sure," she replied.

"I'm Barbara."

Kate nodded politely. "Hi Barbara, what can I do for you?"

"Oh, he obviously hasn't told you about me." She shifted from foot to foot. "I'm an old friend of Mike's and I've heard you two are seeing each other…"

Kate narrowed her eyes. "And?"

"And I'm wondering what the hell you're doing with him. You're young and good-looking. Aren't you out of his league?"

Kate's mouth fell open. "Are you sure you're his friend? Because it sounds to me like you've got a pretty crappy opinion of him."

"What are you after? Is it money, a green card? I just don't want to see him get hurt by the likes of you."

"The likes of me?" she said through gritted teeth, trying to remain calm.

"Yes. I've heard some of the stories going around the paper about your travels around the world. I assume you just jumped from one man's bed to another like a whore. And now you think you can waltz in here, confuse Mike and take whatever you want?"

What she wanted was to slap Barbara across the face. It took all her willpower to resist.

"*You* are confused, Barbara, if you think I'm going to take any of your crap. Now get the hell out of my face before I do something I won't regret."

Barbara flinched but stood firm.

"I mean it, Barbara. Stay away from me and stay away from Mike or you and I are going to have a real problem." Kate barged past her, knocking shoulders with her on the way.

Kate looked into Mike's office. Empty. She stormed towards her desk but noticed Hooper at the photocopier and made a beeline for him instead.

"Who the hell is Barbara?" she demanded.

Startled, he slammed the paper tray shut, forgetting to remove his hand. He yelped.

"Um … there's a Barbara who works upstairs in accounting," he said tentatively. "Why, what happened?" He looked down at his throbbing hand.

"Just the usual office chit-chat: everyone's bitching about me, warned me to stay away from Mike – oh, and she called me a whore."

His eyes widened. "She said what? Oh, she's a piece of work. Surely Mike has told you about her?"

She stared at him. "Nope, he hasn't, but you're going to right now."

He looked over her shoulder into Mike's office.

"He's not there. I already checked. Start talking."

"I can't, he's my best friend—"

"OK then, it seems everyone at this paper likes to talk so I'll just ask someone else." She looked around the office then pointed to a bald-headed man at his computer. "How about that guy over there?"

Hooper was torn, but she was pointing at Frank, the biggest gossip at the paper. He took her aside. "It's better you hear it from me." He shrugged. "Well, it would be better if Mike had been man enough to tell you himself. They've known each other for years – much longer than me and Mike. They started off as friends but around the time I started at the paper her marriage broke up. Mike was already divorced, and they started seeing each other. They were good together at first but after a few months it became obvious that he was more into her than she was into him. Mike and I weren't that close back then, but if we had been, I'd have talked him out of it."

191

"Talked him out of what?"

He leant in close and whispered, "No one else at the paper actually knows how far it got but he asked her to marry him. He bought a ring and everything."

Her jaw dropped.

"But she said no and broke up with him on the spot. He was devastated. It took him a long time to get over her. I can't believe he didn't tell you."

"Me neither, Hooper." She shook her head.

"Don't worry about Barbara. She knows she made a mistake with Mike and now that you two are together she's just jealous because he never looked at her the way he looks at you."

She sighed.

"Barbara's right about one thing. People are talking about you but from what I hear it's mostly good. The women like you: you're friendly, interesting and, hell, you got a job at the *New York Times* with no formal qualifications. I'm still reeling over that, by the way. And the guys are jealous of Mike. They want what he's getting."

She slapped him on the arm. "That's very blunt, Hooper. I think there's meant to be a compliment in there somewhere, so thank you."

"You're welcome, but do me a favour. When you have it out with Mike, don't be too hard on him. I think he's in love with you."

She rolled her eyes. "I've got to get out of here. But thanks, Hooper. I'll see you tomorrow."

She turned to walk away, then stopped. "Oh, and not a word to Mike. He doesn't need to know about this yet."

"You're putting me in a really awkward position.

My loyalty has to be with Mike."

"Fair enough." She squeezed his arm. "You do what you think is best."

***

At his apartment that evening, Mike checked his watch as he wandered aimlessly around the kitchen. He was meant to be preparing dinner, but he couldn't settle. Where was she?

The apartment shook as the front door slammed. He hurried into the living room.

"There you are. I was beginning to get worried."

She walked past him without speaking, set her bag down and took off her jacket.

"I went by your desk. Sulzberger said you left early so I thought you'd be here when I got home. Where have you been all this time?"

"Around," she said coldly.

"Well, I've been calling your cell."

She raised her voice. "Well, maybe I just needed some time by myself."

"Sorry, I was worried. I thought maybe that guy had been hassling you again." He didn't mention that he'd also checked the bedroom to make sure her stuff was still there.

She glared at him.

"Is everything OK, babe?"

"No, it isn't."

"Is there anything I can do to make it better?" He reached for her hand, but she pulled away.

"Did you know that everyone's talking about us at that bloody paper?"

He shrugged. "It's an office – people gossip. It's no big deal."

"Not for you, maybe. But apparently I'm a gold-digger and I can't be trusted. I don't usually care what people think of me, but I thought that you thought more of me."

He opened his mouth to speak but she held her hand up. "Let me finish!" she snapped. "You're very keen on honesty between us, but it's all one-sided. You're constantly asking me to be open and to tell the whole truth, but why are you not doing the same?"

"I'm not sure what you mean. Where is all this coming from?"

"Barbara ambushed me today."

"She what?"

"She warned me off you. I think she still likes you, by the way. Obviously I didn't have a clue who she was, so afterwards I got Hooper to fill me in."

"He never said anything to me." He clenched his fists.

"Because I asked him not to!" she shouted. "And don't you dare be mad at him! The problem is that you never told me about her."

He matched her tone. "Kate, forgive me but I think you're being unreasonable. I've made no secret of the fact that I've had girlfriends since my divorce, but I can't tell you every little thing about my past."

"This isn't little, Mike!" she shouted. "You were in love with her – you asked her to marry you! And she works at the paper, for God's sake. You're bound to have known I'd bump into her at some point. If you'd told me about her I could have been prepared." She took a deep breath and tried to compose herself.

"Instead I had to stand there while she called me a whore in front of the whole office." A tear rolled down her cheek.

He let out a deep sigh and shook his head. "I'm so sorry. I can't believe she spoke to you like that. She's totally out of order. I'll have a word with her."

"Don't bother. I can fight my own battles."

"But you shouldn't have to on my account." He touched her arm. "You're right. I should have told you, but my pride wouldn't let me. I guess it was hard for me to admit that I'd made another mistake."

Was he calling her a mistake? "What do you mean, 'another'?"

He sank down onto the sofa and gestured for her to join him but she remained standing.

"I've never told anyone the real reason my marriage ended, not even Hooper. We told people that we grew apart. Everyone assumed I had an affair, but it wasn't me … it was her."

"What?" She sat down beside him.

"With Rodger."

She grimaced. No wonder he hated going to family events.

"I'd been working late for months. Ironically, the one night I decided to come home early to spend time with my wife, I found her in bed with another guy. The image of his bare ass is permanently imprinted on my brain."

"That's awful. What did you do?"

He shrugged. "What could I do? I left them to it. I went to the kitchen, poured myself a drink and waited. They came in a few minutes later, couldn't stop apologising, then after a while Rodger left and Audrey told me everything. It had been going on for months. She said I loved my job more than her, but I thought I was doing the right thing for my family. I guess we should have talked more. Claire was at a sleepover, so I slept in her room that night and in the morning I packed a bag and went to a hotel. We didn't tell Claire about her mom's affair. She didn't need to know that." He paused to think. "But actually, it was to save face. I didn't want anyone knowing that my wife was cheating on me."

Kate squeezed his hand.

"They got married as soon as we were divorced. That was a hard time for me and Barbara was a really good friend through it all. For the next few years I dated a few women, nothing serious – then Barbara's husband cheated on her. I was there for her like she had been for me. That's when we got together. I thought we stood a chance but I was just her rebound guy. That hurt."

He went silent.

Kate put her arms around him and he rested his head on her shoulder. She wanted to tell him that stories like his were why she had never let anyone get too close to her. She didn't want to give anyone the chance to hurt her. But maybe now wasn't the time.

"You poor thing."

"I'm sorry I didn't tell you about Barbara, but I can't believe how upset you got over it. It looks like nothing fazes you. You seem so confident, it made me forget that maybe you *are* vulnerable after all. I won't forget that again, I promise."

She tutted. "Just because I act like nothing fazes me doesn't mean it's always true, not when it's something or someone I care about."

"So you *do* care about me?" He nudged her.

"Of course I do." She nudged him back. "You're a great guy and I'm really enjoying spending time with you."

His heart sank. That wasn't even close to the answer he wanted. He'd already fallen for her. Even though he knew it was a bad idea, he had to make sure that she knew how he felt. He took a deep breath.

"Kate, I'm falling in love with you."

She leapt up from the sofa and stepped away from him. "Don't!"

"Why not?"

"Because that wasn't the arrangement."

"Why are so you against it? What's so bad about being in love?"

She laughed. "Well, for starters, look what happened to you, twice. I'm never going to give anyone that kind of control over me or my happiness. I control my life and I do what I want, when I want. I answer to no one."

"I think you're confusing love and control."

"I think you're confusing love and sex."

"Is that what we're doing? Just having sex?" He immediately regretted asking.

"No. But whatever we're doing, I'm putting a stop to it right now."

"What?" He jumped up from the couch.

"I'm going to pack my things."

She turned to walk away but he grabbed her arm, desperate to stop her.

"Please don't go. Didn't you hear me? I'm falling in love with you."

She looked him in the eye. "And that's why I have

to go. I don't want to hurt you, but I can't give you what you want. I'd only be able to pretend for so long."

"So you've just been pretending?" His voice wobbled.

"Not with you." She took his hand. "I love being with you, but don't confuse that with me being in love with you. And I certainly don't want the same things as you want – family, a career, a mortgage."

"But we can work all of that out."

"How? I don't want to stay here forever. I don't want to settle down and I would never ask you to give up your life … and I'd never let you offer. I have to go." She was shaking as she hurried off into the bedroom.

Mike finally realised what was going on. He'd been so caught up in his feelings for Kate that he had never stopped to think about why she lived the way she did. It was so obvious to him now: it was fear of abandonment. Her mom was the only stability she'd ever had in life, and she had died. Kate didn't want to feel vulnerable again, so she spent her life actively avoiding commitment, changing her job and where she lived at the drop of a hat.

He went to the bedroom and stood at the closed door. He didn't want to pressure her, but what else could he do? He knew he couldn't let her leave. She'd never come back. He had to put up a fight for her.

Kate's head was spinning as she threw her bag onto the bed. *Love? What the hell was he talking about?* Some people threw that word around like it didn't mean anything, but she didn't think he was one of them. Mike wasn't 'in love' with her, he was infatuated, and she was with him, but it would soon wear off.

She went to the en-suite to get her things. As she reached for her make-up bag, she caught a glimpse of herself in the mirror. She stared at her reflection. *What the hell am I doing?* The thought of leaving and never seeing him again made her feel sick, and what was this pain in her chest? She'd heard the phrase 'love hurts', but surely it didn't mean actual physical pain?

Struggling to catch her breath, she sat on the bed. She knew it couldn't be love, but she did feel something for Mike she'd never felt before. Despite her misgivings, she was trying to convince herself to stay and find out what it was.

There was a knock on the bedroom door, then it opened. Mike stood there in silence. After a while, he spoke. "Please don't go."

She took a deep breath and held out her hand to him. Relief flooded over him as he joined her on the side of the bed. He slid his arm around her waist and she rested her head on his shoulder.

"I'm not going anywhere." She placed her hand on his knee. "I didn't mean it when I said I wasn't in love with you."

He held his breath.

She shook her head. "I'm probably in love with you, but I'm not sure … if that makes sense."

"That makes perfect sense, babe." He moved in to kiss her but she placed her hand on his chest to stop him.

"I've never let myself feel this way before. When my mum died, I didn't want to love anyone again in case—"

"I know." He held her tightly.

199

"Then you should also know that I spent years obsessing about every little ache and pain in my body. I was terrified that I could die at any minute, just like my mum. So that's why I decided just to do whatever the hell I wanted. Screw the consequences."

He laughed. She did too.

"It actually worked out quite well for me … until the day I met Alexander Crawford. Taking his money was the worst decision I ever made."

"It's in the past, babe. You can't change it."

"I know. And if you think about it, that bad decision led me to you – my next bad decision." She winked.

"Hey!" Mike nudged her. "I'm the best decision you ever made."

She narrowed her eyes at him. "We'll see…"

Chapter Fourteen

"Would you mind waiting? I'll try not to be too long."

The cab driver nodded and pointed to the meter, which was running. Kate took a deep breath as she got out of the cab and walked up the path to the front door. She knocked, then straightened her jacket as she waited for the door to be answered.

The door was opened by a woman with short curly grey-blonde hair. She was about the same height as Kate, but much heavier. Dully, she looked at Kate. Kate thought she saw a glimmer of recognition in her eyes.

"Mrs Crawford?"

The woman nodded, and the colour drained from her face.

"My name is Kate. I used to work with your husband Alexander at the paper. Are you OK?" Kate asked.

"Yes, please come in." She held the door open and pointed into the hall.

Suddenly Kate felt uneasy. "I won't stay long. I was in the neighbourhood and wanted to pay my respects."

They walked down the hall to the living room. A dozen or so boxes were stacked against the walls, which were dirty with outlines marking where pictures used to hang.

Mrs Crawford noticed Kate looking at the boxes. "I'm so sorry about the mess. We're moving house."

"Too many memories?" Kate asked.

"Unfortunately not. Money problems. The kids and

I are moving somewhere smaller."

"I'm so sorry to hear that." She felt so guilty that she had taken Crawford's money. Mike had offered to lend her the five thousand dollars. She didn't really want to be indebted to him but the money would mean a lot to Mrs Crawford.

"It's just stuff. It doesn't really matter. In fact, I was just packing up some photos."

She looked through one of the boxes, selected a photo and offered it to Kate. "This is Alexander and a few college buddies last year at the Super Bowl."

Kate felt her chest tighten. She immediately recognised all four faces. She wondered why Mrs Crawford was showing her the photo, but she tried to compose herself.

"Are you OK, Kate?"

"Yes, just a bit shocked to see Alexander. Isn't that Max Davenport?" She pointed to him.

"Yes. It is. Do you know him?"

"Not really, just from work." She pointed to another face. "And him, I saw him on TV. He was Jack Hudson's lawyer, wasn't he?"

"Yes, that's Reuben Rosenblatt." She nodded. "You reporters are so good with faces. They met in college and have been good friends ever since."

"Who's the other guy?" She pointed to the man who had threatened her and killed Ray.

"That's Charley. I can't remember his last name. I've never liked him. He was close to getting kicked out of college when a terrible thing happened. His parents died in an awful accident and he inherited a small fortune. He's burned through it and since then he's been bumming around. He's been on the wrong side of the law a few times."

Kate grimaced. Murder was definitely the 'wrong side of the law'. Mrs Crawford seemed in the mood to talk so she chanced her question. "If you don't mind me asking, what was Alexander doing in London when he died?"

She cleared her throat. "He was covering a story for work."

Kate nodded, even though she knew that was a lie. Mike had said he definitely wasn't covering anything for the paper. "Oh, what story?"

She cleared her throat again. "I can't remember."

Kate sighed. She was sick of getting nowhere. She needed answers – and she thought Mrs Crawford knew a lot more than she was saying.

"I'm sorry, Mrs Crawford, I need to be honest with you. I didn't work with Alexander. I have to tell you something, but it's rather sensitive."

Mrs Crawford motioned for her to continue.

"I think this might come as a shock to you. I'm investigating the death of a friend of mine. I think he was killed, and I feel it was somehow connected to your husband's death. I don't think Alexander killed himself. I think he *was* killed."

She expected a reaction, but Mrs Crawford just stared at her.

"I need to know the real reason Alexander was in London, and don't say work again because I know it wasn't. I'm trying to help you."

Mrs Crawford rubbed her temples and tears started to form in her eyes. "My husband was addicted to gambling. Poker games in Manhattan during the week and at the weekend he would go up to Atlantic City. He would come home after gambling away his salary and swear to me that he'd never do it again. I had to take a second job to pay the bills. One day I was supposed to be going to my mother's after work, but I came home instead and found him on the living-room floor. He had taken a bunch of pills washed down with a bottle of vodka."

Kate looked at her, wide-eyed.

"I got him to hospital. He was OK, but he told me he'd lost all our savings and taken out a second mortgage on the house. The only thing we had left was the kids' college fund which, thank God, he didn't have access to. When he was in hospital, I tried to sort things out. I sold the cars and my jewellery and we had some shares which I cashed in. But it wasn't enough. We were desperate." She took a tissue from her pocket and blew her nose. "When he got home from the hospital, Max came over to see how he was. Alexander explained everything to him and asked for a loan. Max said he'd love to help but he wasn't doing so well either. He'd sunk all of his money into a new company in the hope of a big return, but the deal was about to go sour. He wanted Alexander to help him – and if he did, Max promised he would give him some shares in the company."

Kate narrowed her eyes. "What sort of help?"

"He asked Alexander to go to London for him. I don't know any more than that. I gave him access to the college bank account, he went to London, and the night he died he called and told me that everything was going to be OK. He was so excited and relieved. We talked for ages, until Max arrived to take him out for dinner. The next I heard, he was dead."

Kate sat in silence. *He went out for dinner with Max?* That was impossible. Max wasn't in London at the time. She wondered why Mrs Crawford said he was.

Mrs Crawford cleared her throat, yet again. "I've always wondered why Alexander killed himself when he knew things were going to be OK. Now that I think about it, Max was the last person to see him alive. You said you were looking into the death of your reporter friend – do you think Max could have killed them both?"

Not any more!

Kate was positive she hadn't told Mrs Crawford that her dead friend was a reporter. She felt uneasy and knew she had to get out of there. She looked at her phone. "I'm so sorry to rush off, but I have a cab waiting. I'll give you a call if I find anything out." She picked up her bag and hurried to the door. Her host followed.

"Thank you for stopping by, Kate. I hope I was able to help you. If you need anything else, please give me a call."

"Thank you. I'm sorry for your loss."

They shook hands. Kate didn't wait for the door to close. She practically ran to the cab, then got out her phone with shaking hands and called Mike. She growled in exasperation when he didn't answer. *Bloody meetings.* She left him a message. "You're never going to believe what I found out at Crawford's house. I'm on my way back to the office. Get Hooper. Tell him we got our story."

***

The door of the lift opened and Kate rushed through reception. She saw Hooper at his computer, ran over and startled him by banging the desk. "Come on!" she shouted and hurried towards Mike's office.

"Shut the door, Hooper. Mike, stop what you're doing."

Mike did as instructed. He loved it when she was excited like this.

They listened as she told them everything Mrs Crawford had said.

"Why would Davenport kill Crawford if he was helping him?"

"I'm glad you asked that, Mike." She looked pleased with herself. "Something just didn't sit right with me. I couldn't help wondering why she told me all that when she hadn't mentioned it to anyone before. And don't you think it's a bit strange that the first time someone says that Alexander may have been murdered, she didn't even bat an eyelid? Here's what I think really happened. One, she recognised me as soon as she opened the door. She knew who I was, but she pretended she didn't."

"How?"

"Don't interrupt, Mike." She held her finger up to silence him. He shot Hooper a hurt look. Hooper smirked.

"A photo of me was in Crawford's stuff, wasn't it? She's bound to have gone through it, it's possible she even put it in there. Two, I lied to her and said I knew Crawford from working at the paper. She knows I don't work at the paper! Three, out of the blue she showed me a photo of everyone I suspect is up to something: Crawford, Davenport, Rosenblatt and Charley. That's far too much of a coincidence – she was trying to draw me in."

"Who are Rosenblatt and Charley?" Hooper asked.

"I said, don't interrupt. Four, she told me about London and pretended that Crawford had talked to her on the phone. But she slipped up when she told me that he had met Max for dinner. Max wasn't in London – he was at a conference in Germany with Jack. I know this because he emailed me photos of them there for the company newsletter. Five, she told me that she was the only one who had access to the kids' college fund and that's why he couldn't gamble it away. She had to give him access to the money so he could go to London. That's what got me thinking. If I was her, would I trust my gambling-addict husband with the very last of our cash to go to London on his own and fix things? No, I certainly would not. I would either go with him or I would follow him to make sure he got the job done properly. That's when it hit me. She killed her own husband."

Mike and Hooper looked at one another. "That's a bit far-fetched, don't you think?" Mike said carefully.

"I'm serious. Put yourself in her shoes. Your husband destroys the family financially and then tries to kill himself, leaving you penniless and having to fix the mess he left. She hates him but addiction is an illness so she couldn't be seen to be abandoning him in his hour of need – not that they could even afford to get divorced. Then he gets an opportunity to make a ton of cash. Do you think she's going to let him get his hands on any of that money? He'd just gamble it all away. She knows that he'd tried to overdose before, and she knows that no one will ask too many questions if he tries again. But this time he succeeds. She killed him, I'm sure of it. Then when I come around asking questions, telling her I think he was murdered by the same guy that murdered my friend, she tries to frame Max, to take the heat off her."

"I don't know if you're brilliant or insane," Mike said, looking stunned, "but I think you're reaching."

"I don't buy it either," Hooper said.

Kate glanced back and forth between them and folded her arms.

Mike looked concerned. "Come on, babe, just because I don't agree with you there's no need to sulk." Although he thought she looked incredibly cute when she did. He reached out to take her hand but she pushed him away.

Hooper sniggered. "I think you're sleeping on the couch tonight, old man."

"No, it's OK. You're both entitled to your opinion, even if it is wrong. And I'm not sulking, I'm thinking." She tapped her nail against her teeth.

Mike tried to appease her. "If you're so sure I'm wrong, then you need to give me some evidence."

Evidence? She glanced around the office as if hoping that something would magically jump out at her. Where could she find evidence? At the crime scene – but if it didn't look like a crime, no one would have been looking for evidence. Apart from Ray. She'd told him Alexander had been murdered – maybe what he found out had got him killed.

"Where's that file? The one with all the police photos and press clippings from when Crawford's body was removed from the hotel where he died?" She hunted through a stack of files on the floor, found the one she was looking for and waved it in the air. She opened it and studied the photos, then selected two and set them out on the desk. "*Voilà.*"

Mike and Hooper examined the first photo. It showed the outside of the hotel. A police cordon held back a small crowd as the covered body was wheeled out.

She pointed to a face in the crowd. "Who's that?"

Mike squinted. "That's Helena Crawford."

Kate held out her hands in triumph.

Mike looked sceptical. "But she flew straight to London as soon as she found out."

"Maybe. Now look at this one." She pointed to the second photo, which was of the body being loaded into the coroner's van. "She's not in this photo but you'd agree that it was taken just after the other one?"

Both men nodded. She pointed to the top of the photo. "You can just see the clock on the side of that building. What time does it say?"

"Nine ten."

"Ten past nine in the morning. The police report said his body was discovered at around 10 p.m., so that's eleven hours, give or take, for the body to be identified and next of kin informed. Mrs Crawford then had to book a flight, get to the airport, check in, fly seven hours to London and then get to the hotel through rush-hour traffic. There's no way she could have done it. The day I came here, I booked the flight last minute. I left my flat at 1 p.m. and got to the hotel at 9 p.m. Allowing five hours for the time difference, it took me thirteen hours and I was in a hurry. I couldn't have done it much faster. There's no way she did it in eleven. She was already there."

Mike looked at Hooper in disbelief. "I can't argue with that."

"Me neither," Hooper agreed. They smiled when Kate took a bow. But then the smile left her face and she slumped down into Mike's chair.

"What's wrong, babe?"

"We're still no further on. We can't prove she did it, and the police report said that nothing was found at the scene to suggest foul play." She was silent again for a while, then exclaimed, "That's it, I'm done."

Mike nodded. "Yes, that's enough for today."

"No, not just for today. This is pointless. We have no evidence and no chance of finding any, and there's a killer stalking me. We should just forget the whole thing." She was despondent.

Mike wasn't sure how to react, and looked at Hooper for inspiration. Hooper shrugged.

"Come on, you've worked so hard on this…"

She held up a hand. "And you know what else? It's nothing to do with me any more. I can't be responsible for Crawford's death if his wife killed him. As for Ray, either Mrs Crawford had him killed because he found out about her or Davenport had him killed to stop him printing the story. Either way, it's not my problem any more."

"I know you don't mean that, babe. What did you tell me when we first met?" He waited for an answer, but she just shrugged. "That when you set your sights on something, you usually get it. And I know that's true," he winked, "because you got me."

She shrugged. "Then it must be true. Don't worry, I won't let this go. I'm just tired."

"Good. Put it to the back of your mind until Monday." He tilted his head at her. "You do look tired. I'll take you out for a nice meal tonight and we'll have a relaxing weekend, recharge your batteries."

She nodded but she was still despondent. Mike didn't know what to say or do to lift her spirits. Then it hit him. "I've got something that'll cheer you up." He opened his desk drawer and took out an envelope. He beamed as he offered it to her.

She narrowed her eyes as she opened it. It was a cheque. She looked at it blankly for a moment before noticing the *New York Times* logo.

"Oh my God! Does this mean that I'm a published writer?" she shrieked in excitement.

He nodded. "Your piece will appear on Sunday. It's the lead feature in the travel section."

"Thank you so much!" She jumped up and down, waving the cheque in the air.

"Don't thank me; you did this all on your own. I had to pull some strings to get it made out to cash – just this once. If you're going to write more, you're going to have to get yourself a US bank account. Either way, you need to go down to Personnel and sign some papers. Happy?"

She threw her arms around him and peppered his cheeks with kisses. "I'm happy. Hooper, look at this." Proudly, she offered him the cheque.

Mike tried to stop her, but it was too late. He looked nervous as Hooper examined the cheque. His face was red with anger when he looked up.

"She's getting paid *that*, for one story?"

"She's freelance. They always get a little more," Mike said, trying to defuse the situation.

"It's still too much, isn't it?"

"Nothing to do with me – take it up with Bob."

"If you break it down, I don't get paid that well."

"Maybe because you don't write that well," she taunted, snatching back the cheque which she kissed and slid carefully into her bra.

Hooper pointed at Kate. "Are you going to let her talk to me like that, Mike?"

"Let her? He might be your boss but he's certainly not mine."

"I'll have you know, lady, that I'm a well-respected journalist in this town. I have an MA from Columbia University and fifteen years of newspaper experience. What do you have?"

"I've got the lead feature in the Sunday travel section." She stuck her tongue out at him.

Mike rolled his eyes. "That's enough, guys. You're both talented writers."

They nodded. Neither could argue with that.

"Sorry, Hooper." Playfully, she punched him on the arm. "Mike gave me some of your stuff to read – it's really good."

"Thanks. And if your writing is as good as your cooking, I'm sure you'll win a Pulitzer prize one day. Not before me, though." He winked.

"Wanna bet?"

"Sure. I mean, there's no way you cou—"

"Enough!" Mike whacked a rolled-up magazine against his desk. "No more of this or you'll both be typing classifieds until your fingers are sore."

They looked at him like school children who had been told off by their teacher.

"It's just banter, Mike."

"Yeah, Mike, lighten up. Is he always this serious, Hooper?"

"Yeah, but not as much since he met you." He

nudged her.

She blushed. "OK, I'm off to cash my first pay cheque and I'll go to the grocery store and get something nice for dinner."

"I said I'd take you out tonight, babe."

"Nope. Cooking relaxes me. I'd much rather stay in." She gave him a suggestive glance.

Mike bit his lip.

Hooper tutted at Mike. "So now you've got a girlfriend I'm at O'Malley's by myself on a Friday night?"

Mike shot Kate a hopeful look.

She rolled her eyes. "You're very welcome to join us, Hooper. In fact, you can choose. What do you like?"

Hooper's eyes lit up. "Mexican food – do you know how to make enchiladas?"

Mike cleared his throat. "How come he gets what he likes?"

"You can have what you like for dessert … as long as Hooper knows when to leave. Enchiladas it is. Arrive no earlier than half six." She picked up her jacket and handbag.

"What?"

"That's British for six thirty, Hooper." Mike laughed, then looked at his watch. It was two thirty. "Kate, work?"

She pointed to herself. "Kate, freelance." She blew him a kiss and ran out of the door.

Mike shook his head, turned to Hooper and narrowed his eyes. "I didn't get to speak to you this morning. I wanted to thank you for dropping me in it with the Barbara thing. What gives?"

"Sorry, Mike, I had to tell her. She was going to ask

Frank, and I played down your heartbreak way more than that drama queen would have. How'd it go anyway?"

"Awful. She threatened to leave."

"What? Because of Barbara?"

"No, because of my big mouth."

"What did you say?" Hooper groaned.

Mike bit the inside of his cheek. "I told her I was falling in love with her."

"What the hell did you say that for?" He whacked Mike on the arm. "Have I taught you nothing? A woman like Kate doesn't want to hear that kind of sentimental bullshit. She's independent and unconventional. You don't use the word 'love' around a woman like that unless she uses it first. I'm starting to see a trend here. Why do you have to bring love into your relationships?"

"Because I'm not you, Hooper. And this isn't just love. It isn't how I felt when I proposed to Barbara. I never even felt this way about Audrey. I can't describe it. I just know Kate and I are meant to be together."

"Are you drunk? Get a grip, old man, and just think about it like this: you're getting regular sex from a beautiful woman and she's still here even after your lame declaration of never-ending love. I think that's a good sign. It's a good job I'm coming over tonight. I'll stop you dusting off Barbara's engagement ring."

"I couldn't even if I wanted to. I gave it to Claire — she had earrings made from the diamonds. Just remember: no jokes tonight, play it cool."

"I think you should take your own advice, old man."

Mike looked at his watch. "Don't you have a deadline?"

When Kate let him in to the apartment that evening, Hooper did a double take. "I can't get used to you opening the door."

She pointed to the kitchen. "You know where the beer is."

"Sure do." As he passed, he held up a bottle of tequila and a bag of lemons.

"Thanks." She groaned. "I just sent Mike to get some. You must have just missed each other."

They walked into the kitchen and he helped himself to a beer as Kate set the table.

"This all smells great. But enough of the small talk. Mike told me you had 'the talk' last night. Have you made your exit plan yet?"

She screwed up her face. "My what?"

"Your exit plan. I think you and I have a very similar approach to relationships. I always make an exit plan when I suspect a chick is getting too attached."

She reached for her wine glass and took a sip. "I don't have an exit plan and I probably won't tell Mike you called him a chick."

"OK, that's a good start." He laughed. "I was sceptical about you at first but now I know you're good for him. He's definitely happier than I've ever seen him and he's been missing work, going to parties and not wearing ties. Don't even get me started on that stupid grin he's been wearing – it's creepy. He's head over heels in love with you, Kate. But if you're going to bail, do it now, before it gets any worse."

She grabbed the wine bottle and filled her glass. "I don't intend to bail." She omitted to say 'any more'.

"I've never met anyone like Mike before and I really want to make this work, but it's not as simple as everyone thinks. Yes, he's a great guy, but he comes with baggage. I can cope with the ex-wife and even the grandson, but his daughter hates me and I don't need that kind of aggravation. Plus, I'm not sure if New York is where I want to be forever but he would never want to leave, so … in a way I'd end up living *his* life."

"You'll get your own life. There's a job for you at the paper, unless this article you wrote bombs, in which case you'll find something else to do. You guys have stuff to work out, but I think you can do it."

She put her hand on his arm. "Thank you. Mike's lucky to have a friend like you. Hey, maybe one day I'll be able to call you a friend too."

"Sure, but if things don't work out with Mike maybe we could be more than just friends." He raised his eyebrows.

She glared at him. "You're so not my type."

"I'm eligible and good-looking." He puffed out his chest. "What does Mike have that I don't, apart from more wrinkles?"

"A conscience. And they're not wrinkles, they're definitions of character."

They heard the front door open and close.

"Whatever helps you sleep at night, Kate."

She threw a napkin at him. "I sleep like a log; Mike sees to that."

"Ew." He put his hands over his ears.

They fell silent as Mike came in. He set a bottle of tequila and a bag of lemons on the counter next to the other bottle of tequila and bag of lemons.

"Is there anything I can do to help with dinner?" he

asked, kissing Kate on the cheek.

"Yes, please. Put that stuff on the table and then sit down. It's ready."

He carried the food to the table: chicken and beef enchiladas, a corn salad and homemade guacamole, *tamale* and *pico de gallo*. "You've outdone yourself again, babe. Honestly, you didn't have to go to all this trouble."

Hooper elbowed him as he helped bring the food to the table. "Ssh, I've never eaten this well."

Kate set a plate of lemon wedges on the table. "Who's for tequila?"

After dinner and more than half a bottle of tequila, they chatted in the living room. Mike and Kate snuggled on the sofa and Hooper sat in the armchair. Soon the conversation had veered towards work. Hooper, who couldn't wait until Sunday, was trying to get a preview of Kate's feature, but she refused to give any spoilers.

"You won't be disappointed," Mike offered in consolation.

She blushed.

"I mean it. If you put your mind to it, you could make a lot of money from writing and when you get this Hudson story, you'll really get your name out there."

She sighed.

"You're going to crack it," he assured her.

"Of course I am, but I don't want to talk about it until Monday. I'm taking the weekend off."

Mike whispered into her ear, "Let's not get out of bed."

"Sounds good..." She giggled as he kissed her neck.

"And that's my cue to go." Hooper jumped up from

the armchair. "Thanks for dinner, Kate."

Suddenly realising how inappropriate their behaviour was, they composed themselves. "But it's early, Hooper, and there's tequila to finish."

"I hope you two enjoy it. This gooseberry is going home."

Mike and Kate smirked like teenagers.

"See you Monday." Mike waved at Hooper, not taking his eyes off Kate.

"Ahem, I think you mean Sunday, old man. Tee time?"

"Oh, golf – can I come?" Kate asked.

Mike's eyes widened. "You play?"

She nodded. "I'll show you both a thing or two … at the nineteenth hole." She giggled.

"Tee time's 10 a.m., babe."

"I can have a mimosa with brunch while I read the *Times*. I'll be signing copies."

"OK, Mr and Mrs Kelly, see you on Sunday. I'll let myself out." Hooper chuckled as he walked to the door.

Mike tensed as he looked at Kate but was relieved to find she was still laughing. She looked beautiful and relaxed – until she made a face.

"Are you all right, babe?"

She rubbed her head. "Just feel a little light-headed. Too much tequila."

"I'll get you a glass of water." He kissed her hand. "I'll be right back."

She was lying on the sofa when he arrived with the water. He stroked her hair.

"Tired?"

"Yeah, I have been tired lately. I've probably been doing too much exercise," she joked, "or the whole nine-to-five thing is too much for me."

He couldn't believe his ears. "What? Most of the five days you've worked at the paper, you've spent so much time talking to people that it's eleven o'clock before you get to your desk, then you leave at three. I'd hardly call that nine to five, babe. And most people start at eight."

"OK, boss, I didn't know you were time-keeping."

"I'm not, but cut me some slack. Everyone knows we're together, and you can't be seen to be getting special treatment. I mean, if you're out getting a story that's fine, but when you're in the office you're meant to be working, not socialising."

"Then it's nine to five from now on, but is it OK if sometimes I just sit at my desk and play Candy Crush?"

"Yeah – that's what everyone else does anyway," he said, defeated.

"They think you don't notice." She rubbed her chest.

He stroked her thigh. "Are you sure you're OK?"

"Yes, I've probably just eaten too much spicy food."

"But you're pale."

"I'm a redhead. I'm always pale."

"Paler than usual. I'll get you some antacids and make us some tea. Why don't you see if there's anything you want to watch on TV? We'll cuddle for a while before bed."

"Perfect."

He went into the kitchen and she snuggled into the sofa.

She took a deep breath as she looked around the room, feeling loved and cared for. Everything *was* perfect. Maybe this relationship thing wasn't going to be so bad after all.

Chapter Fifteen

The time on her computer screen said 09.23 and there was no Candy Crush in sight. If Mike hadn't been at his Monday morning meeting already, he would have been proud. She might have got to her desk earlier if so many people hadn't stopped to congratulate her on her story in the previous day's paper.

She washed down two antacids with the last of her coffee and stared at a blank page entitled *Story Two* until she was joined by Chen from the finance section.

"Hey Kate, I'm really sorry I didn't get back to you last week about the Biomes documents you gave me. I had to go out of town. Family emergency."

"I heard about your mother. Is she OK?"

"She's fine, thanks. So, I finally got a chance to look at that stuff."

She sat up straight. "What did you find out?"

"It's research and development costings and projected profit margins for a new product they're developing."

"Oh, so not really interesting?" She slumped back in her chair. "I already know it's going to be a big money-spinner."

"Whatever it is, they're expecting demand to be high. Their sales projections are through the roof."

She waved her hand dismissively. "It's just a medicine."

"Oh, OK. I'm sorry there wasn't anything juicy. I also did a little research into Biomes. It's been struggling financially for years and their shares were worth virtually nothing. They couldn't give them away."

"Interesting," she said, uninterested.

"Then some parts of the company were sold off last year. It only really exists on paper at the minute, but a few months ago all the shares were bought by a single investor."

Her ears perked up. Mrs Crawford said Max had told her he'd sunk all his money into a company. It had to be him.

"Max Davenport?" she asked, excited.

"No."

She tutted.

"The investor was a corporate partnership made up of Reuben Rosenblatt and Charles Hackett."

She sat up in her chair, stunned.

"You've heard of them?"

"They're friends of Davenport's." She tapped her finger on the table. "I'm just thinking out loud here … Davenport gets Jack Hudson out of the way so he can award the contract to his friends' company, which then charges Hudson Inc. whatever it wants and they all split the profit?" She nodded. "That's a nice little scam."

"You would be right, but Biomes don't have a factory any more, so how are they going to make the drug?"

They stared at each other in silence. Kate wanted to scream. Here she was going around in circles again. But maybe she couldn't find anything because there was nothing to find. *Maybe there wasn't even a drug?*

"Chen, if there was no drug could they still make money?"

He grimaced. "Not really. Even if they were paid

upfront, when they didn't deliver it would be a breach of contract and they'd get sued."

"But what if they didn't have the money any more? Say they spent it?"

"There would be assets and paper trails." He shook his head. "But don't forget, Hudson Inc. would only be paying Biomes to manufacture the drug – the predicted huge profit is the revenue from the actual sale of the drug. They can't sell something they don't have."

"You're right. And when I talked to Jack Hudson, he seemed passionate about the drug. It has to exist."

She replayed her conversation with Jack in her head. He had said there was a company, Medibond, which had new technology that meant they could make the drug for a fraction of the cost Biomes could. So, in order to maximise profit, Max Davenport – as Hudson Inc. – awarded the contract to his friends' company, Biomes. But they didn't have a production plant any more.

"There's no reason Biomes couldn't subcontract to another company, is there?"

He shook his head. "No, it's done all the time."

"So Biomes subcontract to Medibond and make an astronomical saving on the manufacturing costs – and leave Rosenblatt and Hackett with a small fortune to split between them. Then when Hudson Inc. sells the product at the higher price, rather than the cost price Jack wanted, Davenport gets his payoff. He's going to make billions. No wonder he's killing people."

Chen swallowed. "He's what?"

"Sorry. It's a big story we're working on. Forget I said that."

Chen looked around the office and lowered his

voice. "If there's killing involved, I don't want any part in it. All I've been hearing about recently is dead reporters."

She cleared her throat. "Thanks. Chen, I really owe you one."

"Great. How about we get a drink after work one day, and maybe a bite to eat?" He held his breath and waited for her response.

"You do know that Mike and I are together, don't you?"

His jaw dropped. "I thought that was just a rumour."

"Not a rumour—" She saw Mike going into his office and patted Chen on the shoulder. "I gotta go. Thanks." She rushed over to Hooper's desk.

He looked up at her and then at the clock. "Mike said he was going to talk to you about your time-keeping. I can't believe he actually had the balls."

"Very funny, Hooper." She beckoned to him. "Follow me."

Mike almost jumped out of his chair when Kate and Hooper burst through the door.

"Where's the fire?"

"I'm about to start one." She told Mike and Hooper what Chen had told her.

"How come they left Crawford out of the deal?" Hooper asked.

"I don't know. Maybe they thought he was a liability. They've been friends since college, so they probably knew about his gambling."

"So, Mrs Crawford isn't a murderer then?" Mike enquired.

Kate glanced at him. Was he patronising her?

"No, I still think she did it. I just can't figure out if she's involved in the whole thing with Max and Charley or if she did it for her own agenda."

She replayed their meeting again and remembered the boxes she'd seen at the house. Mrs Crawford said they had money problems and they had to downsize, but if she was due a windfall from Davenport, why was she still moving house? What if Max was trying to get out of the deal? She held up her hand.

"I've got to make a phone call."

She picked up Mike's phone and dialled a number.

"Hi, is that Noreen? It's Kate Turner from the London office. How are you? Really? That's not so good. I'm sure he'll call. Just give him a few days. Now, I have a really quick question. Remember you told me there was a woman arguing with Max at the office the other week? Do you remember her name or what she looked like? Uh-huh … and can you remember anything else about it?" She nodded along, smiling as she listened. "Thanks, Noreen. That's really helpful. Yeah, sure we can go for a drink sometime. I'll give you a call tomorrow. Bye."

She set down the phone and slowly traced her finger over the receiver.

Mike and Hooper waited.

"Babe, you're killing me…"

She gave them a smug look. "Looks like Mrs Crawford was down at Hudson Inc. on the Monday of the trial, fighting with Max. When she left, she threatened him. She said that he couldn't treat her like that and his days were numbered. It's obvious – Mrs Crawford wants her money but with her husband gone,

Max thinks he doesn't have to pay up. She wants revenge – that's why she's trying to frame him for her husband's murder." She looked around the room and saw Crawford's boxes on the floor. "That's why she came straight to you, Mike, and got you involved in her little story and asked you for help. She sent you boxes containing all the information that you would need to uncover the plot and lead you to Davenport!"

"Well, it's a good thing you're here, babe, because honestly I wouldn't have paid that much attention to them."

She rubbed her temples. "This is too big for us."

Mike let out a sigh of relief. "I agree. We should go to the police."

"And tell them what?" She imitated Mike's voice. *"We think some people murdered some other people, but we don't have any proof."*

Mike wasn't amused but Hooper thought it was hilarious.

"No, what I meant was, we're trying to do too much. We don't have to prove everything – not two murders, embezzlement and the drug scam. I'm going back to my desk to think. You two do the same." She slammed the door behind her.

Mike sat down behind his desk. "I think I made a mistake with Kate."

Hooper pulled out a chair and sat opposite him. "What? You guys are doing great."

"I don't mean that – I mean this situation. When this all started I didn't really think she had anything solid, I was just humouring her because I liked having her around. But the more she dug, the more she uncovered. If it's all true and Davenport and his partners are killing to protect their investments, that puts Kate in real danger. She said she was going to drop it and I stupidly talked her out of it but now I'm thinking maybe she should. I think we should go to the police and tell them everything we know, then let them decide who's guilty."

Hooper's mouth fell open. "And give up our exclusive? Are you crazy? You know if you do, she'll never forgive you. She'll be on the first plane out of here and you'll never see her again." He shook his head. "She's about to crack this and I can't wait to see her do it."

"All of a sudden you're her biggest fan?" Mike scoffed.

"Well, she's certainly my new favourite travel writer."

"Be serious, Hooper. What do you think we should do?"

"I think we should do what she told us or we'll be in trouble. There's bound to be a way forward."

They sat and looked at each other in silence.

"Am I the only one who does any work around here?" she said as she stormed back into the office. "Nap time's over – let's get back to work."

They glared at her. She'd only been gone for ten minutes.

"I've been at my desk thinking. You're right, Mike. We need to go to the police."

"That's the smartest thing you've said all day." He beamed.

She pouted. "You didn't let me finish. There was going to be a 'but'."

"Oh."

"But wouldn't it be better if we had hard evidence, just a tiny little bit? We have the motives for murder and embezzlement now, we just need the proof. Ray is dead, Crawford is dead, so they can't back up any of my story. It would be my word against Max's or Mrs Crawford's or whoever's. The easiest thing to prove is the embezzlement, then everything else will fall into place. Max is bound to have some incriminating evidence in his office, so I need to get to his computer. I'll go down there tonight and use my key card to get through security. It should still work. I'll go to his office and search his computer…" She stopped. She didn't know his password. "Forget that. I'll go to his house. His home computer will almost certainly be networked to the office one, so if I—"

"That's not going to work," Mike said.

She glared at him. "I'm amazed you've been so successful in your career as it seems to me that you give up at the first hurdle. No wonder I always do these things alone."

"These things? How many of 'these things' have you done?"

"This is just the second one … Mike, you're a genius."

"I am?"

"Yes. It's the simple things that work, like booking the 'electrician' in London to get Crawford into Jack's office. Keep it simple, Kate. We don't need a complicated plan – all we need is a diversion. A distraction to get him away from his desk. If he's like everyone else, his passwords will be in a little book in his top drawer." She folded her arms, looking pleased with herself.

"So, what's your distraction?"

"I don't know."

"I'm sure you'll figure it out, babe. I've got a meeting."

"Bye, Mike." Without even giving him a kiss goodbye, she took Hooper by the hand and led him out. "Let's get some coffee and think of a plan."

Mike shook his head as they left the office. He should have been happy that Hooper was with her so she wouldn't be able to run off and do something stupid. But by the sound of it, Hooper was just as eager as she was to get to the bottom of this without involving the police. He had an uneasy feeling that something bad was about to happen.

**

She tried to steady her breathing as the lift approached the eleventh floor. When the doors opened, she stepped out into the reception area.

"Hi, Kate, are you here for our drink? I don't get off until five, but you can wait here."

"Oh, sorry, I'm actually here to see Max."

The smile faded from Noreen's face. "I didn't see an appointment in the book."

"I don't have one but I'm sure he'll see me." She winked.

"I'll call through." Noreen picked up the phone. "Mr Davenport, Kate Turner from the London office is here to see you. OK." She hung up. "Take a seat. He will be with you shortly."

The phone rang again and Noreen answered

quickly. It was obviously a personal call as she started to whisper down the phone.

Kate sat with her hands on her knees and desperately tried to stop her legs from shaking. Her pulse was racing and the pain in her chest was back. Actually, it hadn't gone away. She'd had enough of all this; the suspense was too much. She was going to confront him, accuse him directly and see what he said.

She got her mobile from her handbag. She would get the evidence she needed if she recorded the meeting. From what she'd seen on TV, she knew it probably wouldn't stand up in court, but it would at least be something for the police to follow up, then the whole thing would be over. She set her phone to record and put it in her jacket pocket, then waited.

After a few minutes the office door opened. Max stuck his head out and looked over to the reception desk. He sighed when he saw Noreen on the phone. "What have I told you about personal calls?" he snapped.

Noreen quickly hung up.

He turned to Kate. "I'm so sorry to keep you waiting. Please come in." He held the door open. She forced a smile as she walked into the office.

"I hope you're here for our dinner." He closed the door and gestured towards the chair in front of his desk. "You said you'd call. I was worried."

"Cut the crap, Max. I'm on to you. I know exactly what you've been up to."

She'd done it. She had actually surprised herself.

Although she had expected him to be shocked, he looked calm.

He gestured for her to continue.

"I know all about your plan to get rid of Jack so you can use your friends' company to bump up the price on that medication. And I know you killed Ray Freers, but I can't work out who killed your old friend Alexander Crawford. Was it you?"

He laughed. "Are you serious? I don't kill people."

"Oh, I'm so sorry. Let me rephrase that: you have people killed. I know you use your friend Charley!"

Now she had his full attention. He got up from his chair and walked around the desk so he was towering over her.

"Hand it over," he demanded.

"What?"

"Your cell."

"No."

He reached for her and she pulled away. He grabbed her arm and dragged her off the chair and shoved her against the wall. She trembled as he patted her down, then froze when he got to her pocket. He took out her phone and saw that it was recording.

"Nice try." He switched it off and threw it onto his desk. He leant in so close to her that she could smell the coffee on his breath. "You think you're so smart, don't you? You think you've had the upper hand the whole time, but I was on to you the second I saw you on TV at the courthouse. I knew who you were, so that's why I sent Charley to keep an eye on you. He asked you nicely to drop this, but you didn't listen, did you? You just had to keep on snooping around. Now here we are, and what am I going to do with you?" He looked around the room anxiously, then pointed to the chair. "Sit down."

There was no way she was going to sit down. What if she needed to get to the door? "I'm fine standing."

"I said sit down!"

She sat down.

He paced the room a few times then walked over to a wall. He removed a picture to reveal a safe, and typed in the combination. He reached inside and produced a gun, opened the chamber and angled it so that she could see the copper bullets inside. It was fully loaded.

She flinched then quickly regained her composure. He wasn't going to hurt her; he was just trying to scare her. After all, Noreen was just outside the door if she needed to shout for help.

"We have a serious problem here. You're getting in the way of my business and I've got investors depending on me to get this deal done. There's a lot of money at stake. By now I assume you know the lengths that people will go to for money." He placed the gun on the table and rubbed his head. "I didn't want anyone to get hurt over this, I swear to you. I'm a businessman. All I wanted was Jack out of the way so I could make my deal. If he'd listened to Reuben, he wouldn't even have gone to prison. But Charley … he's invested in this too and let's just say that sometimes he gets a bit carried away."

Her eyes widened. *That's the understatement of the century*.

He went back to the safe and pulled out two bundles of cash which he set on the table. "I hear that you're open to bribery. I'm going to make you an offer you can't refuse. That's twenty grand. All you have to do is keep your mouth shut, ditch that reporter and get out of town. And to prove there's no hard feelings I'll wire you another twenty when you're safely back in London and the deal is done. It's easy money, Kate."

"What if I don't go?"

"Then I won't be able to guarantee your safety."

She forced a laugh. "You're bluffing."

"I'm not bluffing, and it's more serious than you think. You know Charley's been following you. He knows all about your boyfriend's daughter and grandson. He has some … unorthodox ways to make people do what he wants."

She swallowed. "I'll go. As long as no one else gets hurt, I won't say a word." She stood up. Her hands shook as she accepted the cash.

Max seemed genuinely relieved. "Good decision. I'll have my driver meet you downstairs and take you straight to the airport."

She shook her head. "I have to go and get my stuff."

He pointed to the cash in her hand. "Buy new stuff."

"I won't be able to leave the country without my passport, genius."

"OK, I'll have him take you to your apartment to get your things, but if your boyfriend is there you know what you have to do."

She nodded. "It's OK. He'll still be at work." At least, she hoped he would be.

"Good. I'll walk you down to the car. Just do as I say and it'll all be OK. But I swear, if I see your face again, I'll make sure that little boy's body is the last thing your boyfriend sees before he becomes dead reporter number three."

She squared up to him. "Don't you dare."

"Not me; Charley's been the one killing people. Between you and me, I think he caused the accident that killed his parents, so I don't think he's going to worry too much about a little boy he doesn't even know." He took her arm. "Smile nicely at Noreen on the way past."

She tried to pull her arm from his grasp, but he held her tightly and marched her out of the office.

When they came out of Max's office, Noreen looked up from her computer. "It's nearly five. I won't be too much longer."

Kate swallowed and managed a smile. "I'm so sorry, Noreen, but I have to go back to London tonight. Max has been nice enough to offer me a lift to the airport. I'll give you a call next time I'm in town."

Noreen tutted and shook her head as Max led Kate into the lift.

***

She called out as she opened the door to the apartment. "Mike, are you home?"

There was no answer.

She went straight into the bedroom, got her bag from the cupboard and threw it on the bed. She opened the top drawer and grabbed her passport and underwear, then went to the wardrobe, ripped her dresses from their hangers and shoved them into the bag.

There was a noise outside the door. She braced herself as it opened. It was Mike. Without making eye contact with him, she continued to pack.

"What are you doing?" he asked as she zipped the bag closed.

"I'm getting out of here. I'm done with the Hudson thing and I'm going back to London."

"I'm glad to hear about the Hudson thing, but why are you going back to London?"

She turned to him and took his hand. "I'm sorry. I needed information and a place to stay. I thought sleeping with you would be an easy way to get both. Everyone was right about me; I was just using you."

He shook his head. "I don't believe you."

She sighed. "You have to. You're a great guy and I've had a lot of fun with you but that's all it's been."

"Why are you saying this?"

"Because it's true." She gave him a gentle kiss. "I have to go." She picked up her bag and turned to the door.

"Don't go! We need to talk about this."

"There's nothing to talk about. I was just using you."

He slammed the bedroom door shut. "Damn it, Kate! Don't lie to me!"

She froze. She'd never seen him angry before.

Seeing that he'd made her nervous, he tried to calm himself. "I know you better than that. Something has changed. Tell me what happened." He waited for her to reply but she stood there in silence. *"Tell me."*

She flinched. "It's that guy, Charley. Davenport says he'll kill us if we don't leave things alone. I believe him."

He sighed and rubbed his chin, his hand shaking. "More idle threats."

"Not idle, not this time. He threatened Claire and Michael too."

The blood drained from his face. "I'll kill him."

"You won't go near him." She put her hand on his

235

arm. "I've made a deal with Davenport. Everyone's going to be fine. Promise me you'll leave it alone."

"What sort of deal?" he demanded.

"He gave me twenty grand and told me to get out of town and no one will get hurt. That's exactly what I'm going to do."

He gave a nervous laugh. "You were going to walk right out of my life without even saying a word? I suppose for twenty grand it was an easy choice."

"It's not easy and it's not about the money." She pointed to the cash, which sat on the dresser. "Keep it, give it away, I don't care. I can't let anyone else get hurt because of my stupid mistake. If something happened to you or your family because of me, I couldn't bear it." She reached out and touched his arm. "I have to go. There's a limo downstairs waiting for me."

He positioned himself in front of the door and said calmly, "You're not going anywhere."

"Get out of my way, Mike."

"No." He stood resolute.

She tried to push past but he didn't move.

"I'm not letting you go."

"You have to, for your family."

She tried to get past again, but he stood firm.

She was shaking. He was too. They stood in silence, staring at each other, knowing there was no way that the other would back down.

Mike was the first to speak. "I'm going to do what I should have done this morning. I'm calling the police." He reached into his pocket and got his phone. She grabbed it from him and threw it onto the bed.

"No, that won't work! Once we publicly point the finger, it's over. We don't have any proof. Davenport and Charley can still talk their way out of everything and then they *will* kill us."

"Then we need to get some proof, now."

"How? Have you got a plan, Mike?"

"No. I'm waiting for you to tell me yours."

She rolled her eyes. "I went down there to talk to him, to try and get him to admit to something. I had my mobile recording to catch him out, but he was on to me and it didn't work."

He screwed up his face. "That was your plan?"

"You didn't let me finish…" She raised her eyebrows at him. "I got Hooper to follow me down there and told him to wait and see what Davenport did after I left. Where he went and who he talked to. See if we can flush something out or see if he leads us to Charley or whatever they're planning next."

Mike reeled. "*You* were the distraction?"

"Yes!"

He sighed and wrapped his arms around her. "That was really stupid, babe. Why didn't you let me in on the plan?"

"Because I knew you wouldn't let me do it. I wanted to keep you out of it, to keep you safe."

"I can look after myself. Hey, what about Hooper? Don't you care if anything happens to him?"

She shrugged. "Not really."

He pulled away and looked at her, open-mouthed. *Did she really just say that?*

She punched him on the arm. "I'm kidding. I just told him to watch the guy. He's not going to do anything risky."

"This isn't the time for jokes."

"Sorry. Davenport's driver is downstairs waiting. If I

237

don't go down he'll come up and get me and there will be trouble. I'll let him take me to the airport as planned and I'll hang round there for an hour then come back into the city. Don't call Hooper in case he's undercover; just send him a text and tell him what's happening and to wait until he hears from us."

Mike nodded. "OK, but I'm following you in a cab."

"No," she warned, "it's safe to say he's watching your apartment, so he's seen you coming home. A few minutes after I leave, go out and buy a bottle of whisky, look angry and upset, look like I broke your heart. Come back here and wait for my call and I'll tell you where to meet me."

It did sound like an OK plan, but he wasn't so sure. "I don't like this, Kate."

"It'll be fine. We'll talk to Hooper and see what he finds out, and even if he gets nothing we'll go to the police. I promise, this ends tonight."

Her choice of words didn't reassure him. Was she deliberately trying to make him nervous?

"I have to go. I'll call you when I get to the airport." She put her arms around him and rested her head on his chest. She felt his heart beating against her cheek as his grip around her tightened.

After a few moments she tapped him on the back. "Time to go."

He kissed her on the forehead. "Be careful." Reluctantly, he let go of her.

She picked up her bag and hurried out of the door. He grabbed his phone and followed her into the living room. She opened the door.

"Kate?"

"What is it, Mike? I have to go." She turned and

saw the look on his face. She had never imagined he could look so vulnerable.

They stared at each other in silence.

"Kate, I—"

"Stop," she instructed. She set her bag down and they rushed to meet each other. He wrapped his arms around her.

She looked up at him. "I know what you're going to say..."

He nodded and opened his mouth to speak but she placed her finger over his lips. "I feel the same way, but I've never said those words before, and I don't want to say them as I'm running out the door. Save it for later."

He tightened his grip on her. "I'm not letting you go. I won't let you put yourself in danger."

"I'm getting myself out of danger. Davenport obviously doesn't want to hurt me or I wouldn't be here. He just wants me out of the way. If he believes I'm gone he'll get Charley to leave you and your family alone. Then we meet up with Hooper and take everything we know to the police."

"Let's just call the police now."

"No!" she snapped. "You know I have to do this. I'll see you in a few hours. There's no danger, Mike, I promise. Have I ever lied to you?" She bit her lip and tried not to laugh.

"You're not funny, babe."

She made sad eyes at him. "I'm a little bit funny. See you later." She kissed him on the lips and went back to the door, giving him one last smile as she closed it behind her.

He went to the kitchen, picked up the bottle of whisky and a glass, brought them into the living room and set them on the coffee table. He pulled his phone out of his pocket and placed it beside the bottle.

She was right. If they went to the police with no evidence, those guys would definitely get away with murder. This was the only option. The thought didn't make him feel any better about the fact that he had just let the woman he loved put herself in danger. He sank his head in his hands. He should have told her to get on the first plane. At least she would have been safe. Better yet, he should have locked her in the bathroom and taken away the key.

His hand was shaking as he opened the bottle, poured himself a generous measure and swallowed it in a single mouthful. He picked up his phone and texted Hooper the plan, then placed a call.

As the call was answered, he took a deep breath and tried to sound calm.

"Hi honey. No, everything's fine. I just thought I'd check in. Is everything OK? Is Steve at home? OK, good. Oh OK, you get back to dinner. I'll talk to you tomorrow. Tell Michael Gramps loves him. I love you too, honey. Bye." He set the phone down and poured another drink.

***

She flinched as the limo door closed behind her. She looked out of the window. As the car pulled away from the apartment building, she felt sick. She took a few deep breaths and tried to calm herself. She wished that Mike hadn't come home when he did. She really didn't want him involved – or Hooper. This was her mess, and she had to be the one to put it right.

She tried to work out what they should do next.

She decided to text Hooper to see what he had found out and arrange where they could meet. Reaching into her pocket for her mobile, she felt a wave of nausea. She raised her hand to her mouth and tried hard to stop herself being sick. Her phone wasn't there. It was in Max's office – she could picture it on the desk. *How will I text Hooper? How will I call Mike? What am I going to do?*

Then it hit her. She pulled her purse out of her bag and rifled through her cards, receipts and cash. Where was Mike's business card? More sentimental than she cared to admit, she knew she hadn't thrown it away. It had to be there... Finally she had it in her hand. Yes! His mobile number was on it. She shoved everything back into her bag.

She sat back in the cold leather seat and tried to relax. When she looked out of the window, she noticed they were heading towards the Bronx. She knocked on the partition. "Hello? This isn't the way to JFK. What airport are you going to?"

There was no answer.

Her geography of New York wasn't great, but she was pretty sure there was no airport in the Bronx – not one that she wanted to go to anyway. She banged on the partition again. "Oy! Where are you taking me?"

There was no answer. She pounded on the partition until her fists were sore. She tried the handles and windows on both sides, but they were locked. If the glass hadn't been blacked out she could have caught the attention of another driver. Out of breath, she gave the partition one last thump. "Stop this car now and let me out!"

The driver kept on driving.

She hunted through her bag for something to use to defend herself but there was nothing but clothes. Why hadn't she taken her make-up bag? She could see it on the shelf in the en-suite: it had scissors, tweezers, antiperspirant … useful things.

She searched through her handbag. The only thing that might be any use was a small bottle of perfume, which she shoved into her jacket pocket. There was nothing else. She knew the perfume wasn't going to be enough.

She would have to try and run as soon as the door was opened, but she wouldn't get far in her heels so she reached down and unfastened the leather straps. She took off a shoe and examined it. The heel was sharp enough to use as a weapon, she decided. And she had two of them.

With the shoes on her knee, she waited. How could she have been so stupid? Of course Max wasn't going to let her go. The last thing she wanted to hear was Mike saying 'I told you so' as he rescued her but, in this situation, it would be music to her ears.

After a few minutes, the car slowed. She looked out of the window as the limo turned into a private driveway and stopped in front of a building. The driver stepped out, holding his mobile to his ear. Kate strained to listen but couldn't quite make out what he was saying. As he finished the call, she prepared herself, gripping a shoe in each hand. She waited.

The door to the building opened and she was not entirely surprised to see Max Davenport approach the car. He nodded to the driver as he opened the rear door.

"Hello Kate, would you like to come with me?"

He reached into the car and grabbed her arm. As she squirmed to break his hold, she lost her balance and fell out of the car. She scrambled on the tarmac to retrieve one of her shoes, then sat up and looked around. It was the grounds of an old factory. She could see one other car.

Max pointed to her bare feet. "You wouldn't have gotten far like that." He offered his hand to help her up but she cowered away. "Don't worry. I'm not going to hurt you – but I can't speak for Charley."

He extended his hand again. When he bent down to her, she jammed the heel of her shoe into his ankle.

He cried out in pain and clutched at his ankle.

She scrambled to her feet, but as she turned to run she felt her knee buckle. A quick glance revealed that it was cut and bleeding from her fall. She stumbled, then regained her balance. Just as she was about to run she felt a blow to the face. She hit the ground again.

She lay flat on her back. The pain in her head was tremendous. As she tried to focus, she was lifted to her feet. Max was on one side and the driver on the other. She looked between the two. *Which of you bastards punched me? That really hurts!*

They marched her into the building through a dimly lit reception area and down a dark narrow corridor before stopping at a closed door.

"You can go now," Max said. He waited until the driver had gone back up the corridor before opening the door and pushing her inside.

Her vision was blurred by the blow, and it took her a while to focus. The room contained a few machines, a desk and a chair. At the back of the room a figure was standing over something on the floor. Horrified, she realised the figure was Charley and … was that Hooper on the floor?

When he saw her, Hooper's eyes widened. He tried to shout something, but his words were muffled by the tape over his mouth. He was propped up against the wall, his wrists bound on either side of him with cable ties attached to a pipe that ran the width of the room. His eye was bruised and there was dried blood around his nose.

She ran to him and knelt down beside him. "Are you OK?"

He nodded. She squeezed his arm to reassure him, took a deep breath, stood up straight and turned to face Max and Charley.

"What the hell are you doing? Let us go!"

Max sighed and pointed to Hooper. "I was going to let you go but then I found this guy following me and a text on his cell from your boyfriend telling me your plan. I didn't want anyone else to get hurt, but now I have no choice."

"Of course you have a choice! This is all my fault. I didn't believe you when you said you'd kill me, but now that I know you mean it, I'll definitely go. Just cut Hooper loose and we'll forget any of this ever happened. Right, Hooper?"

Hooper nodded furiously.

Max sighed. "No. This is the only way." He took the gun out of his pocket.

Frantically, Hooper tried to break free.

Her heart sank. She couldn't let Hooper get hurt

because of her mistake. "OK, you can kill me. I won't even put up a fight if you let Hooper go. He has nothing to do with this."

"No way. We have to tie up all loose ends."

She felt her chest tighten. She struggled to steady her breathing but deep down she knew Max wasn't a murderer and decided it wouldn't hurt to call his bluff. *After all, things can't get any worse.*

"Well, what are you waiting for? If you're going to kill us, just get it over with."

Hooper shouted something inaudible and continued to struggle with his restraints.

"Not yet – we're still waiting for our last guest to arrive." Max looked at his watch. "He's on his way." He took Hooper's phone out of his pocket and waved it at her. "I texted your boyfriend and told him there was a change of plan. He should be here any minute." He threw the phone onto the table.

Shit, I was wrong. Things are worse. Mike's on his way. This is all my fault. If only I'd let Mike call the police. The police! I have an idea.

"OK, Max, I gave you a chance to let us go but now you're really in trouble. Hooper's job was to follow you, and if I had known what an amateur he was" – she shot an accusing look at Hooper – "I'd have got someone else to do it. But Mike is a professional and his job is to bring the police with him. I'll bet they're outside right now."

Max's eyes darted to the door.

Charley laughed. "She's bluffing, Max. Look at her, she's shaking like a leaf. The police aren't coming."

Max edged towards the door. "Are you sure? Because if she's not bluffing, we might still have time to get out of here."

"The police aren't coming." Charley stepped up to Kate and ran his hand down her cheek. "No one's going to save you, sweetheart."

She slapped his hand away. "Don't you dare touch me."

Max sighed. "Leave her alone, Charley. It's your fault we're in this mess. The plan was to frame Jack, not kill people. Just tie her up beside him while I go and check there's no police. Don't forget to use the cable ties – they'll burn up nicely."

She swallowed. "Burn?"

Max shrugged. "I know. Awful, isn't it? I've been meaning to get the electrics fixed. This place is a death trap." He left and closed the door behind him.

Charley stepped so close to Kate that she could smell the stale smoke on his breath. "Looks like it's just you and me."

She took a step backwards and found herself up against the wall. "Didn't you hear your boss tell you to leave me alone?"

"He's not my boss; we're partners."

"Really?" she said with contempt. "Then you must be the sleeping one."

He raised his hand to hit her, but she put her hands up in defence. Instead he pulled a gun from behind his back and rammed it into her chest, then took a cable tie from his pocket and offered it to her. "Put your hands in there and tighten it with your teeth."

Trembling, she reached out to take it. Desperately, she searched the room for something she could use as a weapon, then spotted a fire extinguisher on the floor near the desk. She let the cable tie drop onto the floor and shrugged. "Oops."

Charley gritted his teeth. When he bent to pick up the cable tie, she retrieved the bottle of perfume from her pocket, flicked off the lid and waited for him to straighten up. As soon as his eyes drew level with her hand, she sprayed.

He brought his hands to his face in pain and shouted obscenities. She grabbed him by the shoulders and, with as much force as she could summon, dug her knee into his groin. He dropped to his knees. She bolted for the fire extinguisher. He was already starting to get up when she swung it at him.

He fell to the floor.

She wasn't sure where she'd hit him as she'd had her eyes closed, but he looked unconscious. *Should I hit him again?* She nudged him with her foot, then saw the dropped cable tie. She bound his wrists together, picked up his gun and ran over to Hooper. She tore the tape off his lips and tried to release the cable ties.

"Just go and get help. My cell's on the table."

"No – if Max comes back he'll kill you! We've only got one gun. We'll be safer together. You don't happen to have a penknife, do you?"

He shook his head and they looked around the room for something they could use to cut the restraints. She looked at the gun in her hand and then at the pipe.

"Don't even think about it!" Hooper yelled.

"Oh." She jumped to her feet, hurried back to Charley and searched through his pockets until she found what she was looking for – his lighter. She returned to Hooper and held the lighter where the cable tie met the pipe.

He flinched as the flame caught his arm but the

instant the plastic melted his hand was free. He pointed to her swollen eye as she freed his other hand. "You OK?"

"Yes." She helped him up. "What time did he text Mike? Shouldn't he be here by now?"

"Yeah. Is he really bringing the police?"

She bit her lip. "No."

"I didn't think so." He groaned. "Let's get out of here."

She put her ear up against the door to listen while Hooper got his phone. He joined her at the door.

"You ready?"

He nodded.

She eased the door open. Before she could take a step, Hooper put his hand on her arm to hold her back. Genuinely surprised by his chivalry, she allowed him to go first and they crept towards the reception area. He saw a shadow and gestured for her to stop. They stared at each other, wondering what to do next.

She offered him the gun. "Cover me and be ready for my signal."

He looked at her as if she was crazy. "Cover you? No, you cover me."

"I know he's not going to hurt me. I can't say the same about you … but get him in your sights just in case." She took a deep breath and squeezed his arm on the way past.

She crept out from behind the wall to find Max pointing a gun at Mike. They turned to face her, and Mike gasped when he saw her bruised eye.

"Are you OK?" He started to move towards her.

"*Don't move*," Max instructed, shifting the gun from Mike to Kate and then back again.

Knowing that she had to distract Max so Hooper could get a shot, she took a step closer to Mike. "I can't believe you let yourself get captured."

His eyes widened. "Isn't that what you're doing here?"

She took another step closer to him. "Yes, but I was dragged in here kicking and screaming. Looks like you just walked in through the bloody door."

"*Quiet!* I need to think," Max snapped.

Kate noticed tiny beads of sweat on Max's forehead. She was right about him – he wasn't a killer, but she didn't want to antagonise him too much, just in case. "It's over, Max." She stepped even closer to Mike. "Charley's down and Hooper is outside calling the police. Just let us go." She took another step.

"No, he isn't. This is the only way out."

Her next step forced Max to turn his back to the corridor. "Listen to me, Max. You're going to put the gun down and we're going to walk out of here, all three of us."

His voice wobbled. "I can't."

She kept inching towards Mike. "Yes, you can. You haven't done anything wrong – well, not *really* wrong. I know Charley killed Ray. I don't know who killed Crawford, but I know it wasn't you because you were in Germany with Jack. You're off the hook! Just let us go and we'll pretend nothing happened. Right, Mike?" She looked at Mike and signalled to the wall Hooper was hiding behind.

He nodded. "Sure, babe." He looked at Max. "Kate's right, you haven't done anything wrong. Let's all walk

249

out of here." He saw Hooper come out of the corridor and point the gun towards Max.

Max shifted his gun between them. "No, you guys have ruined everything. At least one of you is going to die – who wants to go first?"

"Shoot him first. I can wait," Kate said casually to buy some time as Hooper crept up behind Max.

Mike shook his head. "No, shoot her first, she got me and Hooper into this mess. Babe, I thought you said Hooper was outside?"

"No, honey, he's right there holding a gun to Max's head."

Max froze as he felt the barrel of a gun against the back of his head. Slowly, he lowered his gun.

"I said you had a choice." Kate took the gun from him and looked him in the eye. "You made the right one." She patted his shoulder.

Hooper gestured to the wall with the gun. "Get over there."

Max went into the corner and slid down the wall, curling up into a ball on the floor.

She took a deep breath and examined the gun. "That was close."

Mike held out his hand. "Give me the gun."

She narrowed her eyes as she handed it to him. "Please don't do anything stupid. Claire and Michael will be fine."

"Oh, I know. I just didn't want you to be holding a gun when you found out I called the police."

He gestured for her to listen. All of a sudden she heard sirens. They were getting closer.

She glared at him. "What the hell did you do that for?"

"Because I'm not an idiot. When I got the text from Hooper, with appalling punctuation, telling me to come to an abandoned warehouse in the Bronx, it set off some alarm bells. It just took the cops a bit longer to get here than I'd hoped."

She tilted her head. "But you came in anyway?"

"I had to. You were in here." He held his hand out to her, but she slapped him on the arm.

"I can't believe you called the police when I specifically asked you not to."

"You can't be mad at me over this…"

"I'm not." She giggled. "I knew you'd call the police; I was counting on it." She wrapped her arms around his neck. "Just like I knew you'd fall in love with me. It was all part of my plan."

He tried to suppress his grin. "Really?"

"No! But that's what we're going to tell people."

She squeezed him as hard as she could until he broke away.

"OK, but now can I tell you that I love—"

"In a minute, Mike." She pushed past him and walked over to Max. She knelt down beside him. "Settle something for me, would you?"

He looked at her as if she was crazy. "No."

"Oh, come on. You'll have to tell the police anyway." She pointed at Mike and Hooper. "These guys didn't believe me when I told them Mrs Crawford killed her husband. Tell them I'm right."

He shook his head. "You're wrong. Charley got him drunk and gave him the pills."

"He did?" She tutted. "I was sure it was her. Then why was she in London?"

"She was with Charley. They'd been fooling around

for a while."

"Then that makes her an accessory, so technically I was right." She stood up and took a bow.

"Very technically," Hooper scoffed.

Kate was reaching to slap him on the arm when Mike cleared this throat. She looked up to find him with a stern look on his face. He beckoned her over.

She took a deep breath, straightened her skirt and prepared herself to hear the three little words she never thought she'd want to hear. Simultaneously excited and terrified, she approached him and slid her arms around his neck.

His heart was pounding as he wrapped his arms around her waist. He gazed into her beautiful brown eyes. Just as he opened his mouth to speak, the NYPD stormed through the door.

Chapter Sixteen

Mike sat on the edge of the hospital bed and watched Hooper type frantically into his phone.

"The police said it's OK for us to leave. Go down to the office – you look ridiculous trying to type that on your cell."

"I thought I'd keep you company until Kate gets back. She's going to love this," Hooper said as he continued to type.

"You mean you want to see the pretty doctor again? Get the hell out of here."

"OK, old man." He stood up and picked up his jacket. "I told you that girl was trouble. For a minute there I thought it was lights out..."

"Don't!" Mike shuddered. "When I think what could have happened... But it didn't, and we got one hell of an exclusive."

Hooper squinted. "*We? You mean Kate and I. All you did was call the cops." He pulled open the curtain and turned back to Mike. "I wish you'd seen her in there, Mike. She was really brave. She saved my ass. Looks like you were right – seems like there really is nothing she can't do. Don't screw it up this time." He walked off, chuckling.

Don't screw it up? Mike rubbed his temples. He'd screwed up the previous times he'd been in love. Audrey had cheated on him because he hadn't paid her enough attention and Barbara wouldn't marry him because he'd given her too much. In just three weeks he'd developed feelings for Kate that were far stronger than his feelings for Audrey and Barbara put together. He was head over heels in love with her and he knew he wouldn't screw up this time. He couldn't.

Then the curtain was pulled back. Mike looked up, expecting to see Kate, but it was the doctor. She pulled the curtain closed behind her.

"Hey, doc, Kate's not back from X-ray yet. I know you guys are busy, but she's been gone a long time."

"I'm so sorry to keep you waiting." Her expression was grave. "I've had a call from upstairs. Kate has been rushed to surgery."

He jumped up from the bed. "Surgery? Her eye looked bad, but not *that* bad."

"It's not her eye."

Mike's stomach churned in fear. "What happened?"

"She had a heart attack when she was waiting for the X-ray."

"What?" He felt dizzy and had to put his hand on the bed to steady himself. "A heart attack? That's not possible. She's young, she's healthy, she…" He felt a wave of nausea. "Her mother died of a heart attack when Kate was fifteen."

The doctor nodded. "That's useful to know. Was it CHD, arrhythmia?"

He buried his head in his hands. "I don't know."

"Was Kate taking any medication?"

"Not that I know of."

"It's possible that it's hereditary, or it could have been brought on by stress or other factors. I won't know more until I speak to the surgeon. Either way, she's extremely lucky she was here when it happened."

"I need to see her."

"You can't. She's still in surgery."

"Please! I need to see her."

She put her hand on his arm. "All right. I'll take you up there, show you where you can wait."

"How long will it take?"

"I'm sorry, I don't know."

"She is going to be OK, isn't she?" he asked, his voice shaking.

She pulled the curtain open. "Let's get you upstairs."

***

The door opened and the automatic lights flickered on. A doctor approached the bed. He picked up the chart and scanned it.

Mike, who was asleep in the armchair, stirred. He sat up and looked at Kate, but his hopeful expression faded when he realised it was just the doctor who had disturbed him.

"I'm sorry, I didn't mean to wake you. Have you still not been home?"

Mike looked down at the suit he'd been wearing for three days and shook his head.

The doctor smiled. "From what I can see, she's doing really well: breathing on her own, her vitals look great. We've stopped the sedation and she should wake up naturally soon."

Mike nodded. "Is she going to be OK?"

"She's going to be fine." He glanced at the clock on the wall. "I've got to go. Give the nurse a call as soon as she wakes up."

Mike took Kate's hand. He wouldn't allow himself

to believe she was OK until she was awake and could tell him herself. He watched her chest rise and fall beneath the sheet and tried to ignore the tubes and machines that surrounded her.

He was desperate for her to wake up so he could tell her he loved her and he wanted to be with her – on any terms. He'd done a lot of thinking over the last two days. He had decided that he didn't have to work at the *Times*. He could go back to writing, but freelance, and work when and where he chose. He didn't have to live in New York either, or even America. Claire was grown up and had a family of her own. He could Skype or FaceTime her every day if he wanted to. For the first time in his life, he didn't have a plan for his future. He'd make a plan, with Kate.

Her eyelids flickered then opened slowly. She looked around the dark room. It took a few seconds for her to realise she was in a hospital bed. She tried to sit up but was too weak to move. Scared and confused, she panicked until she noticed the armchair and its occupant, who was sound asleep. His presence reassured her and she closed her eyes, listened to the sound of his breathing, and fell back to sleep.

It was daylight when she woke again. She looked towards the armchair, where Mike was still asleep. As she watched him, she tried to remember what had happened. When she'd been waiting for her X-ray, she'd felt a tightness in her chest which had spread quickly to her neck, then her jaw. She couldn't remember much of what had happened next, only that she had wanted Mike to hold her and tell her everything would be OK.

While she summoned the energy to move, she watched him sleep. He was the most incredible man she'd ever met. Why had she tried so hard not to fall in love with him? It turned out that falling for him was the easiest thing she'd ever done. She didn't regret the way she'd lived her life before she met him. But those days were gone. She wanted nothing more than to be with Mike.

She pulled her hand from under his and rested it on his arm. She tried to nudge him but she was too weak to disturb him. She wanted to scream but could only manage a whisper. "Mike."

Nothing.

Her mouth was dry, and she swallowed painfully. "*Mike*."

He raised his head and squinted at her. A wave of relief rushed over him as he realised she was awake. He sat bolt upright and looked into her eyes.

"Morning, babe." He reached for her hand and pressed it firmly against his lips before cradling it against his cheek.

She couldn't stop tears welling up, and she struggled to breathe.

"It's OK," he murmured as she tried to catch her breath. "The doctor says you're going to be fine. You just need to get your strength back." He kissed her hand again. "I'm sorry I fell asleep. I wanted to be here for you when you woke up. I should call a nurse, tell them you're awake."

He reached for the call button but she whispered, "No."

He stroked her cheek instead. "How do you feel?"

"Numb."

"That's probably normal, but I'm calling the nurse just in case."

Before she could stop him, he had pressed the call button.

"Do you remember what happened?"

She gathered the energy to speak. "Pain," was all she could manage.

He nodded. "You had a heart attack." He held back the bit about the bypass surgery. "But you're going to be fine."

He perched on the side of the bed and wiped away the tear that rolled down her cheek.

"You gave me quite a scare. I've only just found you, and I was terrified I was going to lose you. I've been sitting here for two days rehearsing exactly what I was going to say to you, and it was perfect. I told you a hundred times when you were sleeping but now that you're awake I can't remember a damn word."

She looked into his eyes and tried to squeeze his hand. "Simple."

"OK." He smiled. "I think the two main points were, in no particular order, one, I can't imagine my life without you, so wherever you go, I go. Two – now, what was the second thing again?" He scratched his head. "Oh yes. I love you."

Tears rolled down her cheeks. She wanted to throw her arms around him, tell him she loved him too and she had already decided she was going to stay in New York. She opened her mouth to speak but he placed a finger on her lips.

"I don't want the first time you say those words to be in a hospital bed, so save it for later."

As he kissed her hand the door opened and a nurse came in.

After the nurse had checked Kate and left to fetch the doctor, Mike thought he should fill Kate in on his plans for her while she was too weak to argue.

"I know you had planned to go home but you're far too ill to travel. Looks like you're stuck with me for a bit longer."

She tried her best to roll her eyes at him.

"I talked to Bob. I'm taking a leave of absence from the paper and I've rented us a little cottage in the Hamptons. I'm going to take you there to nurse you back to health. When you're back on your feet, you're free to go wherever you want" – he paused – "and I don't care whether you want to live in London or Lebanon, I'm going to be right there with you. I'll figure it out."

She tried to shake her head then motioned for him to come closer to her. She whispered into his ear, "We're staying here."

"No…" He narrowed his eyes at her. "That has to be the drugs talking."

She tried to suppress a yawn.

"See, you're exhausted. No more talking – I've got a lot to tell you." He made himself comfortable in his chair. "Max and Charley have both been charged with two counts of false imprisonment, for starters. The NYPD are liaising with the police in London about how to proceed with the murder investigations. Helena Crawford has been questioned and will probably be charged as an accessory. And your old friend Jack Hudson just filed for an appeal. Hooper wrote a great story about it all in the paper and I saved you a copy.

How about I read it to you? Just listen and try to relax."

He got up and picked up the paper and his glasses from the windowsill. Before he sat down, he held up the front page for her to see.

Her photo was on the cover of the *New York Times*. The headline read:

Former Hudson Employee Uncovers Deadly Plot to Prevent Affordable Medication for Millions Worldwide

"Oh, and guess what?" He beamed. "Hooper shared the byline with you."

She managed a small smile, but it soon faded. "That was our story."

"It's OK, babe." He stroked her cheek. "We'll get another story."

Chapter Seventeen

Four weeks later: Montauk, New York

Kate sat in an armchair by the open window, her laptop on her knee. She breathed in the fresh sea air and gazed out at the waves as they crashed on the shore. She was recalling the day she met Mike, remembering how good his arms felt around her when she heard him behind her.

"Morning, babe. It's after ten. Why didn't you wake me?" Mike kissed her cheek and pulled up a chair beside her.

She greeted him with a huge smile. "I thought you could use the sleep; you must have got in late last night. Productive day?"

"Very. I spent a few hours at the office. Bob said he loved your feature and he'll run it on Sunday. Everyone else says hi and there's a million cards and presents for you in the car. I went to the apartment and got the stuff you wanted, then I did a few errands. It's amazing what builds up when you're gone for three weeks." He let out a long sigh. "And I met with that immigration lawyer. I've got some stuff for you to read and some forms to sign. It's a long process – I won't bore you with it right now."

"Don't worry, honey." She held her hand out to him and he locked fingers with her. "There's nothing I can't do." She kissed his hand.

"I'm sorry I was gone the whole day. Were you OK

on your own?"

"Yes, I barely had time to miss you. Mrs Carmichael brought me food and checked in on me a hundred times, and with you gone I got so much writing done. My heroine just met a handsome reporter."

He drew a sharp breath. "I hope somebody warns the poor guy..."

She shot him a dirty look and he laughed.

"I really missed you yesterday. It was so weird being at the paper and the apartment without you. And I'm sorry, but I'll have to leave you on your own again. I have to nip into town this morning and get a few things."

"I'll come with you."

He shook his head. "Nope, you need to save your strength for this afternoon."

"Why? What's happening this afternoon?"

"A walk on the beach. It's a beautiful day. I know it's a little cold, but I'll wrap you up nice and warm."

"You don't have to sell it to me – it sounds great."

"Good. Is that coffee I smell?"

She screwed up her face. "No, it's decaf."

***

As they walked arm in arm along the deserted beach Kate noticed a small table with two chairs. She smiled to herself as she looked around for the young lovers it was obviously intended for, but when Mike directed her towards it, she realised that it was for them. Her grip on his arm tightened.

"You did this?"

"Not just me." He pulled out a chair and invited her

to sit. "I asked Mrs Carmichael where the most romantic spot on the beach was and she suggested this place. She helped me put it all together."

She ran her hand along the table to straighten the gingham tablecloth, which had been disturbed by the light breeze. "It's the most romantic thing anyone's ever done for me."

"She'll be pleased to hear that," he joked and pulled a blanket from under the table.

She groaned as he put it over her knees.

He took her hand. "Are you OK?"

"Yes, just a bit tired from all the walking."

"You walked for about three minutes, babe."

"Well, it's the most I've walked in four weeks. It was exhausting."

"I'm sorry. I drove as far as I could, but I did offer to carry you."

She rolled her eyes and looked at the picnic basket under the table. "Please tell me there's food in there. I'm starving."

He took a stick of French bread from the basket, tore off a chunk and offered it to her.

"Oh, my favourite – carbs."

"And to go with the carbs..." He placed two round packages on the table. "Brie you love and pâté I know you're going to love." He reached into the basket again and brought out a salad. "Caesar, extra dressing."

She rubbed her hands together. "Perfect."

"And to drink..."

"There'd better be a flask of whisky in there."

"No Scotch, but this should warm you up a little." He reached into the basket and produced a bottle of champagne and two flutes. "I know you're not supposed to be drinking, but a few sips won't hurt."

"Who brings a bottle of Dom Perignon to a Halloween beach picnic?" she teased.

"A man who wants to spoil the love of his life." He reached for her hand and kissed it. "And I was hoping it would be more than just a picnic…"

"If you're suggesting sex on the beach, it's a great idea but it's broad daylight and I'm in no fit state."

"No… I thought it could be our engagement party."

Her jaw dropped. "Our what?"

Reaching into his coat pocket, he produced a small box. He got up from his chair and knelt in the sand in front of her, taking her hand as he offered her the box. "Will you marry me, Kate?"

Her hand shook as she brought it to her mouth, overcome. She knew he would propose sometime, but she had no idea it would be so soon. She'd lied earlier when she said she'd been too busy to miss him yesterday. She'd pined nearly the whole day and was only able to fall asleep without him due to sheer exhaustion. She wanted to marry him more than anything else in the world, but she tried to wait a reasonable amount of time before she answered. "Yes."

He nearly fell over in the sand. "Yes?"

"Yes."

"That easy? No calling me crazy, no protests, no conditions?"

She held up her index finger. "Just the one condition."

He took a deep breath. "Oh, thank God. I was worried there. Hit me with it."

"I don't want a big fuss. As soon as I'm well enough, let's elope."

He shook his head. "No. I can't agree to that. You're getting a fuss. Your one and only wedding day is going to be perfect." He gestured for her to look around. "How do you like it here?"

"In Montauk?"

"More specifically, here on the beach?"

She looked around at the gleaming white sand and rolling dunes, and sighed in happiness. "It's absolutely beautiful."

"Good, because we're getting married right here next Friday. Unless it rains" – he pointed over her shoulder to the cliff top – "then we'll get married in that lighthouse."

She gasped. "We're getting married next Friday?"

"I know it's quick, but after speaking to the immigration lawyer I thought marriage would help things along." He squeezed her hand. "But I need you to know that's not why I'm doing this. I'm doing it because I love you, but if you need more time, we can do it next month, next year, in two years..."

"Next Friday sounds perfect." She placed her hands on his cheeks and pulled him in for a kiss. "I can't wait to be Mrs Michael Kelly."

He pulled away and made a face. "You're going to take my name? I had no idea you'd be so traditional."

"I thought you'd learned to expect surprises from me." She clapped her hands. "Now let me see the ring."

He opened the box to reveal a platinum band with a huge classic-cut diamond solitaire. She gasped.

"I hope it fits." They held their breath as he slid it onto her finger. He sighed when he saw it was a bit too big.

"It's just a little loose, but I've lost a few pounds so

a few more carbs and it should be perfect." She held out her hand to admire it. "It's so beautiful, Mike, but you really shouldn't have. You know I don't need big romantic gestures."

"I know, but if you're going to be my wife, you better get used to them. You've given up the world for me, babe, and I'm going to spend every day proving to you that I'm worth the sacrifice."

She looked down at him kneeling in the sand, his beautiful blue eyes welling with tears. She'd never imagined that she could be so in love. "I already know," she whispered as her lips met his.

She draped her arms around his neck. As she melted into the kiss she remembered their first, outside the hotel. At that moment she had wanted to melt into him so they could never be separated, and now here on the beach she knew they never would be.

He ran his hand through her hair, enjoying the taste of her lips and the warmth of her breath. He'd savoured moments like this before when he was preparing for her to leave, but this kiss was different; he felt free to enjoy it as he knew there would be many more to come.

He stood up and dusted the sand off his trousers, then opened the bottle of champagne and filled the flutes. He gave Kate a soft kiss as he handed her a glass and pulled his chair closer to hers. He held his glass out to her and proposed a toast.

"Here's to next Friday."

She shook her head as she clinked her glass with his. "To next Friday. You know how to put a girl under pressure. That's just ten days away and I have nothing to wear…"

"I've made most of the arrangements, subject to your approval, of course. All you have to do is turn up and say 'I do'."

She squinted at him.

"That's what I was doing all day yesterday. You know Edwin and Stella, the fashion editors at the paper?"

"Who doesn't? They're amazing."

"They know your shape and size and they're coming here on Saturday with a selection of wedding gowns and some accessories. You'll have plenty to choose from. I've arranged a girl from a salon in town to come and do any treatments you want – not that you need any, babe. I met Claire for lunch – you really won her over when they were here last weekend. I told her my plans and she's excited to help organise flowers, music and so on. She'll call you tomorrow about colour schemes. My best man Hooper is organising the reception in the golf club over there, even though he's furious that there's no bachelor party."

She shook her head. "That all sounds perfect, but I'm not sure I'm up to a reception."

"It's small – just the people I've mentioned plus a few from the paper. And my brother and his wife are flying in – they're going to love you. And—"

"Stop, this is too much." She wiped a tear from her eye.

"Just one more thing. I called Nick and Diane. You may not approve, but I felt I had to ask for their permission to marry you. Of course they said yes and they wouldn't miss it for the world, so I'm picking them up at the airport next week. Nick wants to give you away, and Diane is trying to get hold of your best friend to be your maid of honour. But she's in the Himalayas or something, so if she can't make it, Diane will take her place."

Tears ran down her cheeks. She held him close to her. "I can't believe you've done all this. But what would you have done if I'd said no?"

He looked lovingly at her. "The thought didn't even cross my mind. We're meant to be together, babe."

She nodded. "You know I don't usually subscribe to that kind of crap, but I've been thinking. Neither of us was meant to be at the courthouse that day. We shouldn't even have met but we both made a conscious decision to be there. Then I end up in a hospital at the exact moment I have a heart attack. What are the odds? I really wonder if we were meant to be together."

"We are," he said, as if it was obvious.

"So *you're* the one I was waiting for."

"I'm so glad you did. One last thing…"

She held up her hand. "You said there was no more."

He took her hand and cradled it in his. "You're too ill for a honeymoon right now but when you're well enough, I'll take you anywhere you want to go. The world is our oyster."

"Italy," she said without thinking. "The Amalfi Coast. You'll absolutely love it. After that we could swing by London – I have to collect some stuff. Then we can stop over in Belfast so I can show you where I was born, before we come home to New York."

He smiled. "You do know that New York doesn't have to be home? I've told you I'll live anywhere with you, absolutely anywhere."

"I know, but the past few weeks have made me

realise that the only thing in this world that I really want is to be with you. Your home is here, so mine is too. I feel grounded here."

"Really?" He got up and stood in front of her. "Because I feel like I'm in heaven." He held his hand out to her. "May I have this dance?"

She laughed. "But there's no music."

"We don't need music, babe."

He helped her to her feet, then lifted the fallen blanket and draped it around her shoulders. They gazed into each other's eyes, wrapped their arms around each other and danced slowly to the sound of the waves.

Acknowledgments

I began my writing journey in secret. Fear of failure prevented me from sharing my dream with anyone other than my husband. But as I progressed and my story began to come together, I felt more confident about opening up to friends and family. The encouragement and support I received was completely unexpected. I thank each and every one of you for believing in me.

The writing and publishing process was by no means easy, and a huge thank you goes out to the writing community on Twitter. There are far too many people to mention individually, but you have been both a great support and an invaluable resource.

A special thank you goes to the wonderful Jennifer Suzanne, whose notes on my draft manuscript helped me make sense of my own story.

Finally, I would like to thank you for taking a chance on my book. I hope you like it as much as I do – now that it's finished. Please leave a review, or pop by and say hello on your preferred social media channel.

About the Author

Catherine Morrison lives in Lisburn, Northern Ireland with her husband and two children. When she's not at her paid job or spending time with her family, she is writing or thinking about writing. So please don't ask her about the latest mini-series because she doesn't have time to watch TV.

Despite graduating from the University of Ulster in 2002 with a BA in English Literature and Media Studies, Catherine did not put pen to paper until she was certain she had forgotten absolutely everything she had learned during her degree.

One night in 2018, she had a dream. A dream she couldn't shake. For reasons she still can't explain, she decided to try to get that dream down onto paper. It wasn't easy. But just over a year later, she independently published her debut novel, The Hook.

She didn't stop there. In March 2021, Catherine published her second novel, Waiting for Saturday: A new friendship turns a woman's life upside down.

catherinemorrisonauthor

wouldbewriter

@would_bewriter

Printed in Great Britain
by Amazon